SCARED

Pyanfar stared at Tully a long time, and he just looked scared. Scared and on the other side of a half-functioning translator . . . and the gulf of other minds.

"Goldtooth's got a Personage breathing down his neck," she said flatly. "They want to get you, Tully, because they wanted trade. I'll bet on that. And those human ships weren't getting through. *Ijir's* no common trader, no way. They wanted to get you to a rendezvous—find out what humanity's up to. That was the game. But they found out too gods-rotted much and now Goldtooth's scared. Scared, understand? *Kif*, the mahe can handle. But if *knnn* have their small black feet in this—o gods, Tully—you lunatics."

"Got a lot of ships coming—a lot, Pyanfar. Got fight *kif*, got make stop *knnn*."

"No one *fights* the *knnn*! Gods and thunders, you don't pick a fight with something you can't talk to!"

CHANUR'S VENTURE

C.J. CHERRYH

DAW BOOKS, INC.
DONALD A. WOLLHEIM, FOUNDER
375 Hudson Street, New York, NY 10014

ELIZABETH R. WOLLHEIM
SHEILA E. GILBERT
PUBLISHERS

Dedication
To Diane Nancy

First DAW Printing, January 1985

7   8   9   10   11

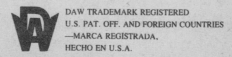

DAW TRADEMARK REGISTERED
U.S. PAT. OFF. AND FOREIGN COUNTRIES
—MARCA REGISTRADA.
HECHO EN U.S.A.

PRINTED IN THE U.S.A.

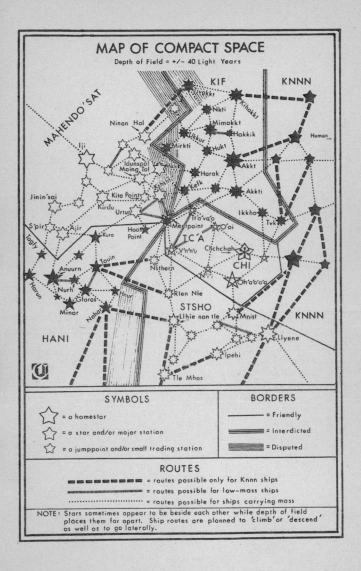

MAP OF COMPACT SPACE

Depth of Field = +/– 40 Light Years

KIF

KNNN

MAHENDO'SAT

Trokkt

Nkti

Ninan Hol

Ikktl

Mimakkt

Iji

Hakkik

Hakkik

Human

Mirkti

Ukkur

Hukt

Idunspol
Maing Tol

Akkts

Akkt

Harak

Jinin'sai

Kita Points

Kefk

Akkti

Kirdu

Urtur

Ikkho

Tvk

S'pir

Ajir

Hoas
Point

Meetpoint

It'a'va'o

Tagly

Kura

IC'A

O'oi

Harun

Anuurn

Touin

V'n'n'u

Clchchah

CHI

Nurh

Nsthern

Oh'a'b'o'a

Gfaras

Minar

Anur

Nahal

Rlen Nle

STSHO

Llhie nan tle

Mnist

KNNN

HANI

Llyene

Ipehi

Tle Mhos

SYMBOLS

☆ = a homestar

☆ = a star and/or major station

☆ = a jumppoint and/or small trading station

BORDERS

——— = Friendly

≡≡≡ = Interdicted

≣≣≣ = Disputed

ROUTES

▬ ▬ ▬ = routes possible only for Knnn ships

▬▬▬ = routes possible for low-mass ships

········· = routes possible for ships carrying mass

NOTE: Stars sometimes appear to be beside each other while depth of field places them far apart. Ship routes are planned to 'climb' or 'descend' as well as to go laterally.

Chapter One

The encounter of old friends was common enough on Meetpoint Station, where half a dozen species came to trade; and one such old friend came walking Pyanfar Chanur's way when she had no more than put *The Pride* in dock. She was hani, Pyanfar Chanur, maned and bearded in curling red-gold, sleek of pelt. Her left ear bore the gold rings of successful voyages along its rim, and the bottommost ring had a monstrous gaudy teardrop pearl. Her red blousing breeches were silk, with the faintest striping of orange; and wrapped about the waist was a belt whose dangling ties were finished in precious stones and gold and bronze. She was not quiet, this Pynafar. She exuded

1

wealth and dignity, and drew eyes wherever she went.

And rounding a collection of canisters awaiting dockside pickup, she spied a dark-furred, all but naked shape: mahendo'sat—ordinary encounter anywhere on Meetpoint. But this one flung wide his arms. His eyes lit up, his broad mahen face broke into a charming grin that showed blunt primate fangs all capped in gold.

"Pyanfar!" he cried.

"You!" Pyanfar stopped dead in her tracks. "You!" She slapped aside the offered embrace and stalked past at a good clip, to make the mahendo'sat exert himself.

"Ha, hani captain," the mahe called after her. "You want deal?"

She turned about again, planted hands on hips and let the mahe overtake her against all better judgment. A heavy hand descended on her shoulder and the mahe resumed his gilt-edged grin.

"Long time," Goldtooth said.

"Gods rot you, don't grin at me. You want a smile from me, you mahen bastard? How'd you get in port?"

"Just docked. Find my good friend here. Give surprise, a?" He laughed, slapped her on the back, seized her about the shoulders in one lank, coarse-pelted arm and propelled her toward the ship berths. "Got present, hani."

"Present!" Pyanfar dug claws into the deck-plates, resisting this camaraderie, aware of probable witnesses, of a whole row of grinning mahendo'sat lazing in front of a canister-surrounded loading area. A ship access gaped ahead. *Mahijiru*, doubtless. "You owe me, mahe, owe me for tools and two good welders, for fake repairs, for doublecross—"

"Good friend, Pyanfar Chanur." A powerful arm shoved her rampward through the gathered mahendo'sat, and she spun about and cast an indignant look back before Goldtooth wrapped his arm into a tighter grip and hastened her up the ramp. "Good friend. Remember I save your neck, a?"

"Present," she muttered, stalking along the accessway. "Present." But she went, and stopped inside the lock, while some of the mahendo'sat who had trooped after them poured past into the interior corridors. Goldtooth turned sober for the moment, and she liked that less. Her ears were flat. "What kind present, huh?"

The mahe winked, decidedly a wink, this trader who was no trader, who played what he was not, with *Mahijiru* which was not the slow-moving freighter it looked to be. "Good see you one piece, hani."

"Huh." Her mouth pursed in better humor, in deliberate good humor. She slapped the mahe on the arm, claws not quite pulled. "Same good

3

see you, Ana Ismehanan-min. You still play merchant?"

"We trade sometime, keep us same honest."

"Present, a?"

The mahe looked to his left where the towering black wall of mahe crew parted. Pyanfar looked—and her ears went up and her mouth fell open at the gangling stsho-cloaked apparition in the doorway to *Mahijiru's* inmost corridors. A mostly hairless face with mane and beard like spun daylight; a face like nothing in civilized space.

"O gods," she said, and whirled about, heading for the airlock, but the mahendo'sat had it packed.

"Pyanfar," the human said.

She turned, ears flat. "Tully," she said in despair, and lost the rest of her dignity as the human hastened to fling his arms about her. His clothes reeked of mahen incense.

"Pyanfar," Tully said, and straightened up and towered over her, grinning like a mahe and trying to stop it, for he knew better. *"Py-an-far."* In evident delight.

That was the limit of his conversation. That mouth was never made for hani speech. Goldtooth set his hand possessively on Tully's shoulder and squeezed.

"Fine present, a, Pyanfar?"

"Where'd you find him?"

The mahen captain shrugged. "Come all the way mahen trader name *Ijir*, long time mahen ship, all time want you, Pyanfar Chanur, crazy mad human. Come find you, come find you, all he know."

She looked up at Tully, who stood there with something brimming over in him, who had no possible business where he was, in mahendo'sat transport, light-years from human territory, in a zone where humankind was banned.

"No," she said to Goldtooth. "No. Absolutely not. He's your problem."

"He want find you," Goldtooth said. "Friend. Where your sentiment?"

"Gods rot you—gods rot you, Goldtooth. Why? For what? What's he want?"

"Want talk you. Your friend, hani, good friend, a?"

"Friend. You earless, mangy bastard. I just got my papers clear—*You know what it cost?*"

"Trade." Goldtooth came close and put his arm conspiratorially about her shoulders. She stood like rock, laid back her ears and grinned into his face in chill reception. "Trade, hani. You want make deal?"

"You want to lose that arm?"

Primate fangs gleamed gold. "Rich, hani. Rich—and powerful. You want this human trade? Got. —Look this face—"

"Have I got a choice?"

5

A wider grin. "Loyal friend. Want you do a thing for me. Want you make this human happy, a? Want you take him to Personage. Want you take him to the *han*. Make all round happy. Got trade, hani. Profits."

"Sure, profits." She shoved back at arm's length and stared up at that earnest mahen face. "Profits like last time, like bills up to the overhead, like hani barred six months from Meetpoint and *The Pride* out a gods-rotted year—"

"Like stsho got lot gratitude hani save their hides, a?"

"Same as the mahendo'sat. Same as the mahe who double-crossed me—"

Black palms lifted. "Not my fault, not my fault. Stsho close Meetpoint, what I do?"

"Snatch the trade, what else? What route you been running?"

"You take him, a?"

"You brought him here. Friend. It's all yours. So's the lawsuit. *You* explain it to the stsho!"

"Got *trade*, Pyanfar—"

"And get embargoed? Gods rot, you earless lunatic! You try to do for the rest of my business? The stsho—"

"Pyanfar." He took her by both shoulders. "Pyanfar. I tell you, one paper this human got, he read for you this paper. They send him, this humanity. They got trade. Big business, maybe

6

much big thing the Compact ever see. You got share."

She drew a deep, long, mahe-flavored breath. "Favors, Goldtooth?"

"A," he laughed, and hugged her shoulder with bone-crushing force. "Promise, hani. I make promise, keep. Got business. Got go. You take this human. Don't I make promise you get share human trade? I keep. This human come to me, I find my old friend Pyanfar for him. You want share, you take. But you got do this thing."

"Now we get to it. Why?"

"Got business. Got go fix."

"Got business—*How'd* you get here? How'd you just happen to pull in on my tail?"

"Know you come, old friend. I lie off and wait."

"How'd you know? *I* didn't, till the papers cleared at Kura."

"Got contacts. Know you got that stsho business clear. So you come here soon."

"Gods rot your hide, mahe. That's a lie."

Dark eyes glittered, shifted. "Say then I follow you from Urtur."

"With *him*? Out of mahen space? No way, egg-sucker. How'd you arrange it?"

The hand dropped from her shoulder. "You sharp dealer, hani."

"What say instead the stsho kept *Mahijiru* off Meetpoint docking lists. Say you were here all along, blocked off the lists. Waiting for me."

"You got lot suspicion."

"I got gods-rotted plenty suspicion, you earless foundling bastard. Give me the truth."

"Might say."

"Might say. Might say— The stsho know he's here?"

"Know."

"Then who are you hiding from?" And on a second thought: "*O gods!*"

"Got kif trouble."

"Gods rot you, then *you* take him! You take this whole business and—"

"Good, brave friend. Kif spies already here. *Han* spies too. Got *han* deputy ship in port. Know we meet. After this they got plenty curiosity. So you got risk already, hani. Don't want profit too? Besides, you hurt his feeling. Hurt mine."

She stood still, a long, long time. Her claws flexed out. She drew them in, with a long slow breath. "Gods rot your—"

"Give you fair deal, Pyanfar. Number one fine deal. Know you got troubles. You got *han* trouble. You promise human trade, you don't got. Lose face. You got mate troubles—"

"Shut up."

"I keep promise, Pyanfar. You want share profit, you got share risk."

"Share suicide. What you think I am?"

"You get human trade, your enemies can't

8

touch you, a, hani captain? The *han*—don't like you lose face. You get rich, keep your brother life, keep your mate. Keep *The Pride*."

A narrow darkness closed in on her sight, hunter-vision set on Goldtooth. It was difficult to hear, so tight her ears were folded. She deliberately raised them, looked about her, at Tully's distressed face.

"I take him," she said to Goldtooth, a small, strangled breath. "*If*—"

"If?"

"—if we get letter of credit at mahe facilities. Good anywhere. Unlimited."

"God! You think I Personage?"

"I think you next best thing, you rag-eared conniving bastard! I think you got that power, I think you got any gods-rotted credit you want, like what you pulled on me at Kirdu, like—"

"You dream." Goldtooth laid a blunt-clawed hand on his breast. "I captain. Got no credit like that."

"Good-bye." She faced about, bared teeth at the crowd blocking her retreat. "You going to move this lot? Or do I move them for you?"

"I write," he said.

She faced him with ears flat. Held out her hand.

He held out his to one of the mahe at his side. "Tablet," he said, and that one vanished

9

hurriedly into the inner corridor with a spatter of bare mahen feet and non-retracting claws.

"Better," said Pyanfar.

Goldtooth scowled, took the tablet the breathless mahe brought back to him, removed its stylus and wrote. He withdrew a Signature from the belt that crossed his chest and inserted it; the tablet spat out its seal-stamped document. He held it.

"I'll translate that," Pyanfar said, "first thing."

"You one bastard, Pyanfar." Goldtooth's grin looked astonishingly hani in his dark mahen face. "One sure bastard. No—" He drew it back as she held out her hand; he turned and handed it instead to Tully, who looked at them both confusedly. "Let *him* hold. He bring. With other documents."

"If that paper doesn't say what it had better say—"

"You do what? Toss good friend Tully out airlock? You no do."

"Oh, no. No such thing. I pay debts where they're due, old friend."

Goldtooth's grin spread. He thrust the tablet into a crewman's hands and clapped her on the arm. "You thank me someday."

"You can bet I will. Everything I owe. I find a way. How you going to get him to *The Pride*? Tell me that! You walk him up to my lock, I fix your ears."

"Got special canister." Goldtooth held out his hand. "Customs papers," he said, and a crewman held out another tablet and stylus. "You take cargo, a? *Shishu* fruit. Dried fish. Got four cans. One all rigged, number one good lifesupport. Pass him that way."

She shook her head to clear it, stared at him afresh. "I'm going mad. That trick's got white hairs. Why don't you just roll him up in a carpet, for the gods' sake, and dump him on my deck? Deliver him in a basket, why don't you? Good gods, what am I doing here?"

"Still good trick. You want this honest citizen, you pay duty, ha?"

She drew her ears down tight, snatched the tablet and furiously appended her own signature, handwritten. She shoved it back at the mahe crewman who dared no expression at her at all.

"Fish," she said in disgust.

"Cheapest duty. What you want, pay more? I tell you, got thing fixed."

"I'll bet you do."

"Customs ask no question. Number one fixed."

"I've got questions. I've got plenty of questions. You set me up, you egg-sucking bastard. So I take this deal. But by-the-gods you tell me everything you know. *What* kif trouble? Where are they working? Are they on your tail right now?"

"Always got kif at Meetpoint."

"Then why come here, for the gods' sakes? What are you doing here? The kif know what you've got?"

Goldtooth shrugged. "Maybe."

"From how long? How long you been at this?"

A second shrug. "Packet. In packet got paper tell you. Tully bring in canister. You take, you read all. You run fast. Go Maing Tol, go Personage. Get plenty help from there."

"They on your tail?"

A third shrug.

"Goldtooth, you bastard, how tight?"

"Got trouble," Goldtooth said.

She weighed that. *Mahijiru* in trouble. A mahen hunter-ship with more kif troubles than it could handle. "So you got. Where you go now?"

"Best thing you don't ask."

"Human space?"

"Maybe deep in stsho territory. Read packet. Read packet. Friend."

"Rot you."

"Rot you too," Goldtooth said soberly. His ears stayed up. There were fine wrinkles round his dark eyes. "God save us. Need you, Pyanfar. Need bad."

"Huh." She flicked her ears up with a light chiming of their rings. "I'm not a gods-blessed warship, mahe."

"Know that."

"Sure. Sure." She walked off a pace to get clear breath, looked at Tully, who understood— perhaps a little. Always more than he spoke.

Tully would not lie to her. That much she believed. His silence, his level, unflinching stare now, that vouched for his own honesty in this.

"When bring to you?" Goldtooth asked.

She turned back to him. "Got an appointment in station office. Got to make that. Got to advise my crew. Got to tell them— You give me lot of problems, hear? And you be careful." She extruded a claw and poked Goldtooth hard in the chest, so she saw him wince. "You be careful this package. You be gods-rotted careful, hear?" She meant two things.

"Hear," Goldtooth said, full soberly. He heard both things. She knew.

"Got three days this port," she said. "Got stall three days with gods-rotted kif sniffing round. I pull *The Pride* out sooner, big trouble. Lot of attention. When you go?"

"Deliver package, wait awhile, then go. Got no cargo but fake cans I give to you."

"So." She turned away, met Tully's eyes, patted him very gently on his arm, recalling his fragile skin. "*Safe*, understand. You do what they say. No fear. These mahendo'sat bring you to me. Understand?"

"Yes," Tully said, and looked at her in that way he had, his pale stare desperately intense.

Her ears twitched, her nostrils widened with
the scent of something more than Meetpoint-
sized amiss, more than a corrupt stsho and
closed routes and xenophobe stsho councils
back in Llyene, atwitter over humanity that
wanted *through* stsho space. Mahen connivances.
Kif greed. She looked back at Goldtooth. "Pres-
ents. One fine present. Ha!"

Goldtooth lifted his head, his brown eyes
half-lidded. "Tell you this, old friend. Kif don't
forget. They hunt me. Soon hunt you. Not
revenge. Kif-thought. *Skikkik*. Hunt me, hunt
you. Tully come here— Got one fine trouble
this time. This business Tully bring us only—
hurry things. Make timetable ours, not kif's."

"Huh," she said. "So I take this gift. I don't
like things coming at my back. You watch
yourself. You run far, mahe. You do good. Wish
you luck."

"You got," Goldtooth said. "Wish you luck,
hani."

She flicked her ears, indecisive, turned and
stalked out the airlock through the parting crowd
of tall mahendo'sat.

Luck.

Luck indeed.

Her mind was not in it as she walked on
down the dock. It kept sorting troubles past
and troubles future—*dangerous*, she thought,

catching a whiff of some scent not mahendo'sat nor stsho, but something she could not, in this large, cold space . . . identify.

Cargo, maybe. Maybe something else. It set her nose to twitching and set an itch between her shoulderblades.

She did not look about, here on Meetpoint's docks, padding along the cold deckplates, beside the gapings of ship accesses, out of which wafted more friendly scents. There were other hani ships at Meetpoint. She had read the list before she had put *The Pride* into dock: *Marrar's Golden Sun; Ayhar's Prosperity;* oh, yes, and *Ehrran's Vigilance.* That ship. *That* one, that Goldtooth had mentioned, but not by name . . . that *han's* eyes, which were doubtless on other business at the moment, but which were capable of catching small furtive moves—like a Chanur captain paying calls on mahen ships.

There were a dozen other mahen vessels in port: *Tigimiransi, Catimin-shai, Hamarandar* were some she had known for years. And familiar stsho names, like *Assustsi, E Mnestsist, Heshtmit* and *Tstaarsem Nai.* Round the wheel of Meetpoint, beyond the great lock that separated oxy- from methane-breathers, ships went by stranger titles: tc'a and knnn and chi names, if knnn had names at all. *Tho'o'oo* and *T'T' Tmmmi* were tc'a/chi ships she had seen on docking lists before.

And kif. Of course there were kif. She had made a particular point to know those names before she put *The Pride* in dock ... names like *Kekt* and *Harukk*, *Tikkukkar*, *Pakakkt*, *Maktikkh*, *Nankktsikkt*, *Ikhoikttr*. Kif names, she memorized wherever she found them, a matter of policy—to recall their routes, their dockings, where they went and trading what.

The kif watched her routes with as much interest this last year. She was very sure of that.

She did not loiter on the docks, but she made no particular haste which might attract attention on its own. She stared at this and that with normal curiosity, and at the same general pace she strolled up to the nearest com booth along the row of dockside offices, keyed up Chanur credit and punched in the code for the station comlink to *The Pride*'s bridge. She waited. The com whistled and clicked through nine cycles unanswered.

There was a kif on the docks. She spied the tall, black-robed form standing over shipside in conversation with a stsho, whose pale arms waved emphatically. She stood with her back to the plastic wall and watched this exchange past the veil of other traffic, the passing of service vehicles, of pedestrians, mostly stsho, pale-robed and elegant; here and there mahendo'sat, dark and sleek. Something winged whip-

16

ped past, small and upward bound for the heights of the tall, cold dock.

Gods only knew what *that* was.

Click. "*Pride of Chanur,*" the voice finally answered. "Deck officer speaking."

"Haral, gods rot you, how long does it take?"

"Captain?"

"Who's out?"

"Outside?"

"*I want that cargo inventoried.* Hear? I want all of you on it, right now. No liberties. If anyone's out, get her back. Right now."

"Aye," the voice came back, diffident. "Aye, Captain." There was question in the voice.

"Just do it!"

"Aye. But—Captain?"

"What?"

"*Na* Khym's out."

"*Gods* and thunders!" Her heart fell through her feet. "Where'd he go?"

"Don't know. To the free market, I think— There some kind of trouble?"

"I'm coming back. *Get him,* Haral. I want him found."

"Aye, Captain."

She slammed the receiver down and headed back toward the ship in haste.

Khym, for the gods' sake. Her mate, gone strolling out in fullest confidence that papers in order meant safety . . . on a stsho trading station, where weapons were banned, as he had gone out of ship at Urtur and Hoas among mahendo'sat; as he had gone wandering wherever he liked through the last two markets—male, and duty-less and bored.

Gods. O gods.

She remembered the kif then, looked back, one injudicious glance over her shoulder, breaking the rest of her precautions.

The kif was still there, looking her way beyond the gesticulating stsho, looking black and grim and interested.

She flung around again and moved as fast as a walk could carry her, past *Mahijiru* behind its darkened (malfunctioning?) registry board, past one berth and the other in the chill, stsho-made air.

She was panting in earnest when she came within sight of *The Pride's* berth. Everything was stopped there. The machinery that ought to be offloading stood still with cans still on the ramp. Haral was outside waiting for her, red-gold figure in blue breeches; and spying her, came her way with scurrying haste.

"Captain—" Haral skidded up and braked, claws raking on the plates. "We're looking."

"Kif are out," Pyanfar said. That was enough. Haral's ears went flat and her eyes went wide. "With Ehrran clan in port. I want him *back*, Haral. Where'd he talk about going? Doing what?"

"Didn't talk, Captain. We were all busy. He was there by us at the ramp. When we looked round—gone."

"Gods rot him!"

"Can't have gotten far."

"Sure he can't." She took the pocket com Haral offered her and clipped it to her belt to match what Haral had. "Who's on bridge?"

"No one. I stayed. Alone."

"Hilfy's out there."

"First."

"Lock up. Come with me."

"Aye!" Haral snapped, spun on her heel and ran.

Pyanfar strode on.

Market, she reckoned. Meetpoint's famed Free Market was far and away the likeliest place to look. Baubles and exotics. Things to see.

He might have tried the restaurants before the market.

Or the bars of the Rows.

Gods rot him. Gods rot her soft-headedness in ever taking him aboard. On Anuurn they called her mad. At times like this she believed it, all the way.

She was breathing in great side-aching gasps when Haral came pelting back to fall in at her side.

"He's not here," Hilfy said—youngest of *The Pride*: her left ear one-ringed, her beard only

19

beginning, her breeches the tough blue cloth of hani crew, though she was ker Hilfy, Chanur's someday heir. She met Tirun Araun between two aisles of the dock bazaar, among the stacks of cloth, foodstuffs, the fluttering of stsho merchants. Fluting cries of exotic nonsapients legal here for trade, the shouts of traders and passersby, music from the bars of the Rows alongside the market—echoed off the lofty overhead in one commingled roar. Smells abounded, drowning other scents. Color rioted. "I've been down every aisle, Tirun—"

"Try the Rows," said Tirun, older spacer. Her beard was full; her mane hung wild about her shoulders. Her left ear flicked, clashing half a dozen rings. "Come on. I take evens, you take odds. Hit every bar on the Rows. He might have, gods only know."

Hilfy gulped air and went, not questioning the orders as Haral herself had not questioned what had happened, except that something had gone wrong. Very wrong. That had been a coded call to get off the docks. At once. Her ears kept lying back on their own; she pricked them up with spasmodic efforts, seeking a hani voice through the din, from out of the row of spacer bars that lined the marketplace.

No sign of any hani in the first bar on the row. It was all mahendo'sat inside, honking music and the raucous screech and stamp of drunken spacers.

She crossed Tirun's path on the walk on the way out and they split again into the third and fourth bar.

Stsho, this den. But she spotted the red-gold of hani backs clustered about a bowl-table, dived through and slid to her knees on the rim. A senior hani spacer turned round and eyed her; other eyes turned her way, all round the table. She bobbed a hasty bow with hands gripping the rim.

"Hilfy Chanur par Faha, gods look on you— you seen a hani male?"

Ears laid back and pricked in non-sobriety all round the table, six pairs of ears heavy with rings. "Gods—what you been drinking, kid?"

"Sorry." That was a mistake. She scrambled to her feet and started away; but the spacer swayed erect, waved wildly for balance as she clawed her unsteady way up the plastic bowlseat to catch her arm. "Hani male, hey? Need help, Chanur? Where you see this vision, hey?"

There were derisive laughs, curses—someone was trodden on. The rest of the hani came up on the seat and scrambled out of the pit. Hilfy tore loose and fled. "Hey," she heard at her back, hani-cough, a drunken roar.

"Pay!" A shrill stsho warble from another side. "Pay, hani bastard—"

"Charge it to Ayhar's Prosperity!"

"O gods!" Hilfy dived for the exit, just as a

pair of kifish patrons loomed in the doorway. Black musty robes brushed her with a smell that sent the wind up her back. She did not look back or pause as she dived past them both. "*Hani rabble!*" she heard hissed behind her, the noise of drunken encounter mingled with kifish voices.

She darted through the outer doors into the light of the market, blinked, hesitating on one foot, hearing above the market noise the sound of hani in full chase behind her—no sight of Tirun. She leaned into a run and plunged into the next odd-numbered bar—stsho again, not a sight of hani. She pelted back out the doors, through the incoming mass of Ayhar clan, who began a turnabout in that doorway in merry disorder.

Still no Tirun. She dived into the next odd-number, another stsho den, saw a tall red shape, and heard the voices, a deeper hani voice than this port had ever heard, the chitter of stsho curses, the snarl of mahendo'sat.

"*Na* Khym," she cried in profoundest relief. "*Na* Khym!" She eeled her way through the towering crowd at the bar and grabbed him by the arm. "Uncle—thank the gods. Pyanfar wants you. Now. Right now, *na* Khym."

"Hilfy?" he said, far from focused. He swayed there, a head taller than she, twice her breadth of shoulder, his broad, scarred nose wrinkled in confusion. "Trying to explain to these fellows—"

"Uncle, for the gods' sakes—"

"He *is*," a hani voice cried from the door. "By the gods—what's *he* doing here?"

Khym flinched, faced about with his back to the bar, starting with misgiving at the drunken Ayhar spacers.

"Hey!" —A second hani voice, from among the Ayhar. "Chanur! You crazy, Chanur? What are you up to, huh, bringing him out here? You got no regard for him?"

"Come on," Hilfy pleaded. "*Na* Khym—" She tugged at a massive arm, felt the tension in it. "For gods' sake, *na* Khym—we've got an emergency."

Maybe that got through. Khym shivered, one sharp tremor, like an earthquake through solid stone.

"Get, get, get!" a stsho shrilled in pidgin. "Get out he my bar!"

Hilfy pulled with all her might. Khym yielded and kept walking, through the hani crowd that drew aside wide-eyed and muttering, past the black wall of curious mahendo'sat and the glitter of their gold.

Another black wall formed athwart the brighter, outside light. Billowing robes blocked the path to the door, two tall, ungainly shapes.

"Chanur," said a kif, a dry clicking voice. "Chanur brings its males out. It needs help."

Hilfy stopped. Khym had, with a rumbling in his throat. "Don't," Hilfy said, "don't do it—Khym, for gods' sakes, just let's get out of here. We don't want a fight."

"Run," the kif hissed. "*Run*, Chanur. You run from kif before."

"Come on." Hilfy wrapped her arm tightly about Khym's elbow. She guided him through the crowd toward the doorway, past the first brush of robes, trying to look noncombatant, trying to watch the whereabouts of dark kifish hands beneath the dusky cloth.

"Hilfy," said Khym.

She looked up. The whole doorway had filled with kif.

"It's got a knife!" A hani voice. "*Look out, kid—*"

Something flew, trailing beer and froth, and hit a kifish head. "Got!" A mahen voice crowed delight. Kif lunged, Khym lunged. Hilfy hit a kif with claws bared and bodies tangled in the doorway. *Yiiii-yinnnnn!* a stsho voice wailed above the din. "*Yeeiei-yi!* Police, police, police!"

"Yaooo!" (The mahendo'sat).

"*Na Khym!*"

Tirun's voice, a roar from outside the tangled doorway, inbound. "Hilfy! *Na Khym! Chanur!*"

"*Ayhar, ai Ayhar!*"

"*Catimin-shai!*"

Mugs and bottles sailed.

*　　*　　*

"He's on the Rows! Hurry!" Haral's voice came from the pocket com; and Pyanfar, delaying for a check of eat-shops outside the market, started to run for all she was worth, past startled mahendo'sat and stsho who leapt from her path, herself dodging round the confused course of a methane-breather vehicle that zigged away on another tack.

Sirens sounded. The three-story bulkhead doors of the market sector were blinking with red warning lights. She put on a final burst of speed and dived through asprawl as the valves began to move. The edges met with a boom and airshock that shook the deck, drowning the din of howls beyond, and she gathered herself up off the deck plates and ran without even a backward look.

The whole market was in turmoil. Merchants or looters snatched armfuls of whatever they could; aisles jammed. Animals screeched above the roar. A black thing darted past Pyanfar's legs and yelped at being trodden on. She vaulted a counter, scrambled on a rolling scatter of trinkets, found a clear aisle and ran toward the Rows where a moment's clear sight showed a heaving mass in the doorway. Stsho darted from that crowd, pale and gibbering; drunken mahendo'sat stayed to yell odds—a pair of hani arrived from the other direction: Chur and Geran headed full tilt toward the mass.

She jerked spectators this way and that, care-
less of her claws. Mahendo'sat howled outrage and moved. A kif-shape darted past her,
moving faster than clear sight. She caught at it
and got only robe as she broke through to the
center of the mob. Plastic splintered. Glass broke,
bodies rolled underfoot.

More kif ran from the scene, a scatter of
black-robed streaks outward bound at speed.

"Khym!" Pyanfar yelled and flung herself in
the path of his wild-eyed rush after the kif.
Behind him Haral and Geran added themselves;
Chur and Tirun followed. Hilfy jumped last,
atop the heap on Khym's shoulders as it all
came down in front of her.

They stopped him. They held him down until the struggles ceased.

There was mahen laughter, quickly hushed.
In prudence, mahe drew back to perimeters,
while the noise of looting went on in the market,
the crash of glass, the splintering of plastics,
the polyglot wails of outrage and avarice.

"Gods rot you!" Pyanfar yelled, with a claws-
out swipe at anything too near. "Get!"

Mahendo'sat gave her room. A small knot of
hani spacers stood facing her. Ears were back.
The Pride's crew gained their feet, Haral foremost, ears laid back and grinning. Khym levered himself to his feet with Tirun holding fast
to his right arm and Hilfy locked to the other

side. The last sounds of combat died inside the bar. A last glass broke.

"Pyanfar Chanur," a broadnosed hani said in stark, disapproving tones.

"Tell it to your captain," said Pyanfar. "Tell it proper. He's my husband. You hear? *Na Khym nef Mahn*. Hear me?"

Ears flicked. Eyes showed whites. The news had not gotten this far out, what lunacy she had done. Now it did. "Sure," a younger hani said, backing up. "Sure, captain."

And Chur, at her back: "Captain—we'd better get out of here."

She heard the sirens. She looked about past the melting crowd, who sought other bars. Trampled bodies stirred within the doorway.

There were cars coming up the dock, with the white strobe flash of Security.

Chapter Two

The door hissed back and revealed two guards, which at Meetpoint might have been any oxy-breathing kind but stsho, considering the stsho's congenital distrust of violence. They hired all their security. Fortunately for the peace at present, these were both mahendo'sat.

Pyanfar stopped in her pacing of the narrow room—*waiting area*, they had called it: stsho euphemism. Other species had other names for such small rooms with doorlocks facing outward. "Where's my crew?" she spat at the mahendo'sat forthwith, ears flattened despite herself. "Gods rot it, where are they?"

"Director wants," one said, standing aside from the door. "You come now, hani captain."

She pulled in her claws and came, since something finally seemed in movement, and since neither of the two mahendo'sat were armed with more than nature gave them and showed no desire for confrontation. They would not talk, not this pair; not threaten or swerve from duty: mahendo'sat at punctilious, honest best.

"Here," was their only other word, at a lift door some distance through the maze.

More traveling. The lift went a long zigzag distance through Meetpoint's bowels, and let them out again in white, pastel-decorated halls. Lights obtruded here and there in seeming random—stsho, this section, not making apology to other species' tastes, all pastels and opal colors, vast spaces, odd-angled panels riddled with random holes and alcoves. The tall black-furred, black-kilted mahen guards and the splash of her own scarlet trousers and red-gold hide were equally alien here.

A last door, a last hallway of twisting plasti-form shapes. She flicked her ears so that the rings chimed, flexed her claws with one deep breath as if she contemplated a leap from some height, and let herself be shown into a pearl-toned hall, a splendor of bizarre walls and white-upholstered depressions in the level, gleaming floor. One gossamer-clad stsho stood to meet them, recorder in hand. Another sat serenely important in the central bowl. *Gtst*—(stsho had three sexes at one time, and neither he, she, nor it was really adequate) *gtst* was ornamented in subtlest colors ranging into hues invisible to hani eyes, but detectible at the verges, whites with low violet shimmerings on the folds. *Gtst* tattooings were equally illusory on *gtst* naturally pearly skin, and shaded off into green and violets. Pearl-toned plumes nodded from augmented brows, shading moonstone eyes. The small mouth was clamped in disapproving straightness and nostrils flared in busy alternation.

Pyanfar bowed before this elegance, once and shortly. The stsho waved a languid hand and the servant-translator, it must be, came and stood near, *gtst* own robes floating free on invisible breezes—stsho-silk and expensive.

"Ndisthe," Pyanfar said, "sstissei asem sisth an zis—" with the right amount of respect, she reckoned. Feathery eyebrows fluttered. The assistant clutched *gtst* recorder and drew back in indecision.

"Shiss." The Director motioned with one elegant jeweled hand. The translator stopped in *gtst* retreat. "Shiss. Os histhe Chanur nos schensi noss' spitense sthshosi chisemsthi."

"Far from fluent," Pyanfar agreed.

The Director drew breath. *Gtst* plumes all nodded in profound agitation. "Sto shisis ho weisse gti nurussthe din?"

"Did you know—" The translator flung gtstself into belated action. "—the riot in the market took four hours to stop?"

"—ni shi canth-men horshti nin."

"—Forty-five individuals are treated in infirmary—"

Pyanfar kept her ears erect, her expression sympathetic.

"Ni hoi shisisi ma gnisthe."

"—and extensive pilferage has taken place."

"I do share," said Pyanfar, drawing down her mouth in yet more distress, "your outrage at this disregard for stsho authority. My crew likewise suffered from this kifish banditry."

That got rendered, with much fluttering of hands.

"Shossmemn ti szosthenshi hos! Ti mahenthesai cisfe llyesthe to mistheth hos!"

"—You and your mahendo'sat co-conspirators have wreaked havoc—"

"Spithi no hasse cifise sif nan hos!"

"—involved the kif—"

"Shossei onniste stshoni no misthi th'sa has lles nan shi math!"

"—A tc'a ship has undocked and fled during the riot. Doubtless the chi are disturbed—"

"Ha nos thei no llen llche knnni na slastheni hos!"

"—Who knows but what this may also agitate the knnn?"

"Nan nos misthei hoisthe ifsthen noni ellyes-
theme to Nifenne hassthe shasth!"

"—You and your crew within three hours of
docking have created havoc with every species
of the Compact!"

Pyanfar set her hands at her belt and lowered
her ears deliberately. "As well say all victims
of crime are guilty of incitement! Is this a new
philosophy?"

A long silence once that was translated. Then:

"—I am put in mind of papers lately recovered, hani captain. I am in mind of heavy fines
and penalties. Who will recompense our market?
Who will see to our damages?"

"It's true," Pyanfar said with a direct, baleful
stare. "Who dares charge the kif—excepting
hani. Excepting us, esteemed Director. Tell me,
what would happen without hani traffic here?
Without mahendo'sat? How would the kif be-
have at Meetpoint then? Not simple pilferage,
I'll warrant!"

Plumes fluttered. Round eyes stared, dark
centered. "—You make threats without teeth.
The han does not bend at your breath. Less so
the mahendo'sat."

"Neither will the han look with favor on a
hani ship beset, on a hani captain detained—I
omit mention of the locked door!"

"—Have you such confidence you will relate
to the han how a Chanur captain suffered such

embarrassment? I have heard otherwise. I have heard Chanur's affairs are less than stable with the *han* in these days."

Pyanfar drew a long, long breath, wrinkling up her nose so that the translator drew back a pace. "There is no profit in such a wager, esteemed Director."

"—What profit to any dealing with Chanur? We restore your papers and see how you repay us. Where are our damages? Where will you obtain the funds, who claim to be a terror to the kif? We fine you. You dare take nothing from them."

"They by the gods steal nothing from *us* except where we have relied on stsho authority."

The moonstone eyes acquired wider, darker centers. "—You have brought a male of your kind here. I hesitate to breach this delicacy, but it is well known that this gender of your species is unstable. This surely contributed—"

"This is a hani affair."

"—Other hani find the state of affairs on your ship disturbing and improper."

"A hani matter."

"—A deputy of the *han* has shown concern. The deputy has assured me that this is not new policy, that the *han* deplores this action—"

"It's none of the deputy's gods-rotted business. Or anyone else's. Let's stay to the issue of safety on the docks."

"—Hani have not found it wise to bring their males into foreign contacts, for which they are naturally unsuited and unprepared. Other hani are shocked at your provocation."

"The docks, esteemed director. And public safety."

"—You have violated law. You have brought this person—"

"A member of my crew."

"—This person has a license?"

"He's got a temporary. All in order. Ask your own security."

"—A permit granted at Gaohn station. By a Chanur ally, doubtless under pressure. He is here without permissions—"

"Since when does Compact law require permissions for listed crew?"

"—Since when does listed crew take liberty during unloading and visit bars?"

"This is my ship and my affair!"

"—It became a stsho affair."

"Indeed it did! And any other question is utter persiflage. Let us stay to the issue: a kif attack on personnel of my ship; on *personnel of my ship*, who relied on the security assured by stsho law and custom. We have suffered outrage; *I* have suffered personal outrage in being detained for hours while kif assassins doubtless do as they please on the docks, to the hazard of life and property, some of which is mine—and who guarantees the safety of my goods waiting loading, when we are the victims of this outrage? I hold the station responsible. Where are my crew, esteemed Director? And who pays the indemnities we're due?"

This was perhaps too much. The translator wrung gtst hands and stammered on the words, bowed like a reed in the wind on receiving the reply.

"—Why not ask the mahendo'sat you conferred with?"

Pyanfar's ears went tight against her skull. She brought them up with utmost effort, smoothed her nose and assumed a bland expression. "Would the director mean perhaps the mahendo'sat whose registry board malfunctioned in this well-ordered station?"

Another exchange. The translator's skin lost its pearly sheen and went dead white. "—The director says gtst knows about this board. A subordinate has been disapproved in this malfunction."

"It would be impolite to suggest higher connections. It would be stupid to doubt them."

The translator made several gasps for air and performed, with further hand-wringing. "—The subordinate in question had no inkling of higher complicities, such as you and your co-conspirators arranged. This mahen ship has elected departure during the disturbance. The disturbance reached also to the methane-breathers. The director asks—are you aware of this? Are you aware of hazards with tc'a and chi?"

"Not my affair. Absolutely not my affair."

"—The director asks—do you want the merchandise this person left?"

Pyanfar took in her breath, feeling an impact in the gut.

"—It is," the translator rendered the next remark, "perishable."

"I take it then station will deliver this merchandise . . . recognizing its obligation."

"—There are entanglements. There is, for instance, the question of our damages. This shipment is impounded."

"*I refuse to be held to account for thieving kif!* Take it up with the mahendo'sat you dealt with!"

"I cannot translate this," the translator said. *Gtst* eyes were round. "I beg the esteemed hani captain—"

"Tell *gtst* if I behaved as the kif did *gtst* would not be speaking to me about damages."

"*Ashosh!*" the Director said: the translator turned and folded *gtst* hands on *gtst* breast, lisped in softest tones, turned with moonlike eyes at widest.

"—We will speak of damages later. Now this merchandise, this—*perishable* merchandise."

Pyanfar set her hands within her belt, stood

with feet set. "In the estimable Director's personal keeping, I trust."

"—Four canisters. Am I a menial, to keep such goods personally?"

"Gods rot it—" She amended that, flicking up her ears, trying for a quieter tone. "Considering they are perishable, I trust there is some care being taken."

The translator relayed it. The Director waved a negligent hand. *Gtst* eyes were unblinking, hard. "—Customs matters. Unfortunately the consignor in his haste for departure left papers in disarray, lacking official stamps. Have you suggestions, hani captain, that would prevent this property being sold at public auction? There would, I am certain, be interested bidders—some very rich. Some with backers. Unless the esteemed Chanur captain takes personal responsibility."

A blackness closed about the edges of the room, on everything but the graceful nodding stsho.

"—Also," the stsho continued, "the matter of papers lately cleared. This station is dismayed . . . utterly dismayed at the betrayal of its trust. I am personally distressed."

"Let's talk," Pyanfar said, "about things good merchants like us both understand. Like fair trade. Like *deal*. Like I take my small difficulty out of Meetpoint within a few hours after getting my cargo in order, and I take it elsewhere without a word to anyone about bribes and mahendo'sat. You want to talk trouble, esteemed Director? You want to talk kif trouble, and word of this getting back to your upper echelons? Or do you want to talk about the merchandise, and finding my crew, and letting me take this off your hands—*with* my permits in order—before it gets more expensive for your station than it already is?"

The translator winced, turned and began to render it in one hand-waving spate.

"Ashosh!" the Director said; and other things. A flush came and went over *gtst* skin, mottlings of nacre. The nostrils flared in rapid unison. "Chanur sosshis na thosthsi cnisste znei ctehtsi canth hos."

Another flinch from the translator, a rounding of round shoulders as *gtst* turned.

"Tell *gtst*," Pyanfar said without waiting, "*gtst* is in personal danger. From the kif, of course. *Say it!*"

It was rendered. The Director's skin went white. "—Unacceptable. There is a debt which in your doubtless adequate if unimaginative perception you must acknowledge was incurred by your crew, to have released a member of your species widely acknowledged to be unstable—"

"A member of my crew and my mate, you fluttering bastard!"

Nostrils flared. "—The debt stands. No agreement embraced such damages."

She drew her own breaths with difficulty, trying to think, hearing words that sent small fine tendrils into quite different territory. *Goldtooth, blast you— There was a setup, all the way. . . .*

And her ears sank, so that the translator edged back a pace, gtst eyes wide and showing the whites about the moonstone round of them. The director's plumes fluttered, hands moved nervously.

"I make you a deal," she said. "We get that cargo, we get the money for you."

"—You will sign affidavits of responsibility."

"Don't push it, stsho."

"—Your visa is canceled," the answer came back. "And the visas of your crew and this male hani, under whatever pretext you secured civilized permits for this unstable person. You will forfeit your permission to enter our docks and forfeit any Chanur ship's clearance to dock here until this debt is paid!"

"And this cargo?"

"Do you doubt us? I make you a gift of it. In appreciation for your own damages, of course."

Pyanfar bowed. Gtst waved a hand at gtst attendant.

"Sthes!"

It was not at all the courteous farewell.

*   *   *

More corridors. There was an affidavit to be signed, the terms of which set a cold misery at her stomach. She looked up from the counter and the stsho clerk backed all the way around the desk dropping papers as gtst went.

"That do it?" she asked with, she thought, remarkable calm.

The stsho babbled, refusing to come closer.

"—Gtst say got more," one of the guards translated. She had heard that much. She wrinkled her nose and the stsho dropped more papers, gathered them, gave them to the mahendo'sat to avoid bringing gtstself closer.

"Customs release, hani captain. All fine you sign this."

"Wait, hani captain. Must secure permission to leave."

She drew small even breaths, signed this, signed that, kept directing no more than baleful stares at the stsho official and gtst fluttering aides.

At last: "No more forms?"

"No, hani captain. All got."

"Crew," she demanded, for the third time and this time with a broad, broad smile.

"Ship, hani captain; they long time got release. Same got release Ayhar clan. We go you ship now."

"Huh," she said then, and took the open

41

door, stalked out, with her mahen escort to key
the lift for her.

No other word. None seemed apt. She stared
at the uninteresting pearl-gray of the lift doors
while the lift zigged and zagged its way through
Meetpoint station.

She thought, during that interval. Thought
very dark wordless thoughts that involved stsho
hides and a certain mahe's neck, until the lift
stopped and opened its doors on the cold air
and noise of dockside.

She oriented herself with a quick glance at
the nearest registry board, a black, green-lit
square above the number 14 berth: *Assustsi*.
She drew a cold, wide-nostriled breath of the
dockside taint—oil and coolants, cargo and food-
smells and all the mongrel effluvium of Meetpoint, like and unlike every other station of the
Compact.

Leftward was *Vigilance*'s berth, number 18.
Ehrran clan ship. Doubtless someone of the
deputy's staff was nosedeep in reports, writing
it all up for the *han* in the worst possible light.
Gods knew what that white-skinned bastard
had spilled to willing ears.

Or what Ayhar had had to say, to save its
own skin. Gods-be-bound that *Prosperity* and
Ayhar would never claim responsibility, financial or otherwise.

Chanur's enemies in council would pounce on it, first chance.

She started walking, constantly aware of the two dark shadows that stalked behind her, but ignoring them. Gantries towered and tilted in the curved perspectives of the station wheel. The dock unfurled down off the curtaining horizon as she walked, and she made out *The Pride*'s berth, counting down from fourteen to six.

There should have been canisters outside *The Pride*'s berth. She made out none, and thought further dark thoughts, still not looking back.

She passed berth 10, which had been *Mahijiru*. That berth was sealed completely, the gantry drawn back with its lines in store-position. Number ten board remained dark, not listing the name or registry of the outbound ship.

Malfunction. Indeed, malfunction.

Connivances, mahendo'sat with stsho—with stsho who ran before every wind that blew—and now, with *Mahijiru* on the run and Goldtooth unable to break the director's neck in person—was the prevailing wind kif-tainted?

It rankled, gods, it rankled, that stsho had dared confront her, stsho, that she could break with one swipe of her arm. And dared not. That was the crux of it. Stsho showed one face to the kif, one to the mahendo'sat—yet a third to hani: *non-spacing*, stsho law had regarded hani till a century ago, because (though hani preferred not to recall the fact) it was the mahendo'sat had given hani ships. *An artificially accelerated culture.* Hani were still banned from stsho space, on their very border. Trade was at Meetpoint only, or inside non-stsho space.

And hani in their good nature were patient with these fluttering dilettantes who bought and sold—everything. They backed Chanur to the wall. It was stsho doing. Everything. And the *han* being political, and the *han* being short-sighted, and most of all because she was a fool who expected otherwise, Chanur was in trouble at home. Of course the stsho knew it, sure as birds knew carrion—had gotten news even a hani ship like *Prosperity* had not; and threw it up in her face at first chance.

Gods, that the *han* fed stsho bigotry and wielded it for a weapon—

A deputy of the han *has shown concern*—

Or—a cold, fully sensible fear got past the outrage: the stsho had independent sources and played everyone for a fool—Goldtooth, the *han*, even the kif. They were capable of that. Thoroughgoing xenophobes and slippery as oiled glass. Lately the stsho had a new xenophobia to keep them busy. They had humankind to worry about, with concerns and motives worldbound hani had no least idea of.

Goldtooth, rot you, how much does gtst know? How much the bribe? Nothing holds a stsho that's already paid.

Nothing persuades one against gtst own profit.

She walked past nine, eight, seven. She saw no activity outside *The Pride*. No sign of any loaders, the cargo ramp withdrawn, the canisters missing. The cans were inside, she hoped. She kept alert for any sight of kif on the docks and found none. The few passersby with business on the dock were mostly stsho, a few mahendo'sat, no hani. If they noticed the rare spectacle of a hani captain being trailed by two hulking mahendo'sat station guards, they gave no sign of it. This was Meetpoint, after all, where folk minded their business, knowing well how trouble tended to travel down line of sight. At the upward-curved limit of the horizon, only its bottom third visible, the great seal of the market zone was still shut, on gods knew what kind of damage. Money was being lost while that market was out of action. Hourly the tab went up.

The Pride's ramp access gaped ahead, berth six. She ignored her escort, not even looking back at them as she took out the pocket com. "Haral. I'm coming in."

No answer.

"Haral." She walked up the rampway into the chill, yellow-lighted access, hearing no footsteps behind—walked warily, thinking of kif ambush even here. Ambush and stsho treacheries.

She met a shut hatch beyond the bend of the tube. She had expected that, and hit the bar of the com unit in the accessway. "Haral. Haral, gods rot it, it's Pyanfar. Open up."

The hatch shot open at once, with a waft of warmer, familiar air. Tirun was there; and Chur, appearing armed from the lower-deck ops room down the corridor. Both showed the plasmed seams of recent wounds on their red-brown hides, Chur with a stripe of plasm visible across the leather of her nose, a painful kind of cut.

"Huh." She walked in past the lock. "Close that. Everyone aboard?"

"All accounted for, nothing serious."

She came to a stop and gave Tirun one long stare. "Nothing serious. *Gods and thunders*, cousin!"

Tirun's ears fell. "On our side," Tirun said.

"Huh." She turned and stalked for the lift, with their company as the inner lock hissed shut at her back. "Where's Khym?"

"*Na* Khym's up in his quarters."

"Good." She shoved that distress to the hindmost, swung about in the lift as they got in with her. Chur anticipated her reach for the button, tucked her arm behind her again in haste when she had pushed it. Pyanfar glared at her. "What else is wrong? What's Haral doing up there?"

"Got a lot of messages in," said Tirun. "Still coming. Board's jammed."

"Huh." The lift slammed upward. Pyanfar studied the door in front of her till it opened and spat them out on main, then strode for the bridge with a cousin on either side. "Who's called in?"

"Stsho, mostly," Chur said. "One message from *Ayhar's Prosperity*. Banny Ayhar requests conference at soonest."

"And some mahen nonsense," said Tirun. "No ship code."

She gave Tirun a second hard look, caught the lowered ears, the tension round the nose. She snorted, walked on into the bridge where Haral stood to meet her, where Hilfy got up from com—o gods, *Hilfy*—with her side patched in bandages. Geran with her right ear plasmed along a rip.

"You all right?" Haral asked. "We got a message from stsho central . . . said you were coming."

"How courteous of them. They give you any trouble?"

"Kept us locked up filling out forms," said Geran. "Sent us out about an hour ago."

"Huh." She sat down in her own place, at *The Pride*'s controls, swung the chair about in its pit to look at the solemn row of faces. Hilfy, her niece, young and white about the eyes just now. Haral and Tirun, tall, wide shouldered, daughters of an elder Chanur cousin; Geran and Chur, wiry and deft, daughters to Jofan Chanur, her third cousins. A row of earnest, sober stares. She gazed last and steadily at her brother Kohan's favorite daughter, at Hilfy Chanur par Faha with a scratch down her comely nose and her ears, gods forfend—plasm on a nick in the left one. Heir to Chanur's mercantile operations, while-and-likely-after Kohan Chanur ruled at home. On the last edge of adolescence. Fearfully proud. Once and silently she wished Hilfy safe at home, but she did not say that. Home was a long, long way away and Chanur interests were at stake.

"I want a watch on com," she said. "I want scan set to alarm if something comes in, if something budges from this station. I don't care what it is. I want to know."

"Aye," said Haral.

"Tully's back."

Ears went up. Eyes went wide. Hilfy sat down. "Good gods," Chur said.

"*Mahijiru*'s here. Was here. Goldtooth's cut loose and run." There were other things to break to them, like being backed into agreements, like a fool of an aging captain who had believed for one moment in a way out of what she had gotten Chanur into, a way into human trade and all it meant. "He was going to slip us a canister with a special cargo. Don't blame me—" She waved a hand. "Goldtooth's originality, gods help us. But the stsho are playing power games. That can's tied up in red tape in customs. I think I've got it fixed."

Chur and Tirun sank into seats where they were, ears back.

"Sorry," Pyanfar said tautly. "Sorry, cousins."

"Got a chance?" Haral asked. Meaning lost trade. Lost chances. A whole variety of things, in loyalty too old to be completely blind. "The mahendo'sat've come through?"

"Don't know. They just headed out and left us the package. There's worse news. The kif are onto it."

"Gods." Geran leaned onto the back of Chur's couch. "And the bar fight—"

"Set up. Absolutely it was a set-up." She recalled with chagrin the kif watcher while she had been on the docks. "Maximum confusion. Goldtooth kited out. Under what circumstances— gods know. Messages were going up and down that dock like chi in a fire drill. Maybe it was a kifish smash-and-grab. Maybe not. Likely it was targeted at the stsho. They've sure got the pressure on."

"The kif know about that can?" Tirun asked.

"Gods-rotted mahe shoved a shipment out in

the middle of bolting dock like their tail was afire—what else could they guess? Gods know who's been bribed. Gods know how long the bribes will hold.—Khym all right, is he?"

Silence for a moment. Haral shrugged uncomfortably. "Guess he is," Haral said.

"He have anything to say?"

"Not much."

"Huh."

"Said he'd be in his quarters."

"Fine." She bit it off. They were blood kin, she and the crew. All Chanur. All with the same at stake, excepting Khym, Mahn-clan, male, past his prime and his reason for living and belonging anywhere. Her brother Kohan Chanur relied on her, back home. Meetpoint in ruins. Kif on the loose. Stsho facing her down. *The Pride* nose-deep in it again. She had gone soft-headed as well as softhearted. Hani everywhere muttered to that effect. Only her long-suffering crew would not say it, even yet. And Hilfy, of course Hilfy. Worship shone undimmed in those young eyes.

Fool kid, she thought. And to the crew at large: "What happened with our cargo out there?"

"Cans on the dock were gone when we got back," Tirun said. "We filed a theft report with station. Cans still inside are safe."

"Kif are *fast*. Power her up. We go on using

station's hookups, but we keep our own on-line. Look sharp, hear? Don't ask me how long this goes on. I don't know. Contact customs. I want to know where that incoming shipment is."

No one mentioned costs or what the stsho might do. No one mentioned licenses, and the docking rights and routes it had cost too much to regain. No one mentioned Khym, a private folly that had long since become a public one. Not a backward look. No protests. Just a quiet moving toward stations, the whine of chairs receiving bodies all about her as she powered her own chair about and keyed in the old com messages.

From a mahendo'sat, unidentified: "I leave paperwork, leave cans same station office. Good voyage. Got go quick. Same you."

She drew one long, quivering breath.

From *Ayhar's Prosperity*: "Banafy Ayhar to Pyanfar Chanur: We have a matter between us. I suggest we keep it private. I suggest you bring your witnesses to my deck. Expecting immediate reply."

"In a mahen hell."

"Captain?"

She restrained herself from violence to the board. "Reply to Ayhar: Tell it to the kif."

"Captain—"

"*Send it.*"

Geran ducked her head and bent to the keys. Other messages crawled past, mostly stsho: a dozen threats of lawsuit from irate bazaar merchants; two scurrilous letters from stsho vessels in port, impugning Chanur sanity; others were rambling. Four were anonymous congratulations in mahen pidgin, some sounding inebriate, one babbling obscure mahen religious slogans and offering support.

From *Vigilance*, not a word.

"Tirun," said Chur behind her. "Got that customs contact." And a moment later:

"Captain," Tirun said. "Got the customs chief on. Claims the papers aren't in order on that shipment."

She spun the chair about. "The Director cleared that! Tell *gtst* so."

"The customs chief says you have to come and sign."

"*I signed that god-rotted thing!*"

Tirun relayed as much, politely phrased. Amber eyes lifted. Ears flicked. "*Gtst* says that was the customs release. Now they want a waiver against claims by the consignor—"

She punched it in on her own com. "This is Pyanfar Chanur. If I come over there I bring my whole ship's company. Hear? And you can explain *that* to the Director, you flat-bottomed bureaucrat!"

Silence from the other end.

She broke the contact. "Tirun: you and Geran get across that dock to that office and watch those cans all the way."

"Kif," Tirun said.

"Gods-rotted right the kif. They've got their bluff in on the stsho."

"Customs is back on," Chur said. "Give it to five." She punched it in. "Well?"

"I have schedule, hani."

"You just put us at the head of it. Hear? I'm sending my own security. I've been robbed once at this forsaken station. Not again!"

She broke the connection, leaned back and exhaled a long, long breath, staring at Tirun. "Get!"

"Aye!" Tirun and Geran scrambled up and headed for the door.

"*Arm and take a pocket com!*" she shouted after them. "And be gods-rotted discreet about it!" She spun the chair left to Haral. "I want that forward hold warmed and pressurized."

"How long's Tully been in there?" Hilfy asked.

Pyanfar shot a glance at the chronometer overhead. "Figure six hours. At least."

"How good's that lifesupport?"

"The way Goldtooth's set up the rest of this mess—who knows?" She shoved her chair around and keyed up comp, hunting cargo lists, mass records. "This list updated?"

"No," Hilfy said.

C. J. Cherryh

"I need that list, gods rot it, niece."

"I'm on it," Chur said. "Scan to your number four, captain."

She smoothed her nose with an effort, twitched her ears and heard the jingling of the several rings. Experience, they meant. Wealth. Successful voyages. She sat and watched for anything untoward, monitoring station com, scan, every pulse and breath of information Meetpoint central let them have. Their own systems showed live in a series of amber lights.

"Pressure's coming up," Haral said.

"Estimate of mass loss to three, captain."

She shunted it to Records. Comp brought up the revision. "Fine that down, Chur. Navcomp's taking main five."

"You've got them."

Nav's five segments unified themselves in comp and shunted other programs to different banks: command screens acquired nav's displays.

Maing Tol. From Meetpoint that was Urtur to Kita Point to Maing Tol at best.

"We can't singlejump," she said at last. "Not with the cargo we've still got, not anything like it."

Silence all round. "Aye," —finally, from Haral.

She sat staring at the graphs.

"Aunt," Hilfy murmured, and turned her chair with a wide-eyed look and the comset pressed

54

in her ear. "Aunt, it's Geran. Says customs has those cans loaded and out already; they have a bunch of mahen security on it, too."

"Good gods. Something's going right. How long?"

"How long?" Hilfy relayed; and her eyes flickered as she listened. "They're coming now."

"How's that pressure?"

"Pressure's good," Haral said.

"Captain—" Chur. "Someone's down at the access com—It's Banny Ayhar, captain. She wants to talk to you."

"Gods rot!" She punched in all-ship com. "Ayhar, get clear, hear me!"

"Who is this?"

"Pyanfar Chanur, rot your eyes, and clear my dock! There's an emergency in progress."

"What emergency? Chanur, I'm not in a mood for more connivances. You hear me, Chanur—"

"I've got no time for this." She spun the chair about and left it. "Haral, stand by to open up that hold. And tell Ayhar get herself out of the way. Hilfy, Chur, come on."

They heeled her down the corridor at an almost run, into the lift for downdecks. She hit the button.

Com snapped from the panel above the lift controls, at the first lurch of the car down. "Captain." Haral's voice. "Geran's on. They've got kif out there."

She put a claw in the slot before the lift had a chance to pass the next level and stopped the car right there, on a level with the airlock. "Hilfy!" she said in leaving, before Hilfy had a chance to follow her and Chur. "Go on below and get that bay opened up."

"Aunt—" One youthful protest, hands lifted, before the door closed between.

They ran all-out, she and Chur, stopping only for the weapons-locker and the com-panel in the hall.

"Get that hatch open!" Pyanfar yelled at Haral, and headed for the lock.

Chapter Three

They hit the access tube running and came round the bend headon into hani coming up the accessway, a broad, scarred hani captain flanked by two senior crew.

Pyanfar evaded collision.

"Gods rot you—" Banny Ayhar yelled, and Chur cursed; there was the thump of impact.

"Gods rot you!" Pyanfar yelled, whirling about, outraged, as Chur recovered from her stagger and spun about at her side. "I told you clear my dock!"

"What's it take to bring Chanur to its senses?" Banny Ayhar yelled. "When's it stop, hey?—You listen to me, ker Pyanfar! I've had enough being put off—"

"We've got *kif* after my crew, blast your eyes."

"*Chanur!*"

She spun and gathered Chur and ran, with the thump of running Ayhar at their heels at least as far as the passageway's exit onto the downward ramp.

"*Cha-nur!*" Banny Ayhar roared at her back, waking echoes off the docks; but Pyanfar never stopped, down the rampway and past the frozen cargo ramp and the gantry that held *The Pride's* skein of station-links.

"*Chanur!*" Far behind them.

There was a curious absence of traffic on the chill, echoing docks, and that silence itself was a warning. Trouble was in sight even from here, around a big can-loader grinding its slow way beside the ship accesses four berths distant.

An odd crowd accompanied it—a half dozen mahendo'sat in station-guard black strode along beside. Two red-pelted hani in faded blue breeches rode the flatbed with the tall white cans, while a dozen black-robed kif stalked along in a tight knot; and if any stsho customs officer was involved at all *gtst* was either barriered inside the cab or fled for safety.

"Come on," Pyanfar said to Chur—no encouragement needed there. Chur kept beside her as they crossed the space at a deliberate jog, not out to provoke trouble, not slow to meet it either. Her hand was in her spacious pocket, clenched about the butt of the gun she tried to keep still and out of sight, and her eyes were constantly on that knot of kif, alert for anything kif-shaped that might show itself from ambushes among the maze of gantries and dockside clutter to the right and the office doors to the left.

"Hai," she yelled with great joviality, when they were a single berth apart. "Hai, you kif bastards, about time you came out to say hello."

The kif had seen them coming too. Their dozen or so scattered instantly all about the moving can-carrier, some of them screened by it. But from the carrier's broad bed, from beside the four huge cans, several mahen guards dropped down to stand at those kif's backs.

"Good to see you," Pyanfar gibed, halting at a comfortable distance. Kifish faces were fixed on her in starkest unfriendliness. "I was worried. I thought you'd forgotten me."

"Fool," one hissed.

She grinned, her hand still in her pocket, her ears up, her eyes taking in all the kif. Two moved, beyond the moving can-carrier, and she shifted to keep them in sight. The smell of them reached her. Their dry-paper scent offended her nostrils with old memories. The long-snouted faces peering from within the hooded robes, the dark-gray hairless skin with its papery wrinkles, the small, red-rimmed eyes—set the hair bristling on her back. "Do something," she wished them. "Foot-lickers. Riffraff. Petty thieves. Did Akkukkakk turn you out? Or is he anywhere these days?"

Kifish faces were hard to read. If that reference to a vanished leader got to them, nothing showed. Only one hooded face lifted, black snout atwitch, and stared at her with directness quite unlike the usual kifish slink. "He is no longer a factor," that one said, while the carrier groaned past under its load of canisters and took itself from between them and four more kif.

More soft impacts hit the deck beside her. From the tail of her eye she saw a red-gold blur. Tirun and Geran had dropped off the flatbed rear. They took up a position at her left as Chur held the right.

"Get back," she said without looking around at her two reinforcements. "Go on with the carrier. Hilfy's in lower ops. Get that cargo inside." The mahen station guards had moved warily into better position, several dark shadows at the peripheries of her vision, two of them remaining in front of her and behind the kif.

"You carry weapons," that foremost kif observed, not in the pidgin even the cleverest of mahe used. This kif had fluency in the hani tongue, spoke with nuances—*dishonorable con-*

cealed weapons, the word meant. "You have difficulties of all kinds. We know, Pyanfar Chanur. We know what you are transporting. We know from whom it comes. We understand your delicate domestic situation, and we know you now possess something that interests us. We make you an offer. I am very rich. I might buy you—absolution from your past misjudgments. Will you risk your ship? For I tell you that ship will be at risk—for the sake of a mahendo'sat who is lost in any case."

She heard the carrier growling its way out of the arena, out of immediate danger. Chur had stayed at her side. So had the six mahendo'sat station guards. "What's your name, kif?"

"Sikkukkut-an'nikktukktin. Sikkukkut to curious hani. You see I've studied you."

"I'll bet you have."

"The public dock is no place to conduct delicate business. And there are specific offers I would make you."

"Of course."

"*Profitable* offers. I would invite you to my ship. Would you accept?"

"Hardly."

"Then I should come to yours." The kif Sikkukkut spread his arms within the cloak, a billowing of black-gray that showed a gleam of gold. "Unarmed, of course."

"Sorry. No invitation."

The kif lowered his arms. Red-rimmed eyes stared at her with liquid thought. "You are discourteous."

"Selective."

The long gray snout acquired a v-form of wrinkles above the nostril slits, a chain slowly building, as at some faint, unpleasant scent. "Afraid of witnesses?"

"No. Just selective."

"Most unwise, Pyanfar Chanur. You are losing what could save you . . . here and at home. A hani ship here has already witnessed—compromising things. Do I hazard a guess what will become of Kohan Chanur—of all that Chanur—precariously—is, if anything should befall The Pride? Kohan Chanur will perish. The name will have never been; the estates will be partitioned, the ships recalled to those who will then take possession of Chanur goods. Oh, you have been imprudent, ker Pyanfar. Everyone knows that. This latest affair will crush you. And whom have you to thank, but the mahendo'sat, but maneuverings and machinations in which hani are not counted important enough to consult?"

The transport's whining was in the distance now. She heard another sound, the hollow escaping-steam noise of the cargo hatch opening up, the whine of a conveyer moving to position and meshing; old sounds, familiar sounds: she knew every tick and clank for what they were. "What maneuverings among kif?" she asked the gray thief. "What machinations— that would interest me, I wonder."

"More than bears discussion here, ker Pyanfar. But things in which a hani in such danger as you are would be interested. In which you may—greatly—be interested, when the news of Meetpoint gets to the han. As it surely will. Remember me. Among kif—I am one who might be disposed toward you, not against. Sikkukkut of Harukk, at your service."

"You set us up, you bastard."

The long snout twitched and acquired new wrinkles in its papery gray hide. Perhaps kif smiled. This one drew a hand from beneath its robe and she stepped back a pace, the hand on the gun in her pocket angling the gun up all at once to fire.

It offered her a bit of gold in its gray, knobbed claws. She stared at it with her finger tight on the trigger.

"A message," it said, "For your—cargo. Give it to him."

"Probably has plague."

"I assure you not. I handle it. See?"

"Something hani-specific, I'm sure."

"It would be a mistake not to know what it is. Trust me, ker Pyanfar."

It was dangerous to thwart a kif in any whim.

She saw this one's pique, the elegant turn of wrist that held the object—it was a small gold ring—before her.

She snatched it, the circlet caught between her claws.

"Mistrustful," said Sikkukkut.

Pyanfar backed a pace. "Chur," she said, and with a back-canted ear heard the whisper of Chur's move back.

Sikkukkut held up his thin, soot-gray palms in token of non-combatancy. His long snout tucked under. The red-rimmed eyes looked lambent fire at her.

"I will see you again," Sikkukkut said. "I will be patient with you, hani fool, in hopes you will not be forever a fool."

She backed up as far as put all the mahen guards between herself and the kif, with Chur close by her. "Don't turn your backs," she advised the mahendo'sat.

"Got order," said the mahe in charge. "You go ship, hani. These fine kif, they go other way."

"There are illicit arms," said another kif in coldest tones. "Ask this hani."

"Ours legal," said the mahe pointedly, who had heard, perhaps, too much of mahendo'sat involvement from this kif. The mahendo'sat stood rock firm: Pyanfar turned her shoulder, taking that chance they offered, collected Chur in haste and headed across the dock, all the while with a twitch between her shoulderblades.

"They're headed off," said Chur, who ventured a quick look over her shoulder. "Gods rot them."

"Come on." Pyanfar set herself to a jog, not quite a run, coming up to *The Pride*'s berth, to the whining noise of the cargo gear. The loader crane had a can suspended in midair, stalled, while three hani shouted and waved angry argument at her crew beside the machinery.

"Ayhar!" Pyanfar thundered. "Gods rot you, *out!*" She charged into the midst and shoved, hard, and Banny Ayhar backed up with round eyes and a stunned look on her broad, scarred face.

"You earless bastard!" Ayhar howled. "You don't lay hands on me!"

She knew what she had done. She stood there with the crane whining away with its burden in fixed position, with Tirun and Chur and Geran lined up beside her as the two Ayhar crew flanked their captain. Thoughts hurtled through her mind, the *han*, alliances, influences brought to bear.

"Apologies." It choked her. "Apologies, Ayhar. And get off my dock. Hear?"

"You're up to something, Pyanfar Chanur. You've got your nose in it for sure, conniving with the mahendo'sat, gods know what—I'm telling you, Chanur, Ayhar won't put up with it. You know what it cost us? You know what your last lunatic foray cost us, while ships of the *han* were banned at Meetpoint, while our docks at Gaohn were shot up and gods be feathered if that mahen indemnity covered it—"

"I'll meet you at Anuurn. We'll talk about this, Banny, over a cup or two."

"A cup or two! Good gods, Chanur!"

"Geran, Tirun, get those cans moving."

"Don't you turn your back on me."

"Ayhar, I haven't time."

"What's the hurry?" A new hani voice, silken, from her side: Ayhar crew's impudence, she thought, and turned on it with her mouth open and the beginnings of an oath.

Another captain stood there, her red-gold mane and beard in curling wisps of elegance; gold arm-band; gold belt; breeches of black silk unrelieved by any banding.

Immune Clan color. Official of the *han.*

"Rhif Ehrran," that one named herself, "captain, *Ehrran's Vigilance.* What's the trouble, Chanur?"

Her heart began slow, painful beats. Blood climbed to her ears and sank toward her heart. "Private," she said in a quiet, controlled tone. "You'll excuse me, captain. I have an internal emergency."

"I'm in port on other business," the *han* agent

said. "But you've almost topped it, ker Chanur. You mind telling me what's going on?"

She could hand it all to the Ehrran, shove the whole thing over onto the *han*'s representative in port.

Give Tully to her. To this. Young, by the gods young, ears un-nicked, bestowed with half a dozen rings. And cold as they came. Godsrotted walking recorder from one of the public service clans, immune to challenging and theoretically nonpartisan.

"I'm on my way home," she said. "I'll take care of it."

Ehrran's nostrils widened and narrowed. "What did the kif give you, Chanur?"

A cold wind went down her back. Distantly she heard the crane whining away, lifting a can into place. "Dropped a ring," she said, "in the riot. Kif returned it." The lie disgusted her. So did the fear the Ehrran roused, and knew she roused. "This what the *han*'s got to? Inquisitions? Gathering bad eggs?"

It scored. Ehrran's ears turned back, forward again. "You've about exited private territory, Chanur. You settle this mess. If there are repercussions with the stsho, *I'll* become involved. Hear me?"

"Clear." Breath was difficult. "Now you mind if I see to my business, captain?"

"You know," Ehrran said, "you're in deep.

Take my advice. Drop off your passenger when you get back to Anuurn."

Her heart nearly stopped while Ehrran turned and walked away; but it was Khym Ehrran had meant. She realized that in half a breath more, and outrage nearly choked her. She glared at Banny Ayhar, just glared, with the reproach due someone who dragged the like of Ehrran in on a private quarrel.

"Not my doing," Ayhar said.

"In a mahen hell."

"I can't reason with you," Ayhar said, flung up her hands and stalked off. Stopped again, to cast a look and a word back. "Time you got out of it, Pyanfar Chanur. Time to pass it on before you ruin that brother of yours for good."

Pyanfar's mouth dropped. Distracted as she was she simply stared as Ayhar spun on her heel a second time and stalked off along the dock with her two crewwomen; and then it was too late to have said anything without yelling it impotently at a retreating Ayhar back.

The first can boomed up the cargo ramp into the cradle; Tirun and Geran kicked their own balky Loader around with expert swiftness, raised the slot's holding sling and snagged it into the moving ratchets that vanished into The Pride's actinic-lighted hold. The can ascended the ramp, while Chur, beside the crane operator on the loader, shouted at the aggrieved mahe, urging her to speed.

"Chur!" Pyanfar yelled, headed for the rampway and the tube beyond. Chur left off and scrambled after, leaving the docksiders to their jobs. Pyanfar jogged the length of The Pride's ramp and felt a stitch in her side as Chur came up beside her in the accessway.

A han agent on their case.

A chance to get rid of Tully into the keeping of that same agent and she had turned it down.

Gods. O gods.

They scrambled through the lock, headed down the short corridor to the lift, inside. The door hissed shut as Pyanfar hit the controls to start the car down, rim-outward of The Pride's passenger-ring.

"Got it?" Haral's voice came to them by com.

"Gods know," she said to the featureless com panel, forcing calm. "Keep an eye on those kif back there—hear me?"

"Looks as if the party's broken up for good out there."

"Huh." It was a small favor. She did not believe it.

"Aye," Haral agreed, and clicked out of contact. The lift slammed into the bottom of the rotation ring and took a sudden jolt afterward for the holds.

"Know which can?" Chur panted beside her, clinging to the rail.

"Gods, no. You think Goldtooth labeled the gods-rotted thing? Couldn't use the small cans, no. Couldn't consign it direct to us. Had to trust the stsho. Gods-rotted mahen lunatic."

The lift accelerated full out, lurched to a second stop and opened its door on a floodlit empty cavern of tracks below the operations platform where they stood. Their breaths frosted instantly. Moisture in the hold's lately acquired air formed a thin frost on all the waiting cans and the machinery. The cold of the deckplates burned bare feet. The gusting blasts of the ventilation system brought no appreciable relief to unprotected hani skin and nose linings.

"Hilfy?" Pyanfar shouted, leaning on the safety railing to look down into the dark. *Hilfy-Hilfy-Hilfy* the echo came back in giant's tones.

"Aunt!" A figure in a padded cold-suit crouched far below the operations scaffold, a glimmer of white in the shadow of the first can to reach its cradle at hold's end. "Aunt, I can't get this cursed lid off! It's securitied!"

"Gods fry that bastard!" Pyanfar ignored the locker with the coldsuits and went thumping down the steps barefoot and barechested. The air burned her lungs, froze her ribs. She heard noise behind her, a locker-door rattle. "*Get those*

suits!'' she yelled at Chur, and her breath was
white in the floodlight glare.

Another can locked through with a sibilance
of pressurized air and a resounding impact with
its receiving cradle as she came down beside
the can-track rails that shone pewter-colored in
the general dark. The incoming can rumbled
past like a white plastic juggernaut and boomed
into the cradle-lock as she arrived. Hilfy scrambled to the side of it and jerked the lever that
secured the lid. Internal-conditions dials glowed
bright and constant on the top-plate.

"Locked too," Hilfy said in despair, rising,
her voice muffled by the cold-mask she wore,
overwhelmed by the crash of another arriving
can headed up the outside ramp. "That Goldtooth give us any key-code?"

"Gods know. The stsho might have it." Pyanfar shivered convulsively as Chur came pelting
up with coldsuits and masks and thrust a set
into her numb hands. She stared distractedly
as the third can locked through, ignoring the
coldsuit, thinking of stsho treachery the while
the can rode the hydraulics down and jolted
into the third cradle. She shouldered aside
Hilfy's move to check its lid and tried it herself.
Locked too.

"Gods-rotted luck," Pyanfar said, rising, fumbling the slot-apertured cold-mask into place
with fingers that refused to set their claws. The

pads of her feet felt the burn of the decking plates. She stared helplessly at Chur, who had gotten her own mask on and held out the cold suit she had dropped. "It has to be the last one, that's all."

"What if there is a key?" Hilfy asked. Her teeth chattered fit to crack, despite the cold-suit. "And the stsho have got it.

"Number four's coming in," Chur yelled over the rising thunder of machinery, and the fourth can locked through and rumbled down the track toward them as they scrambled to meet it. Chur got to it first, crouched down and tugged fruitlessly at the lid. "It's locked too."

"*Gods and thunders!*" Pyanfar yanked her pistol from her pocket and fired past Chur into the lid mechanism, stalked down the row and fired at the next and the next and the next. Maintenance lights on the lids went out. The smoke of burned plastics curled up in the actinic light, mingling gray with their breaths. "Get torches if you have to! Get those lids off."

"It's coming!" Chur cried, tugging at the smoking lid, and Hilfy dived to help, past Pyanfar's own numb-footed advance on the can.

It was fish, a flood of dried fish, that sent its stench into the supercooled air; the next one, dried fruit. The third—

"This is it," said Chur, pawing past the cascade of stinking warm *shishu* fruit, for a second white lid showed through the spilling cargo. She reached it on her knees and wrenched the lock lever down, tugged with all her might at the lid and tumbled back as it came free.

A form like some insect in its cell lifted a pale, breather-masked face in a cloud of steam as the inner air met outer. With a muffled cry Tully began to writhe outward, in a frosting stench of heat and human sweat that almost overcame the fish and fruit. Chur helped, kneeling—seized Tully's white-shirted shoulders and dragged him free in a tumble and slide of fruit, in a cloud of breath and steam from his overheated body.

He gasped, struggled wild-eyed to his feet, hands flailing.

"Tully," Pyanfar said—he was blinded by the lights, she thought; he looked half-drowned in the heat that narrow confinement had contained. "Tully, it's us, it's us, for the gods' sake."

"Pyanfar," he cried and threw himself into her arms. "Pyanfar!" —losing breather-cylinder and hoses and stumbling through the stinking fruit in which he had slid outward. He pressed his steaming self against her, his heartbeat so violent she felt it through his ribs.

"Easy," she said. Hunter instincts. Her heart tried to synch with his. "Careful, Tully." She kept her ears up all the same, carefully disengaged his shaking arms and pushed him back. His eyes were wild with fear. "You safe. Hear? Safe, Tully. On *The Pride*."

He babbled in his own tongue. Water poured from his eyes and froze on his face. "Got," he said. "Got—" and abandoned her to dive back into the can, pawing amid the tangle of discarded breathing apparatus and trampled fruit, to stagger up again with a large packet in his grasp. He held it out to her, wobbling as she took it from his hands.

"Goldtooth," he said, and something else that did not get past his chattering teeth.

"He's going to freeze," said Chur, throwing one of the two coldsuits about his thinly clad, hairless shoulders.

And perhaps he only then recognized the others, for he cried "Chur," and staggered a step to fling his arms about her, shivering visibly as the cold disspated the last of his heat. "Hilfy!"—as Hilfy unmasked herself; he reached for her.

But his legs went and he slid almost to the ground before Hilfy and Chur could save him. "Hil-fy!" —foolishly, from a sitting posture on the burning cold deck, with Hilfy's arms about him.

"Get him up," Pyanfar snapped at them both. "Get him to the lift, for the gods' sakes!" — waving them that way with the packet in one hand, for her feet were freezing and Tully's wet clothes were stiffening, with crystals in his hair.

He made shift to walk when they had pulled him up. He hung on them the long, long course down the tracks to the platform stairs, and labored the metal steps with them supporting him on either side and Pyanfar shoving from behind. He faltered at the top, recovered as they heaved him up with his arms across their shoulders.

"Hang on." Pyanfar reached the lift and punched the button for them, held the door open on that blast of seeming heat and the glare of light while Hilfy and Chur between them dragged Tully in and held him on his feet. A dull white frost formed on the lift surfaces.

"Paper," Tully mumbled, lifting his head.

"Got." She closed the door after her and sent the car hurtling forward. Chur held Tully tight against her body and Hilfy pressed close on the other side as the car reached the forward limit and started its topside climb.

"Get him to sickbay," Pyanfar said as it went. "Get him warm and for the gods' sakes get him washed."

That brought a lifting of Tully's head. His beautiful golden mane was wet with melting frost and clung to the naked skin about his eyes. He stank abysmally of fish and fruit and

75

scared human. "Friend," he said. It was his best word. He offered that, and that frightened look. In distress Pyanfar reached out and patted his shoulder with claws all pulled.

"Sure. Friend."

Gods, not to be sure of them. And to have come this far on hope alone.

"Got—Pyanfar, got—" His teeth chattered, no improvement to his diction. "Come see you—Need—need—"

The lift stopped on lower decks, hissed its doors open. "Take care of him," Pyanfar said, standing firm to stay aboard. "And do it fast. I want you on other business. Hear?"

"Aye," said Chur.

"Pyanfar!" Tully cried as they dragged him out. "Paper—"

"I hear," she said, and held the packet as the door closed between them. "I got it," she muttered to herself; and remembering another matter, put a hand into her pocket and felt the ring beside the gun barrel, a ring made for fingers, not for ears. Only mahendo'sat and stsho wore finger rings, having no under-finger tendon to their non-retractile claws; having one more joint than hani had. Or kif. Not to mention t'ca and knnn and chi.

A human hand was mahe-like. Tully had been in kifish hands once. They had gotten him from them. And gods knew he would not forget it.

Gods-rotted Outsider. A few minutes dealing with him and she was shaking all over. He had a way of doing that to her.

"He's all right?" Haral asked as she arrived sore-footed on the bridge.

"Will be. Shaken. I don't blame him." She settled to her chair, filthy as she was, and curled her frost-singed feet out of contact with the floor. Haral, immaculate, had the diplomacy not to wrinkle her nose. "You hear that Ehrran business?"

"Some."

"Got ourselves one fat report going home, I'll bet. Tirun and Geran in?"

"They're dumping out that fish and fruit. Getting rid of the stuff. Spoiled cargo, we call it. Send it out as garbage."

"Huh." She leaned back into the chair, hooked a claw into the plastic seal of the packet and ripped it open.

"What's that?"

"Expensive," she said.

The fattish packet yielded several clips of papers, a trio of computer spools. She read labels and drew a deep breath at finding the document Goldtooth had given into Tully's hands—virtually indecipherable mahen scrawl, a printed signature, and hand-printed at the top: *Repair authorization* in crabbed Universal Block.

". . . *good repair* . . .", she made out. That the rest of it was unreadable gave her no comfort at all.

Another document, pages thick, swarming with neat humped type in alien alphabet. She flipped through the pages with further misgivings.

Human? She guessed as much.

The third document (typed):

Greeting, it said. *Sorry go now, leave you this. Got lot noise on dock, got kif, got trouble, got one mad stsho give me trouble. I send can customs, trust stsho Stle stles stlen not much far. He Personage on this station, got faint heart, plenty brain. If, Stle stles stlen, you reading this I promise cut out you heart have it for last meal.*

Tully come big trouble. Mahen freighter Ijir same find his ship, human give him come. "Bring Pyanfar," he say, all time "Pyanfar" not got other word. So I bring. One stubborn fellow.

I know he ask hani help. Also I know the han, like you know han, lot politic, lot talk, lot do nothing. Lot make trouble you about this mate business—forgive I mention this, but truth. You stupid, Pyanfar, one stupid-bastard hani give jealous hani chance bite your ankles. That translate? I know what you do. You too long go outworld, got foreign idea, got idea maybe hani

male worth something. You sometime crazy.
You know Chanur got personal enemy, know
got lot hani not like mahendo'sat, same got lot
hani got small brain, not like change custom,
same got hani lot mad with stsho embargo.
What you try, save time, fight all same time?
Hope you get smart, eat their hearts someday.

But someday not now. You go han they make
big mess. I know. You know. You go han they
turn all politic. Instead go mahen Personage
like good friend, take Personage message in
number one tape. Sorry this coded. We all got
little worry.

Now give bad news. Kif hunting you. Old
enemy Akkukkak sure dead, but some kif bastard got ambition take Akkukkak's command.
We got another hakkikt coming up, name
Akkhtimakt. I think this fellow lieutenant to
Akkukkak, got same ugly way make trouble,
want prove self more big than Akkukkak. How
do this? Revenge on knnn not good idea. Revenge on human another kind thing; same revenge on you and me. Ship in port name
Harukk, captain name Sikkukkut. This number
one bastard claim self enemy this Akkhtimakt,
want offer deal. This smell many day dead.

You add all same up, run mahen Personage.
Paper good. You make number one deal mahendo'sat this time. You got big item. Forget
other cargo. Be rich. Promise. You hani enemies not touch.

Wish all same luck. I got business stsho space. Got fix thing.

Goldtooth Ana Ismehanan-min a Hasanan-nan, *same give you my sept name.*

She looked up, ears flat.

"What's it say?" asked Haral, in all diffidence.

"Goldtooth wished us luck. Promises help. He's bribed the stsho. Someone got those papers fixed to get us here and gods-be if any of it was accident." She gnawed a filthy hangnail. It tasted of fish and human. She spat in distaste and clipped the papers into her data bin. "Tell Tirun and Geran get out cargo unloaded. Get Chur on it. Fast."

"All of it?"

She turned a stare Haral's way. It was a question, for sure; but not the one Haral asked aloud. "*All* of it. Call Mnesit. Tell them get an agent down here to identify what's theirs. Tell Sito sell at market and bank what's ours."

"They'll rob us. Captain, we've got guarantees; we've got that Urtur shipment promised—We've got the first good run in a year. If we lose this now—"

"*Gods rot it, Haral, what else can I do?*"

Embarrassed silence then. Haral's ears sank and pricked up again desperately.

So they prepared to run. Prepared—to lose cargo that meant all too much to Chanur in its financial straits, trusting a mahen promise . . .

for the second time. And for the first time in memory Haral Araun disputed orders.

"I'm going for a bath," she said.

"Do what with the incoming cargo?" A faint, subdued voice.

"Offer it to Sito," she said. "Warehouse what he won't take. So maybe things work out and we get back here." Likely the stsho would confiscate it at first chance. She did not say what they both knew. She got out of the chair and headed out of the bridge, no longer steady in the knees, wanting her person clean, her world in order; wanting—

—gods knew what.

Youth, perhaps. Things less complicated.

There was one worry that wanted settling—before baths, before any other thing shunted it aside.

She buzzed the door of number one ten, down the corridor from her own quarters, down the corridor from the bridge. No answer. She buzzed again, feeling a twinge of guilt that set her nerves on edge.

"Khym?"

She buzzed a third time, beginning to think dire thoughts she had had half a score of times on this year-long voyage—like suicide. Like getting no answer at all and opening the door and finding her husband had finally taken that option that she had feared for months he would.

His death would solve things, repair her life; and his; and she knew that, and knew he knew it, in one great guilty thought that laid her ears flat against her skull.

"Khym, blast it!"

The door shot open. Khym towered there, his mane rumpled from recent sleep. He had thrown a wrap about his waist, nothing more.

"Are you all right?" she asked.

"Sure. Fine." His pelt was crossed with angry seams of scratches plasmed together. His ears, his poor ears that Gaohn Station medics had redone with such inventive care and almost restored to normalcy—the left one was ripped and plasmed together again. He had been handsome once . . . still was, in a ruined, fatal way. "You?"

"Good gods." She expelled her breath, brushed past him into his quarters, noting with one sweep of her eye the disarray, the bedclothes of the sleeping-bowl stained with small spots of blood from his scratches. Tapes and galley dishes lay heaped in clutter on the desk. "You can't leave things lying." It was the old, old shipboard safety lecture, delivered with tiresome patience. "Good gods, Khym, don't . . . *don't* do these things."

"I'm sorry," he said, and meant it as he did all the other times.

She looked at him, at what he was, with the old rush of fondness turned to pain. He was the father of her son and daughter, curse them both for fools. Khym once-Mahn, lord Mahn, while he had had a place to belong to. Living in death, when he should have, but for her, died decently at home, the way all old lords died; and youngsters died, who failed to take themselves a place—or wander some male-only reserve like Sanctuary or Hermitage, hunting the hills, fighting other males and dying when the odds got long. *Churrau hanim*. The betterment of the race. Males were what they were, three quarters doomed and the survivors, if briefly, estate lords, pampered and coddled, the brightness of hani lives.

He had been so beautiful. Sun-shining, clear-eyed—clever enough to get his way of his sisters and his wives more often than not. And every hani living would have loved him for what he did at Gaohn, rushing the kif stronghold, an old lord outworn and romantically gallant in the eternal tragedy of males—

But he had lived. And walked about Gaohn station with wonder at ships and stars and foreignness. And found something else to live for. She could not send him home. Not then. Not ever.

"It was a good fight," she said. "Out there."

His nose wrinkled. "Don't patronize, Py."

83

"I'm not. I'm here to tell you it wasn't your fault. I don't care how it started, it wasn't your fault. Kif set it up. Anyone could have walked into it. Me, Haral, anyone."

His ears lifted tentatively.

"We've got one other problem." She folded her arms and leaned against the table edge. "You remember Tully."

"I remember."

"Well, we've got ourselves a passenger. Not for long. We take him to Maing Tol. A little business for the mahendo'sat."

The ears went down again, and her heart clenched. "For the gods' sakes don't be like that. You *know* Tully. He's quiet. You'll hardly know he's here. I just didn't want to spring that on you."

"I'm not 'being like that.' For the gods' sakes I've got some brains. What 'business for the mahendo'sat'? What have you gotten yourself into? *Why?*"

"Look, it's just a business deal. We do a favor for the mahendo'sat, it gets paid off, like maybe a route opens. Like maybe we get ourselves that break we need right now."

"Like the last time."

"Look, I'm tired, I don't want to explain this all. Say it's Goldtooth's fault. I want a bath. I want—gods know what I want. I came to tell you what's happened, that's all."

"That kif business . . . have anything to do with this?"

"I don't know."

"Don't know?"

Aliens and alien things. He was downworlder. Worldbred. "Later. It's under control. Don't worry about it. You going to be all right?"

"Sure."

She started then to go.

"I was remarkable, Py. They arrested me and I didn't kill even one of them. Isn't that fine?"

The bitterness stopped her and sent the wind up her back. "Don't be sarcastic. It doesn't become you."

"I didn't kill anyone, all the same. They were quite surprised."

She turned all the way around and set her hands on her hips. "Gods-rotted stsho bigots. What did they say to you?"

"The ones in the bar or the ones in the office?"

"Either."

"What do you expect?"

"I want an answer, Khym."

"Office wouldn't speak to me. Said I wasn't a citizen. Wanted the crew to keep me quiet. They wanted to put restraints on me. Crew said no. I'd have let them go that far."

She came back and extended a claw, straightened a wayward wisp of mane. He stood a head taller than she; was far broader—they had at least put weight back on him, from that day she had found him, gone to skin and bones, hiding in a hedge outside Chanur grounds. He had been trying to find his death then, had come to see her one more time, in Chanur territory, with their son hunting him to kill him and Kohan apt to do the same . . . if Kohan were not Kohan, and ignoring him for days: gods, the gossip that had courted, male protecting male.

"Listen," she said. "Stsho are xenophobes. They've got three genders and they phase into new pysches when they're cornered. Gods know what's in their heads. You travel enough out here and you don't wonder what a stsho'll do or think tomorrow. It doesn't matter. Hear?"

"You smell like fish," he said. "And gods know what else."

"Sorry." She drew back the hand.

"Human, is it?"

"Yes."

He wrinkled his nose. "I won't kill him either. See, Py? I justify your confidence. So maybe you can tell me what's going on. For once."

"Don't ask."

"They think I'm crazy. For the gods' sakes, Py, you walk in here with news like that. Don't kill the human, please. Never mind the kif. Never mind the gods-be-blasted station's going to sue—"

"They say that?"

"Somewhere in the process. Py—I don't put my nose into Chanur business. But I know accounts. I was good at it. I know what you've put into this trip, I know you've borrowed at Kura for that repair—"

"Don't worry about it." She patted his arm, turned for the door in self-defense, and stopped there, her hand on the switch. She faced about again with a courtesy in her mouth to soften it; and met a sullen, angry look.

"My opinion's not worth much," he said. "I know."

"We'll talk later. Khym, I've got work to do."

"Sure."

"Look." She walked back and jabbed a claw at his chest. "I'll tell you something, na Khym. You're right. We're in a mess and we're short-handed, and you gods-rotted took this trip, on which you've gotten precious few calluses. . . ."

The eyes darkened. "It was your idea."

"No. It was yours. You gods-rotted well chose new things, husband: this isn't Mahn, you're on a working ship, and you can rotted sure make up your mind you're not lying about on cushions with a dozen wives to see to the nastinesses. That's not true anymore. It's a new world. You can't have it half this and half that—you don't want the prejudice, but you gods-rotted well want to lie about and be waited on. Well, I haven't got time. No one's got time. This is a world that *moves*, and the sun doesn't come round every morning to warm your hide. *Work* might do it."

"Have I complained?" The ears sank. The mouth was tight in disaste. "I'm talking about policy."

"When you know the outside you talk about policy. You walk onto this ship after what happened in that bar and you walk into your quarters and shut the door, huh? Fine. That's real fine. This crew saved your hide, gods rot it, not just because you're male. But you sit in this cabin, you've sat in this cabin and done nothing—"

"I'm comfortable enough."

"Sure you are. You preen and eat and sleep. And you're not comfortable. You're eating your gut out."

"What do you want? For me to work docks?"

"*Yes.* Like any of the rest of this crew. You're not lord Mahn any more, Khym."

It was dangerous to have said. So was the rest of it. She saw the fracture-lines, the pain. She had never been so cruel. And to her distress the ears simply sank, defeated. No anger. No violence. "Gods and thunders, Khym. What am I supposed to do with you?"

"Maybe take me home."

"No. That's not an option. You wanted this."

"No. You wanted to take on the *han*. Myself—I just wanted to see the outside once. That's all."

"In a mahen hell it was."

"Maybe it is now."

"Are they right, then?"

"I don't know. It's not *natural*. It's not—"

"You believe that garbage? You think the gods made you crazy?"

He rubbed the broad flat of his nose, turned his shoulder to her, looked back with a rueful stare.

"You believe it, Khym?"

"It's costing you too much. Gods, Py—you're gambling Chanur, you're risking your brother to keep me alive, and that's *wrong*, Py. That's completely wrong. You can't stave off times. I had my years; the young whelp beat me."

"So it was an off day."

"I couldn't come back at him. I didn't have it, Py. It's time. It's age. He's got Mahn. It's the way things work. Do you think you can change that?"

"You didn't see the sense in another fight. In wasting an estate in back and forth wrangling. Your brain always outvoted your glands."

"Maybe that's why I lost. Maybe that's why I'm here. Still running."

"Maybe because you've always known it's nonsense and a waste. What happened to those talks we used to have? What happened to the

89

husband who used to look at the stars and ask me where I went, what I'd seen, what outside the world was like?"

"Outside the world's the same as in. For me. I can't get outside the world. They won't let me."

"Who?"

"You know who. You should have seen their faces, Py."

"Who? The stsho?"

"Ayhar."

"Those godforsaken drunks?"

"Last thing they expected—me in that bar. That's what the stsho owner said. 'Get away from me, get away from my place, don't go crazy here.' "

"Gods rot what they think!"

"So? Did I teach them anything? Stsho didn't want to serve me in the first place. And I'd had—well, two. To prove I wouldn't, you know—go berserk. And then the riot started. What good's that going to do you—or Kohan?"

"Kohan can take care of himself."

"You're asking too much of him. No, Py, I'm going back downworld when we get back."

"To do what?"

"Go to Sanctuary. Do a little hunting."

"—be the target of every young bully who's honing up his skills to go assault his papa, huh?"

"I'm *old*, Py. It catches up with a man faster. It's time to admit it."

"Gods-rotted nonsense! You'll go back to Anuurn with a ring in your ear, by the gods you will."

He gave a smile, taut laugh, ears up. "Good gods, Py. You want my life there to be short, don't you?"

"You're not going downworld."

"I'll beg on the docks till I get passage, then."

"Gods-rotted martyr."

"Let me go home, Py. Give it up. You can't change what is. They won't let you change. Gods know they won't let me. Whatever you're trying, whatever grandstanding nonsense you've gotten into—give it up. Stop now. While there's time. I'm not worth it."

"Good gods. You think the sun swings around you, don't you? Ever occur to you I have other business than you? That I do things that don't have a thing to do with you?"

"No," he said, "because you're desperate. And *that*'s my fault. Gods, Py—" A small, strangled breath, a drawing about the mouth. "It's cost enough."

"You know," she said after a moment, "you know what's kept the System in power? The young expect to win. Never mind that three quarters of them die. Never mind that estates get ruined when some young fluffbrain gets in power over those that know better and tries to prove he's in charge. The young always believe in themselves. And the graynoses flat give up, give up when they've got the estate running at its best—They get beaten and it's downhill again with a new lord at the helm. All the way downhill. You know other species pass things on, like mahendo'sat: they *train* their successors, for the gods' sakes—"

"They're not hani. Py, you don't understand what it feels like. You can't."

"Kohan ignored you right well."

"Sure. Easy. I wasn't much. He still ignores me. How do you think I'm here?"

"Because *I* say so. Because Kohan's too old and too smart to hold his breath till I give in. And by the gods the next time some whelp comes at him with challenge we'll tear the fellow's ears off. First."

"Good gods, Py! You can't do that to him—"

"Keep him alive? You can lay money on it. Me. Rhean. Even his Faha wife. Not to mention his daughters. Maybe some son, who knows? —someday."

"You're joking."

"No."

"Py. You remember the fable of the house and the stick? You pull the one that's loose and it gets another one—"

"Fables are for kids."

"—and another. Pretty soon the whole house comes down and buries you. You start a fight like that in the han and gods know—gods know what it'll do to us."

"Maybe it might be better. You think of that?"

"Py, I can't take this dealing with strangers. I get mad and I can't stand it, I ache, Py. That's biology. We're set up to fight. Millions of years—it's not an intellectual thing. Our circulatory system, our glands—"

"You think I don't get mad? You think I didn't want to kill myself some kif out there? And I by the gods held my temper."

"Nature gave you a better deal, Py. That's all."

"You're scared."

He stared at her, eyes wide in offense.

"Scared and spoiled," she said. "Scared because you're doing what no male's supposed to be able to do; and guilty that maybe that makes you unmasculine; and gods-rotted spoiled by a mother that coddled your tempers instead of boxing your ears the way she did your sister's. He's just a son, huh? Can't be expected to come up to his sister's standard. Let him throw his tantrums, and keep him out of his father's sight. Makes him potent, doesn't it? And gods, never let him trust another male. Rely on your sister, huh?"

"Leave my family out of this."

"Your sister hasn't done one gods-rotted thing to back you. And your worthless daughters—"

"My sister did back me."

"Till you lost."

"What's she supposed to do? Gods, what's it like for her, living in Kara's house with me running about as if I were still—"

"So she's uncomfortable. Isn't that too bad? Spoiled, I say. Both of you, in separate ways."

His ears were back, all the way. He looked younger that way, the scars less obvious.

"You want," she said, "the advantages I have and the privileges you used to have. Well, they don't go together, Khym. And I'm offering you what I've got. Isn't it enough? Or do you want some *special* category?"

"Py, for the gods' sake I can't work on the docks!"

"Meaning in public."

"I'll work aboard." A great, gusting sigh. "Show me what to do."

"All right. You clean up. You get yourself to the bridge and Haral'll show you how to read scan. It's going to take more than five minutes." She sucked at her cheeks. She had not meant to make that gibe. "You can sit monitor on that. Our lives may depend on it. Keep thinking of that."

"Don't give me—"

"—responsibility? Nice, boring, long-attention-span jobs?"

"Gods rot it, Py!"

"You'll do fine." She turned and punched the door button with a thumb claw. "I know you will."

"It's revenge, that's what it is. For the bar."

"No. It's paying your gods-rotted bar bill same as any of us would."

She stalked out. The door hissed shut like a comment at her back.

Chapter Four

Tully was at least on his feet—seemed to be *feeling* like Tully, which meant insisting on cleaning himself up if he wobbled doing it, crashing about the lowerdecks washroom talking to himself (or thinking that he was being understood) and generally insisting on his privacy from females even if they were of different species. Hilfy dithered between communications from Haral topside via the hallway com panel, frantic requests from Chur in the op room down the corridor (Tirun and Geran were busy down in cargo offloading canisters, with attendant booms and thumps up through the deck plates), and the barricaded washroom into which disappeared a pair of Haral's blue trousers and out of which issued steam and the indescribable mingle of human-smell, fruit, fish and disinfectant soap.

"You all right?" Hilfy asked, when a hairless arm snaked the offered trousers from around the corner of the door. "Tully, hurry it up. We've got other problems. Fast? Understand?"

A mumbled answer came back and the door went shut as if he had leaned on the control as soon as she had gotten her arm out. Hilfy looked round in desperation as Chur came trotting back from ops waving a pair of pocket coms and with a third clipped to her drawstring waist. "Got it," Chur said. "Translator's up and running."

"Thank the gods." She pounded on the door again, whisked it open as Chur thrust a pocket com and earplug around the corner to their passenger and drew her arm back. "Tully—" she said to the unit Chur gave her. She put the earplug in with a grimace. "Tully? You hear me now?"

"Yes," the sound came back, mechanical, from the com loop to the translating computer. "Who talk?" The translator's syntax was far from perfect.

"Tully," Chur said, "it's Chur talking. Hilfy and I got other work, understand? Got to go. You hurry it up; we take you to quarters, get you settled in."

"Got talk to Pyanfar."

"Captain's busy, Tully."

"Got talk." The door opened. He leaned in the doorframe, wearing blue hani trousers, which fit, but barely; and shirtless like themselves. His all but hairless skin was flushed from the heat inside and his mane and beard were dripping wet. "Got talk, come # # talk to Pyanfar."

"Tully, we've got troubles," Hilfy said. "Big emergency." She took him by the arm and Chur took the other, drawing him along despite his objections. "Got cargo troubles, all kinds of troubles."

"Kif." He went stiff and stopped cooperating. "Kif are here?"

"We're still at dock," Hilfy said, keeping him moving. "We're sitting at Meetpoint and we're as safe as we're going to be. Come on."

"No, no, no." He turned and seized her arms with his bluntfingered hands, let her go and shook at Chur. "# No # # #"

Hilfy shook her head at the static breakup. The translator missed those words. Or never had them.

"Hilfy, Chur—mahen # take # ship # human. I bring papers from #. They ask # hani make stop these kif. Got danger. We're not safe # Meetpoint."

"What's he mean?" asked Chur, her ears gone lower, up again. "You catch that?"

"Go get hani fight these kif," Tully said.

"Good gods," Hilfy said.

"Friend," he said again, the hani word, that sent garble through the translator, less forgiving of his mangled pronunciation. His strange blue eyes were aflicker with fear and secrets. "Friend."

"Sure," Hilfy said. She felt a cold lump at the pit of her stomach, hearing the clank and whine of cargo at work below. Things clicked into place of a sudden, that her aunt had committed them to something more than running an illegal passenger—being desperate, with Chanur's financial back to the wall.

It was more than human trade Tully brought. Trade might save their hides.

But entanglements with kif, deals with a mahendo'sat who was not the trader he gave out to be—

And the likes of Rhif Ehrran breathing down their backs all the while—she had heard it all from Chur.

The *han* would have their ears.

Pyanfar took the com to the shower with her, hung it on the wall outside. On the day's record so far, she expected calamities.

The first call brought her dripping from shower to the mat outside undried, mane and beard and hide cascading suds.

"Captain." Haral's voice.

"Trouble?"

"*Na* Khym's here. Says you said he should sit scan monitor."

"Show him what he needs."

Dead silence from the other end. Then: "Aye, captain. Sorry to bother you."

Back to the shower then, to wash the suds off. She slicked the mane back, flattened her ears and squinched her eyes and nostrils shut, face-on to the water-jet for one precious self-indulgent second. She sneezed the water clear and cycled from water to drier, fluffing out her mane and beard, enjoying the warmth.

The com beeper went off again.

"Gods rot." She left the heat and stood damp and shivering by the hook, fumbling the answer-slot. "Pyanfar."

"Captain." Haral again. "Got a kifish message couriered in. From one Sikkukkut. Says it's for you personally."

"Open it."

A long silence. "He's offering partnership."

"Good gods." She forgot the physical cold for a deeper shock.

"Says he wants to talk with you face to face. Says—gods—he's talking specifics here. He names ships he says are after us. Says we have mutual enemies. He gets into kifish stuff here— *pukkukkta*."

"Gods-rotted *pukkukkta* changes meaning in every context—get linguistic comp on that. Get it on the whole thing— Keep alert up there."

"Aye, captain. Sorry."

"All right." She sneezed and cut the com off, returned to the shower and recycled the dryer.

"Captain. Captain."

She left the staff and snatched up com. *"For the gods' sake, Haral—"*

"—Captain, sorry. That request for scheduling— It seems we're being sued. Got six lawsuits against us and station says it can't give clearance without—"

She shut her eyes a moment, composed her voice and kept it very calm. "Get the stationmaster online. Tell *gtst* to issue orders."

"By your leave, I've tried, captain. Call won't go through. The stationmaster's office says *gtst* is indisposed. The word was *gstisi.*"

Personality crisis.

"That gods-rotted white-skinned flutterbrain isn't going to Phase on us! Countersue the bastards and start prep for manual undock as soon as they get that cargo clear. Get everyone on it down there. And send a message to the director and say if *gtst* doesn't get this straightened out I'll give *gtst* new personality more damages to worry about, some of them to *gtst* person."

"Aye," Haral said.

She threw clothes on, her third-best trousers, green silk with moiré orange stripes in the weave; a belt with bronze bangles; the pearl for her ear. Her best armlet, the heavy one. The alien ring was on the counter, from the pocket of the red breeches. She considered, dropped it indecisively into her pocket, pocketed the gun again, clipped on the com and pattered out into the hall in haste, claws clenched, headed for the bridge.

"Captain." The pocket com again, this time from her belt. "Captain, I got the stationmaster on."

"I'm coming," she said, and hastened, down the corridor into the open door. Haral looked about; Khym sat at the righthand station, intent on the scan, the light flickering off his dutiful, martyred scowl.

Haral handed her the transcription. "*Gtst* is out. A new individual is in power. I think it's still the last one, in a personality shift. The new Director wants payment in full. Says we got the better of the last director, drove gtst into a crisis that wasn't due for twenty years, and this one's determined to get gtst money up front. Intends to impound all offloaded cargo."

"*Gods rot*—" She swallowed it, seeing the movement of Khym's all-too-hearing ears backward at her voice. She read the demand for payment. "Four hundred million—"

"Nine hundred with the lawsuits. I think *that's* the problem. Someone important has sued and gtst has to do something."

"I could guess who."

"Gods. Kif. Possible." Haral rubbed her scarred nose, looked up from under her brow. "You thinking of breaking port?"

"Maybe."

"If we do it they'll blackball us. Every stsho port. Every stsho facility. They'll never lift the ban."

"Same if we don't pay."

"Aye, captain," Haral said morosely. And lifting her ears: "Captain, we could *offer* them the profit. Earnest money, like. Offer to give them more on next trip. Gods know how we'll pay off the shippers—but that's tomorrow. And it'll be tied up in litigation anyway, soon as it hits Sito's warehouse."

"Maybe." Pyanfar combed her beard with her claws, looked distractedly toward Khym's broad back. Shook her head as at some heavy blow.

"How's that unloading going?" She missed the sound of the conveyors of a sudden. "Finished down there?"

"Sounds like."

"Rot their eyes." Meaning stsho. She sucked in her mustache ends and gnawed at them. "*Pukkukkta.*"

"Captain?"

"*Pukkukkta.* What did comp say it meant?"

"Like trade of services." Haral snatched up a printout and offered it to her hand. "Like revenge. This is the item. Over regular channels, it was."

Greeting, the message said, *Chanur hunter. Beware Parukt; Skikkt; Luskut; Nifakkiti. Most of all beware Akkhtimakt of Kahakt. These aspire; that one aspires most. I Sikkukkut am with you in pukkukkta for this cause and speak to you in words which precisely describe kif, therefore ambiguity of translation lies at your feet.*

I Sikkukkut know about your passenger and likewise say this: wisest to give this passenger to me. You would then be rich. But I Sikkukkut know the sfik of hunter Pyanfar that this passenger has sfik-value and will be defended. Therefore I Sikkukkut say to the sfik of Pyanfar Chanur that she must give this word to this passenger: I Sikkukkut will speak with him at an appropriate time.

Shelter by my side, hunter Pyanfar. Together we might make a fine pukkukkta, and the cost is less today than tomorrow.

Signal me and I Sikkukkut shall come to the dock where we shall find a quiet place to talk.

"Kif bastard," Pyanfar said, and crumpled the paper. "He wants Tully. That's what he wants. That's what would buy him status."

She looked at Khym, who sat listening to it all, saying nothing; but his ears were back. "Consign a can at random to *Harukk*. Tell them and then tell the stsho."

"To the *kif?*" Haral gasped, and Khym turned round at his post with the whites of his eyes showing.

"As a gift. To one Sikkukkut, captain of *Harukk*. Let the stsho sue *him*."

A thoughtful, wicked look came into Haral's eyes, bewilderment to Khym's.

"No one sues the kif," Khym said.

"No," Pyanfar said, "they won't. And let Sikkukkut *and* the station worry what's in that can, whether it's valuable or not. If he won't take it he'll have to wonder. If he does and finds nothing but trade goods—kif have remarkably little sense of humor, where face is involved. *Sfik*. And gods know if he has one of his cronies pick it up he'll have to wonder whether he got all that was in it. Kif don't trust each other. They can't."

"But—" Khym said.

"No time. Do it, Haral."

"Aye." Haral sat down at com, stuck the receiver in her ear and punched out a blinking light. "Captain, that's Tully again. He's called up here a dozen times. Keeps asking something about a packet of papers. He wants to come up here and discuss it with you."

"Gods." She raked at her beard distractedly and stared round her at the bridge, at Khym's broad back as he kept dutifully to the board, proving—proving things to her. Deliberately. Stubbornly.

Then she realized what she was thinking and thrust the thought away. Male and male, same space. Old ways of thinking died hard. *He's not hani, for the gods' sakes. And they're on the same ship.*

"Tell him come up," she said. "Tell everyone get up here soon as they secure the hold. Prep ops for undock. And send that message."

"Aye." Haral's voice droned the communications in sequence. She punched from one to the other channels without amenities. Then in snarling stsho: "Meetpoint Central Control, this is the hani ship *The Pride of Chanur*, berth 6, responding to your notification regarding cargo: must inform you can 23500 has already been consigned to berth 29, *Harukk*—"

"Get through to Sikkukkut," Pyanfar said to her back. "Tell him there's a shipment for him in the hands of the stsho."

"You can't afford to lose that cargo," Khym said, swinging round. "To stsho or to kif. Pyanfar—"

"Captain," she said, folding her arms. His eyes burned. She stood her ground. "You're on the bridge. It's *captain. Eyes to that board.*"

He visibly trembled. The sigh gusted through his nostrils like the breath of a furnace. And he turned back to the board.

"Huh," she said, her worst anticipations overturned.

"The stationmaster wants to talk to you," Haral said. "I think it's gtst interpreter."

"I'll take it." She sat down in her place at controls and stuck a com plug in her ear, leaned toward the board pickup and punched the blinking light. "This is Pyanfar Chanur. Have you a question, esteemed director?"

"The director informs you—" the reply came back "—this high-handed threat will not suffice. We have your signed acknowledgment of responsibility, but this does not cover lawsuits and our liabilities. We wish payment now."

"Is that so?" Her lips drew back as if she had the director in sight. "Tell the director gtst new Phase is a scoundrel, a liar and a pirate."

A pause. "—Our demand is just. The damages of four hundred million must be paid and the lawsuits must be settled—"

"Collect it from the kif."

"—If *The Pride of Chanur* undocks without payment it will violate treaty and application for reparations will go to the *han*. Now this message would be more convenient than usual to deliver."

She sucked in her breath. Gods. For a stsho, the old bastard had a certain flair.

"—Your response."

"Bargain. On the one hand we will countersue. If we lose we will appeal to the court at Llhie nan Tle, to Tpehi, to Llyene, and the case will go on for years—while *gtst* remain legally responsible for holding our goods in warehouse while litigation proceeds."

"—This might be acceptable."

"On the other hand—on the other hand, esteemed director—"

"—Get quickly to this other hand."

"If the request for payment were otherwise phrased, and if Meetpoint makes itself responsible for all present and future lawsuits out of the settlement, money might be forthcoming."

"—Please restate. Was this an offer of payment?"

"The station assumes full financial responsibility for present and future suits and reparations arising from the riot, releases all cargo claims, trades with our factors at listed station exchange rates, and provides us one unified bill for *The Pride's* damage repair."

"Please restate, Chanur captain. This translator understood 'ship damage repair.' "

"You have it right."

A delay. "—This smacks of illegality."

"Absolutely not. We will swear to damages

suffered by *The Pride* during the disturbances. Never mind what kind. I'm sure you have the talent to word it so we can both sign it."

"Please, please, this translator must be correct."

"You've got it. You clear our record, expedite us out, and pad that gods-rotted bill as much as you want. I'll meet you on the dock with the credit authorization in a quarter hour."

"—This is subterfuge. Chanur is known destitute."

"Revise your information, esteemed director. Chanur just called in a debt."

Prolonged silence.

"Well?"

"Excuse, esteemed Chanur captain. This will take consideration."

"You by the gods get me out of here."

More silence. "Please be discreet."

"Would the esteemed director contact me on an unsecure channel? The esteemed director is no fool. It would not be profitable for *gtst* to appeal to the *han*, in whatever form. This would surely tie up the funds in litigation." She turned and motioned furiously at Haral. "*Legal release*," she said into the pickup; and to Haral, and her eyes fell on Khym once-lord-Mahn, on a tense expression turned her way. She motioned at him, listening with one ear to stsho dithering. *Do it*, she mouthed. "—Listen, I told you, pad the bill all you want. I'm not coming to the office again. You're coming to the docks and you're going to sign a release for all damages, hear that?''

There was frantic activity to her right. Haral had comp reeling up legal forms and Khym was leaning over her shoulder muttering corrections and wordings.

By the gods, Mahn's ex-lord, ex-legal counsel. In his element.

She grinned at the mike and listened to more blather. "Simply put," she said to the director, once Stle stles stlen, "you sign ours, we sign yours, we get our papers clear and our cargo sold for top going rate, and you can show the High Director at Nsthen you got full compensation, right? Otherwise you report unpaid damages. Which do you want?''

"The director relays to you *gtst* profound distress that Chanur should have been slandered by fools. *Gtst* is sending you the papers at once and further sends you a gift to make amends for this misunderstanding.''

"Chanur will reciprocate in acknowledgment of the director's wisdom in detecting these slanders." She searched rapidly through the data bin for the appropriate forms, copied those, snagged the one that Haral thrust into her hand, fully printed, bilingual in stshoshi and hani and ready for signature. "Profound gratitude, yes." She broke the contact and flipped the documents looking for key clauses. "Watertight?"

"Full release," Khym said.

"It had better be." She gathered up all the papers, spun the chair on its mechanism. "Eyes back to that scan, hear?"

"You need escort, captain?" Haral asked.

"You stay here. Tell Hilfy meet me at the lock. I gods-rotted don't need protection from the stsho and I want you at controls. In case." She flung herself out of the chair and headed for the door.

Tully was inbound, in great haste. "Pyanfar!" he cried.

"Sorry, Tully, no time." She brushed past, or tried. He caught her arm.

"Got talk! Pyanfar!"

"No time, Tully. Haral—see to him."

"No # listen I # go #!" He snatched again when she broke the grip and tried to overtake her in the hall. "Pyanfar!"

As she left him behind.

"*Pyanfar—*"

She made it into the lift and shut the door between. She punched com. "Haral. Get Tully under wraps. Get him his drugs for jump. And stay by those controls!"

Not the most logical series of orders.

Gods, Tully and Khym loose on the same level of the ship, Haral busy—

The lift stopped on lower deck. The door opened, on Tirun, Chur and Geran, standing at the lift. Haral's voice rang through the lower corridor—"*Who's free down there?*"

"Get topside," Pyanfar said, coming through them, papers in hand. "Move it, hear?" Their fur was draggled, dark-tipped with sweat. They smelled of it. "*Get Tully put somewhere!*"

"Aye."

The door closed and they went up. She headed down the corridor at a long stride, where Hilfy waited at the lock, slant-eared and with the whites showing round her eyes.

"Calm down, imp," she said, meeting that look. "It's just the stsho this time."

But she still had the gun in her pocket. It lately seemed a good idea.

The Pride's area of the dock was quiet now, ghostly quiet, with the giant doors to the market still sealed, with the cargo access shut and the station's cargo ramp drawn back and dark. No cans stood about the dock. Only the gantry remained, the huge air ducts socketed to the vent panel beside the water in- and outflow hoses, but those were in shutdown inside. The sensor-bundle, the sextuple power cables and the com lines: that was all that tied *The Pride* to station now, those and the access tube, the station personnel ramp, and the probe and grapples that, behind that triple-thick wall, added failsafe to *The Pride*'s own steel-armed grip.

Not much, compared to the truck-wide cargo ramp. Not much to hold them now that that link was free. A ship could break away from grapples if it had to, taking damage and trusting station valves and gates to shut. Not even kif had ᵢdone such a thing, reckless as they were of life, but stsho in their paranoia might *think* of such possibilities.

Pyanfar cast one narrowed look at that contact with their docking probe and thought such lawless thoughts.

Like turning pirate.

Like what a desperate hani could do, if she lost a gamble with the mahendo'sat and the *han* and there were nothing left at home. Her crew would stay loyal and to a mahen hell with the *han* if Kohan Chanur died.

Good gods. The thought chilled. It came of advancing age.

Of having a male aboard. Put the mind in different modes. Like *hunt* and *nest* and *kill the intruders* instead of the polite surrender to the *han* on which civilization rested.

Pulling sticks, Khym called it.

Hani ships going far and wide across Compact space with males aboard and all the attendant mindset in the crews. Riot on station docks, interHouse brawls, crews at odds with

other crews and hani born in space, never knowing Anuurn under their feet at all, with no
Hermitage in reach.

Gods, what am I doing here?—standing by
Hilfy, gun in pocket, watching a stsho official
car come humming up the dock. Somehow she
had gotten into this. The steps to it eluded her
at the moment, but the steps that led *from* it—

A kif offered alliance—and for one fleeting
moment it truly looked attractive. She was running out of friends.

The car rolled up and stopped humming;
hummed again in a different key as the door
slid down and Stle stles stlen's current persona
put out a pink-shod foot. The translator got out
the other door and hastened round with a flurry
of robes like rainbow light, to offer *gtst* hand to
the director.

Stle stles stlen (or whatever *gtst* called *gtst*self
this hour) straightened to *gtst* feet and waved
gtst limp-wristed, long-fingered hand. "Shoss."

A paper appeared from some depth of the
translator's robes. *Gtst* offered it, *gtst* mooncol-
ored eyes fluttering in wide nervousness.

"Take it," Pyanfar said to Hilfy, assuming
the loftiness the stsho understood: assistants
traded papers, perused them.

"Bill," Hilfy read in a small strangled voice,
"for 1.2 *billion* credits, aunt."

"I figured. Let me see that."

Hilfy handed it over. Document-reading proceeded to a higher level as Stle stles stlen took the release forms into gtst own pearly hands.

A long rustling of pages while the gantry lines thumped and hissed overhead.

"All right," Pyanfar said.

"Hesth," said Stle stles stlen, and in hani: "Where is this money?"

She held out the appropriate paper. Stle stles stlen took it in gtst own hands, and gtst head came up and gtst eyes went wide.

"Well?" Pyanfar said, keeping her ears up, her expression confident and bland.

"—This is an extravagant power," the translator rendered.

"Of course it is. And I'm sure the esteemed director will want to file that copy. I keep the original."

"Esteemed hani friend," said Stle stles stlen.

"Got a pen?"

Stle stles stlen snatched it from the translator and offered it gtstself. If gtst had had external ears they would have pricked far forward.

She signed; gtst signed; documents changed hands and Chur and the translator signed. Hectic flushes almost to pink chased nacre across Stle stles stlen's pearly skin.

Gtst looked up with adoration in gtst eyes, waved gtst hand and out of the inexhaustible rainbow robes, the translator brought a smallish presentation box, which Stle stles stlen proffered gtstself.

"Accept this trifle."

"Munificent." Pyanfar pocketed the box. "Your files have my manifest: do select a case of Anuurn honey for your table."

"Excellent hani."

"I go first on the departure list."

"Oh, yes." *Gtst* bowed, fluttered. "At earliest." *Gtst* backed toward the car and stopped, looking wide-eyed, then ducked inside.

The translator saw the director inside and the door raised, whisked *gtst* rainbow self around to *gtst* own side.

The car hummed to life, opaqued its windows, and hummed a quick u-turn, off down the docks.

"Aunt—" Hilfy said.

She turned, expecting one of the crew had come outside.

She saw instead a kif between them and the lock, and her hand twitched toward her pocket— prudently stopped with a mere twitch. She stood stiff-legged, hearing Hilfy sotto voce beside her, the belt-com doubtless thumbed: "Haral, for the gods' sakes—*Haral*—there's a kif out here—"

The kif flourished a hand among its robes, billowing the hem like the edge of some dark wing. It sauntered forward with the ease of an old, old friend.

"That you, Sikkukkut?"

"Strange. I can tell hani apart."

"Get off my dockside."

"I came to follow up my message. The ring. How did your passenger receive it?"

"I forgot. Frankly, I forgot."

"Can it be he couldn't receive it? Damaged in shipment, might he be? That would distress me."

"I'm sure it would. Get out of my way."

"Your crewwoman's calling help, is she?"

"You won't want to stay around to see."

The thin wrinkled snout acquired a chain of wrinkles. "So you're putting out. Beware of Kita Point."

"Thanks."

More wrinkles. "Of course. There are such limited ways out of Meetpoint. Except for those the stsho permit. Except for us—who go where we like. I wonder where *Mahijiru* is."

"Don't know, then? Good."

"Your *sfik* will kill you."

"*My* ego, is it?—Come on, Hilfy." She started forward, picking a course to *The Pride* just out of kifish long-armed reach. But he moved to intercept them.

"We are both hunter-kinds, hunter Pyanfar." And with a twitch of that long hairless nose: "Kif are better."

"Hani are smarter." She had stopped, hand in pocket. "*I* have a gun."

Sikkukkut's long black nose gained wrinkles and lost them. "But being hani—you dare not use it unless I prove armed. This is the burden of a species its hosts fear not."

"It's called civilization, you earless bastard."

A dry kifish sniffing, like laughter. "The stsho are grass to us. You will not join with me."

"In a mahen hell."

He lifted both hands, palm outward. "I do not challenge, hunter Pyanfar."

Her hand tensed on the gun, to be quick; but the tall kif turned his black-cloaked back and walked off with that peculiar stalking gait.

"*Sfik*," Hilfy muttered, who was the linguist among them. "Means like *pride*, like *honor*, if the kif had any."

"If," Pyanfar said, staring after the kif and not forgetting a sweep about to see if there were confederates lurking: there were not. "That mouth may speak hani; that brain's pure kif. Move it. Get out of here."

"I have a gun," Hilfy said, backing away as she was told. "Come on, aunt. Let's both get out of here."

"Huh." She backed, turned, grabbed Hilfy by the arm and both of them hastened up the rampway into the access, headon into Tirun and Chur who were coming out.

"Good gods," she said when her heart had restarted.

"Sounded like you had trouble," Tirun said.

"It walked off," she said, and gathered them all up, marched them ahead of her past the safety of the airlock. Chur shut the door.

"Kif?" asked Tirun then.

"Kif," she said, and looked around sharply at movement to her left, where Geran stood, with Tully.

"Got talk," he said.

"Geran, for the gods' sakes I said settle him."

"It's urgent, captain."

"Everything's urgent. Get in line."

"Aunt," Hilfy said, with that kind of look Hilfy could get when something was utterly out of joint.

"Got paper," Tully said, breathless. "Got—" The translator garbled over mangled hani words.

"Get me a plug, will you?" One materialized out of Hilfy's pocket, and she put the audio into her ear. "Tully, what are those papers?"

"Got paper say human come fight kif # # need hani."

"Rot that translator. I'm losing that."

"Human come fight kif."

A very cold lump settled to her stomach. "Why, Tully?"

"Make kif #. *Friend*, Pyanfar. Bring lot human come fight kif."

The cold grew colder still.

"Sounds like," said Tirun, "more than one ship involved."

"They want help," said Hilfy. "*That's* why he came. That's what I think he's saying. It's nothing to do with trade."

"Gods," she muttered, and looked up, at an earnest human face, at four crewwomen with faces taut with the same kind of thoughts. "Kif know this, Tully?"

"Maybe know," he said. He drew a great breath and let it go, held out his hands as if appeal could get past the translator. "Come long way find you. Kif—kif make trouble # one time fight Goldtooth friend."

"Goldtooth," she said. The name was a bad taste in her mouth. "What am I supposed to do with you? Huh?"

"Go Maing Tol. Go Anuurn."

"Gods rot it, Tully, we got *kif* up to our noses!"

His pale eyes locked on hers, desperate. "Fight," he said. "Got make fight, Py-an-far."

She lowered her ears and brought them up again, glancing round at her crew. Scared faces. Looking to her for answers.

"Ought to give him to *Vigilance*," she muttered, "and advertise it to the kif."

No one said anything. She imagined the consequences for herself if she did that. The fragile Compact broken wide open, kif chasing a *han* deputy ship.

Or Ehrran leaving him on a stsho station, where not a hand would be raised to prevent kif from walking in and doing what they liked.

Kif would do anything, if profit in doing it outweighed the profit in restraint.

"Where we taking him?" Tirun asked.

"Maing Tol, Goldtooth says."

"Captain—We do that and that blackbreeches'll have our ears. Begging the captain's pardon."

More questions of her orders. She stared at Tirun, at a cousin, an old comrade; at another Chanur whose life was at risk.

"You want to turn him over to Ehrran, Tirun?"

Tirun stood there with her ears down, with rapid thinking going on behind her eyes. "We could send another can to *Vigilance*," she said. "Let that kif bastard wonder."

The idea struck her fancy. But: "No," she said, thinking of those same consequences. "Can't risk it. Come on." She seized Tully by the arm and dragged him into motion, then abandoned the grip as she headed for the lift. "Get Tully settled. Get his drugs for him and get up to the bridge."

"Go?" Tully asked, close at her heels. "Pyanfar—go Hoas?"

"Urtur," she said, reaching the lift. She looked back as Chur and Hilfy took him by the arms. Tirun punched the door and held it. "Going to

Urtur. Going fast. Take the drugs. Stay out of the way. Understand?"

"Got," he said, and let them pull him off down the hall. She stepped into the lift and Tirun got in and pushed the buttons.

One worried look from Tirun. That was all.

"I know," she said, which summed it up. She pulled the presentation case from the pocket where she had put it, opened it as the car shot upward.

A note. *Beware Ismehanan-min*, it said.

Meaning Goldtooth.

She handed it to Tirun.

The door opened on the upper corridor.

Chapter Five

There was quiet on the bridge, a great deal of calm and quiet, considering the situation, Khym brimming with questions, and a handful of exhausted crew. No one said a word. Six pairs of eyes were on her, expecting her to come up with something remarkably clever.

1.2 billion credits. Hilfy still looked to be in shock.

"Got a few problems," Pyanfar said, sinking into her chair, which was turned to face the bridge at large. "I think we'd better take that docking clearance the stsho promised and get ourselves our of here before they change their minds. Chur, Hilfy, you sure Tully's set, got his drugs, knows to stay put."

"Aye," Chur said.

"I don't promise we get a calm ride out of here. And we're going to push it hard. We're headed for Urtur. We're stripped. We can one-jump it. When we come in there we keep our ears pricked and get the news. Gods send it isn't kif. —Questions?"

Dead quiet.

She picked up a courier cylinder from the document pocket on the side of the chair. "Chur."

"Aye."

"Get one of the docking crew to shoot that through the pneumat. Fast."

Chur took it, whirled and headed out of the bridge with a scrape of claws. So *that* was seen to. If Stle stles stlen did not have all their messages intercepted, rot his pearly hide.

"Crew to stations. —Khym—" She stood up and in the general mill of crew taking seats she took Khym's arm and took him into the small nook of quiet in the corridor outside.

"For this one I recommend the tranquilizer," she said. "Tully takes it. Topside med kit still has it."

"I don't need it," he muttered, his ears gone down. "I don't need—"

"Listen to me. Old hands lose their stomachs in this kind of thing. G like planetary lift; we'll be cycling the vanes—"

"I'm not going to my cabin. Look, you wanted me on the bridge, *work*, you said—"

"You're *not* staying on the bridge."

"There's the observers' seats."

"No."

"Please, Py." His voice sank to its lowest pitch. His amber eyes were quick and large. "*Captain*. Win a ring, you said. In front of them, for the gods' sake, Py. I won't make trouble. Won't."

Her ears fell; her heart went over. "Gods rot it, this isn't a simple hop from port to port."

"Part of the crew. Isn't that what you meant?"

"This isn't a question—"

"Pride's pride, Py. You put me there; you by the gods leave me there. Or do you think the crew won't have it?"

Soft-headed, that was what.

"You take number one observer," she said. "You watch Geran watch scan and if you get sick in the cycles you by the gods reach the bags undercabinet, I don't care what else is going on. If you haven't ridden through a high-v vector change with someone heaving up you haven't seen a mess. Got it?" She jabbed him with one sharp claw, saw him go tight around the nose. "Besides, it fogs the screens."

Without a word he ducked back into the bridge.

She went back behind him, while he set himself into the first of the three observer posts, at Geran's elbow: Geran gave him a look, betraying no dismay, but a look all the same. He fumbled after belts and began fastening them—not nervous, no. He only missed the insert twice.

She slipped into her own place, snapped the restraint one-handed and powered the chair about all in one smooth sequence, because she could, and failed to realize why she did it until she had.

She argued him onto the bridge for one reason and turned surly when he put himself there. And knew it.

Gods.

"Ready to disengage the probe," Haral said.

"Chur's still down there. Hilfy, advise *Vigilance* they've got a message coming."

"Aye." A small delay. "They acknowledge. That's all."

She gave Rhif Ehrran that, she was not prone to destructive chatter.

Advise you, that couriered message said, *kif on our trail. Stop at nothing, even attack on han deputy. Do not attract interest. Station at hazard. Ours more. We take evasive measures, best possible. No explanation possible.*

Well to be out of port when that hit Ehrran's lap.

A series of thumps rang up from the bow, The Pride's own language of clangs and bumps, reliable as her telltales: docking probes had retracted; vents were sealed. Outside the station hull, the grapples disengaged.

"Gantry's clear," Haral said, busy with the prep sequences.

"Where's Chur? She make it?"

Com relayed. "She's coming," Tirun said. "All clear."

"Give me out-schedule."

"Up," Tirun said, and: "Huh."

Banny Ayhar's *Prosperity* was on the list, outbound for Urtur via Hoas Point. So was *Marrar's Golden Sun.*

There went gossip on its way to Anuurn, fast as a loaded merchant ship could travel and carry an Ehrran message.

Likewise a stsho ship had gone outbound half an hour ago, one *E Mnestsist,* Rhus flisth'ess commanding. Hoas-bound for Urtur.

So every ship bound from Meetpoint to mahen-hani space had to go to Urtur via Hoas. Unless they were doing it cargo-stripped, to make Urtur in a single jump. The *Pride*'s own course showed Urtur-via-Hoas, which was a lie.

There were other possibilities from Meetpoint: Nsthen in stsho space, where only stsho and methane-breathers were allowed. The tc'a border-port of V'n'n'u; the tc'a port of Tt'a'va'o: methane-breather/stsho again. The kif port of Kefk, the one kifish corridor to Meetpoint; Kshshti in the Disputed Territories. Messages could go a great many ways from Meetpoint, that being the nature of Meetpoint in its conception.

And a tight-beamed lightspeed message could get to an outbound ship like *E Mnestsist* before it had time to jump. It could still do a vector change . . . if one Stle stles stlen had something *gtst* wanted relayed.

Conniving bastard.

The Pride of Chanur was listed departure ———, without a time. They had been bumped up ahead of *Prosperity* and *Golden Sun*.

That would not sweeten Banny Ayhar's mood, no question at all.

And there was not a single kif listed.

"No telling what's been delayed *off* that list," she muttered. "Could have a raft of kif leaving ten minutes behind us. Station that can't keep its registry boards running dockside, gods know what it does with out-schedules when money changes hands— Power up, Haral: keep us null for outbound."

"Up," Haral said; she heard the distant sound of the pumps delivering their load; the electric whump! of startup normally followed by the louder crash of cylinder-lock going off; but it stayed locked. They would have no G but afterthrust on this system transit. Safer that way. It made sudden moves safer.

She heard the sound of running feet scramble into the bridge at her back; heard a body hit a seat.

"Chur's in."

"Message went," Chur said over the com, above the noise. "Saw it go into the slot."

"Helm to one." Helm to her own board. She pushed buttons, let the auto-interlock stay in during the undock, the computer reckoning their mass and how hard to push to stay inside legal parameters. The holds were empty. The thrust-indicator was way down. The ordinary mark would have hit *The Pride* like a hard kick at an empty can.

"Aunt." That was Hilfy at com one. "Question."

"Ask it."

"That bill—"

"What about that bill?"

"Mahendo'sat paying that?"

"Huh. Yes."

"They know it?"

"Tell you something, imp. There's two strong reasons for one-jumping this. One of them's the kif."

"Gods, aunt—"

"Tirun, you teaching the kid to swear?"

"How do we pay it?"

"It's paid. Goldtooth paid it. He just doesn't know it yet. Stand by the vector shift. We're not going out of here like last time. By the book, at least till we get running room.''

They reached the l-zone limit, two-vectored as they were with station's spin and their own bow-thrust, headed tailfirst across the invisible mark. She gave the port thrust a ten-second burn that slewed the bow about in the same line as spin and gave comp its heading.

"But, aunt—"

The comp did the next burn, trueing up.

"Put it this way. All of you listening? There's a little matter with the mahendo'sat. They're paying the bar bill. Hear? —Put her zero two on mark, Haral. Get the cameras working port-side.''

"Want a look at that kif?"

"Number one right, cousin. Geran, handle that.''

"Got it. Image to your four.''

The image came to fourth screen on her board, clear, fine color, the outside of Meetpoint Station, a portion of its torus shape, the huge painted dock numbers obscured here and there by ships nose-on to station. "Main that,'' she said. The drifting image went to all stations, the strange shape of a stsho trader, the sleek, wicked silhouette of kif, leaner than they had to be; and one, one with uncommonly large vanes and a series of tanks about the waist.

"Those tanks will blow off real easy,'' she

132

said. "Take a good look, Hilfy, Khym. A real good look."

"Hunter-ship," Hilfy said.

"No trader. That's for sure. Gods-rotted kif hunter. That's *Harukk*, no need to look for numbers." She keyed the safety systems to ADVISE ONLY and pushed the mains in hard.

G hit, pressed her elbow into the brace and triggered the over-arm lock that held her hand within reach of the board. New system. It worked. She had rigged *The Pride* with what protections they could afford, since Gaohn; handholds, line-rigs, braces at all boards. A few extra firearms, quietly acquired.

"That's the kif reason," she said against the G. "And the other one for putting a little hurry on—I'd like to beat a certain check to the bank."

"Can we cover it?" Tirun's voice, over com. "—Later?"

"Huh. That's *still* Goldtooth's problem."

"What's going on?" asked Khym.

Silence, except for ship noise, the long misery of acceleration.

"What's going on?" he asked again.

"Just a business arrangement," she said. "Hold onto your stomach. We're coming up on two-range. Going to give ourselves a boost."

"Pyanfar—"

"Tell you later. Haral, set her up."

"Captain, got another ship undocked," Chur said from scan.

"Gods rot. Who?"

"Can't tell yet. Station's not talking. Stand by."

They were not yet far enough and fast enough for *C* to play havoc with information: not far enough and fast yet by far to be out of range of that sleek kif ship back there.

That ship could start out a day late and be waiting for them on Urtur rim. No question. She drew quiet small breaths against the G and calculated. A rush after them made no sense, for a ship that fast.

It was not kif that had undocked. She was willing to bet not kif. It had no need to race, being able to guess their course.

"Ship is *knnn*."

"Oh, good gods."

"What's the matter?" (Khym.)

Knnn. Methane-breathing, dangerous and lunatic in their moves. No one wanted the knnn stirred up.

And kif trouble might. Any trouble might.

"What's the matter?" (Khym again).

"Long explanation," Pyanfar muttered. "Hold the questions, Kyhm. We're busy."

"Com coming up," Hilfy said.

An insane wailing came over com, knnn-song, which announced to the universe and other knnn whatever it was the knnn thought good to say.

Or it was simply singing for its own amusement, and putting it out on com out of thinking as obscure as the rest of its logic.

"Bearing zero two by fourteen."

Askew for them. That meant nothing. Knnn ships obeyed different laws.

"Stand by that cycle," she said, and listened for Haral's acknowledgment. "Take it twice. We're getting out of here."

Vanes cycled in, a brief, stomach-wrenching lurch to a higher energy state. Nausea threatened. Instruments recycled with a flurry of lights, recalibrating. She checked the nav fix on Urtur.

"Knnn no change," Chur said.

Second pulse.

"Helm to one." Controls flashed live under her hands as Haral handed it over. They were up to V, outbound. "Stand by jump. Fix on that knnn to the last gods-rotted second."

Knnn had policy, somewhere in their moves. Black hair-snarls animate on long thin legs, they built good ships—far better ships than oxy-breathers could survive, unless things also went on in them that played games with stress. Nothing could talk to knnn but the leathery, serpentine tc'a, and tc'a brains were manifold matrices.

Nothing could reason with knnn but tc'a.

Time was, knnn took anything they liked, stripped ships in midcourse, raided the earliest stations: so stsho said. It was before the hani came. Tc'a got through the concept of trade—at least so knnn left *something* in their forays. Now they darted manic-fast into methane-breather sectors, deposited some object, which might be anything, and skittered off again with whatever they wanted—which might, again, be *anything*.

Tc'a coped. Chi did, one supposed; but chi, looking like a collection of yellow, rapid-moving sticks, were crazier than knnn. And tc'a themselves were hazy on trade-concepts. Gods knew how they ran their worlds. No outsider did.

"Mark to jump: five minutes."

"How's that knnn?"

"Still— It just cycled, captain."

"I want better news. That's four and counting."

"Continuing to cycle. That's into our lag-time—" Meaning that in the lag of lightspeed information the knnn might be doing other things.

"Rot the book." She shoved the jump cycle in.

—dropped
        —seatfirst—
                —topside down—
      —rightside up

—back again in here and now, and the stomach still wanting to turn itself inside out—

There was that wretched halfway-there, while senses swam, fingers took an hour clenching on controls, instruments underwent a slow ripple of lights that took a subjective day arriving at nothing special at all—

Solidity then, with one focus, sharp-edged and dreadful as the soft uncertainties before, with endless fascination in the angles of counters, the colors, the textures. A mind could get lost in the endless detail of a counter-edge.

Pyanfar swallowed against the dry mouth and copper taste that came with compressed time, flexed hands that had not flexed for three-odd weeks local. The chronometers showed a dubious 3.2 days. The body reacted: would shed hair and old skin within the hour as if entropy had hit, not quite three days' worth, but some: and Tully's drugs would wear off, while the bowels and kidneys had other, later consequences, and blood sugar went through loops and dives, obscuring sense and hazing senses and doing things to the stomach.

Beep went controls.

She shoved the Dump down hard.

Second phasing in and out of hyperspace, bleeding off velocity in the process.

Third.

Her stomach heaved. She held her jaw clenched. The copper taste was worse.

Beep.

"That's Urtur beacon confirmed," Haral read off. "Heading zero, nine, two."

Automatic alarms went off in her skull, memories she had forced there weeks ago. "Geran! 'ware of kif. Do we have company?"

"Checking."

Three subjective days since she had done out-bound at Meetpoint and she felt the ache in her shoulders. "Khym. You all right?"

An incoherent answer; he sounded alive.

"Got Urtur beacon," Haral said. "Tirun. Sort it."

"Aye." That was Urtur beacon information coming in, constant-send, giving incoming ships the exact position of objects insystem so far as known. Course assignment would come, as soon as bounce-back time had delivered their presence to Urtur's robot outrange beacon and its automated systems computed them a lane.

"Advise Beacon," Pyanfar said, "that we're through-traffic. Get your star-fix." Her hands shook. Crew would be in no better state. She wanted a drink, imagined floods of liquid, iced, deluges of flavors. Even tepid. Brackish. Anything.

"Fix on Kirdu," Haral said. "Affirmative. Laying course for Maing Tol via Kita Point."

"Message sent," Hilfy said.

"How long to station signal?"

"About two hours," Tirun said. "That's 2.31. Beacon doesn't show any ship in the range. It's not picking us up."

"Beacon signal," Hilfy said. "Aunt—We're getting a code-call off beacon. We've got a *message* waiting. Stand by."

"Huh." A cold feeling settled to Pyanfar's stomach. "Put it through on one." The beacon robot had output something triggered by *The Pride's* automatic ID, like a tripline. They came into system, beacon affirmed their identity and spat out what it held memory-stored for them. Expensive mail. Very.

And the robot scan was still not showing them added to image of Urtur system. It was not direct scan-image. It was computer-generated; and the computer failed to put their existence on the screen.

"We've got an error," Haral said. "Bastard beacon's giving us Kshshti heading, wants us to take starfix on Maing Tol. Put that lane request through again, Hilfy. It's gone crazy."

"Hold that." Pyanfar stared at the message coming up on her number one screen. She keyed the Print on: it hummed and spat out hardcopy into the documents bin. Strings and strings of codes. More codes. Theirs. . . . *Ana Ismehananmin*, it said, *to good friend. Advise you got bad trouble Kita Point. Beacon give you now new heading. I fix with Urtur authority, number one good.*

Go Kshshti route. Know got close kif, but Kita got too many kif. Mahen ship, kif ship, got two hand number ship. Mahen ship not got be everywhere too quick. Sorry this trouble.

You one-jump Kshshti number one fine, no trouble, no stop middle of dark like Kita. You reach Kshshti you give authorization code Hasano-ma.

You do good; Know you number one quick thinker. Kif not catch.

"You egg-sucking bastard!" The restraint held her seated and half cut off her wind. She took a clawed swipe at the tray and slammed the printout onto the clearspace of the panel; but the screen kept on feeding codes and the printer kept on going in idiot persistence.

"Message from beacon," Hilfy said, carefully unperturbed. "Blinker alarm advises us acknowledge and accept new heading."

She cut the screen output. The printer, undefeated, hummed and spat out yet another sheet.

Second message. More codes. *Urtur station advise you course change big urgent. You not be register on system scan. Beacon blank you image give you cover. Go quick.*

"Beacon's not malfunctioning," she muttered. "It means it. That bastard Goldtooth set something up with Urtur. They're routing us to Kshshti."

"Kshshti's half kif," Geran protested. "We go in there—"

"It's a one-jump. He's right in that, if Kita's blocked. At least we won't be out in the dark nowhere with the kif. . . . Call up Records: what's Kshshti got for muscle?"

"Searching," Chur said. ". . . .Got two hunter-ships assigned from Maing Tol; stats show ten percent stsho calls, sixteen t'ca-chi, thirty-two kif, fifty-one mahendo'sat—I don't get any assurance on those hunter-ships being there. *Based* there, it says."

"Fine." She gnawed at her mustaches and twitched her ears while the beacon went into its Acknowledge-comply routine and com flashed warning lights. Tick-tick. Tick. Tick-tick-tick. Haos was still possible. So was Kura. The stsho. The han. "We go with it. Don't see what else to do. Beacon's going to blow a circuit otherwise."

"We're pretty deep in the well," Haral said, understated caution. The star had them firmly now: vector shift meant total dump. Meant a rough reacquisition, fighting to get more V back than a star wanted to give them.

"Got no choice, have we? Advise Tully. Can't wait around."

Hilfy relayed. "Tully's coherent. He says go."

"Set it," Pyanfar said, and raked the last print-out from the bin.

And stared. It was not the comp readout she had expected. That was on the bottom of the tray. Another beacon-sending had come in, autoed into the printout bin.

No codes this time. Perfect hani.

Hani ship The Pride of Chanur: avoid Kita. Akkhtimakt has established watchers there. You will not come alive through that space.

Be no fool.

A shiver went over her skin.

"Hilfy."

"Aunt?"

"You read that number-three message?"

A silence. Hilfy searched her bin.

"Who sent *that*?" Hilfry wondered, quiet and hoarse.

"Someone fast," she said.

"Brace for dump," Haral said.

The vanes cycled in, a dizzying pulse half-forming their hyperspace bubble, a ripple like vision through oil.

It let them go and Haral began their realspace course-change then, a long sickening hammering of correcting directionals and mains. G hauled at an already outraged gut.

"Got the Maing Tol fix," Haral said. And a long, long while later, when the engines reached null-V and kept burning: "We just passed null."

And later, as bodies ached in one long misery: "Closing on mark."

"Go when ready," Pyanfar said. Urtur's dust had not hit the hull yet, but the place always sent the wind up her back.

Blanked off station scan, for the gods' sake. A ship hurtling dark and unreported through Urtur system with Urtur Station's collusion, a risk to other ships—

Fearing what? Kif insystem?

"Stand by the pulse." Haral's voice cracked with fatigue.

"Want me to take it?"

"I've got it set. Stand by."

Another pulse, another queasy moment neither here nor there. There was the bloody smear of a red light on the board.

"Vane two red," Pyanfar muttered. "Stop it there."

"We're a shade off V."

"What blew?" (Khym, weakly.) "There something wrong?"

"Regulator in the vane column," Pyanfar said, blinking it all into focus again. Her bones ached. "Ship doesn't like all this change of mind. Tirun, I want an interrupt check on that vane."

"Right." Tirun's voice shook with exhaustion. No complaints. "Sure like to know why it didn't cut off."

"Solve it from inside."

"Urtur's no gods-rotted place for a walk."

"We in trouble?" Khym asked.

"Just got a little mechanical problem. Still got one backup left on that system. Regulator ought to have shut the vane down short of blowing what blew. I think our problem's there. That's an in-hull problem. No big trouble." But it was trouble. *Something* made it blow. And Kshshti was a long, long one-jump. Big stress. If that vane went— "What's our transit time?"

"Got—" Haral said, "—48.4 hours to next jump."

"We'll find the glitch by then." She powered the chair back, needing room to breathe. Another quarter turn of the chair and she saw Khym sitting there, head leaned back against the cushion, breathing in slow, careful intakes, looking her way with a bleak curiosity. He had not been sick. Was not. Was plainly determined not to be.

Holding it, she guessed.

"Tully wants to come topside," Chur said.

"Fine." She was numb, with a certain insulation between herself and calamities back at Meetpoint, and the one back there on their tail. She looked aside as all number-four screens acquired an image from *The Pride*'s outside eyes, habit when they arrived at a place. Haral had done that, reflex or a statement: no panic. Just routine operations.

Urtur was spectacle enough, to be sure, one great fried egg of a star and system magnified in their pickup, a yellow star for a yolk that glowed hellishly in the flattened disk of dust that surrounded it. Planets swept dark orbits in the disk, accreted rings of their own. Urtur's worlds were mostly gas giants, with a few well-cratered smaller planets buried in the muck.

No place for a walk indeed. Particles would hole even a hardsuit in short order.

Mahendo'sat owned Urtur system, doing mahen things like poking about in the dust hunting clues to why Urtur was like it was—for pure curiosity, which was why mahendo'sat did a great many peculiar things. But at the same time and practically, they maintained a case for the methane-breathers, who thought methane-dominant Elaji a fine fair place, with its clouds aglow with the constant flicker of lightnings and meteors making streaks by the minute in an atmosphere already greenhoused by previous impacts. Oxy-breathers got photos of the surface. Tc'a revelled in it, and mined rare metals, and had industry in that hell.

Knnn too.

And where, she wondered, considering that deficient scan image, was their own private knnn?

Blocked off scan the same as they, and out of range of their own pickup?

Gone, perhaps. Off their track entirely.

She did not trust that. Not finding the knnn simply meant they had not found it.

The Pride did a minor course correction, a gentle push at her left. For any ship going crosswise to the dust circulation, Urtur transit was a matter of finding the most useful hole in the debris and presenting as little as possible of the vane surface to the particles during ecliptic transit.

They had damage enough to contend with, gods knew.

"Get her set and we go auto for a while. You can do those checks after we get some food in you, Tirun. —Who's on galley?"

"Me," said Hilfy.

"Get on it." And not without thought: "Crew-youngest always gets the extra duty. You help her, Khym."

Khym just stared at her from the oblique, a desperate, half-drowned stare. Hilfy turned her chair, released her restraints and levered herself out of it. Khym moved then, got up like a drunk and held onto the chairback for a moment.

Work, indeed work.

And he followed Hilfy without a backward look, by the gods, the ex-lord of Mahn on galley duty, no complaints.

She drew a long slow breath and remembered youth, Mahn, its fields, the house with the spring.

And a tired elder hani who tried to begin all over. At bottom. In a dimension he hardly understood.

"Going to be one lot of mad shippers," Tirun muttered. "Remember that rush order from that factor?"

"Bet Ayhar nabs it," Chur said.

Pyanfar released her restraints and got to her feet. Her joints ached and there was fire down her back.

She stopped in midstretch. Tully was there in the doorway, ghostlike silent in the white noise of *The Pride's* working. He rested one arm on the doorframe, and stood there, barefoot, in simple crewwoman's breeches and nothing else, looking wan and cold. No more *friend*, no more *Py-anfar*. Just that bruised, cornered look that wondered if anyone had time for him.

"I know," she said. "We get you fed."

"Safe?" he asked. *He* knew ships, enough to feel *The Pride* faltering—and himself alone and knowing all too much. "Ship—" He made a helpless motion. "Break?"

"Got it under control," she said. "Fine. Safe, all fine."

The pale eyes flickered.

"Fix soon," she said. Fear looked back at her, habitual and patient. She beckoned him and he left the door and walked all the way inside. Mobile blue eyes flicked this way and that, scanning monitors for what they could read, quick and furtive move. They centered on her again.

"Got talk." He had gotten a little hani. She grew accustomed to his slurring speech. The translator spat useless static. "Got talk, please got talk."

"Maybe it's time we do." A great uneasiness came over her, things out of joint. Males and tempers and their old friend Tully, whose alien face had that strange, distracted movement of the eyes. Fear of them as well as well as kif? And suspicious reprobate that she was: Lies, Tully? Or plain self-interest from the start?

"Sure," she said. She stank, reeked; she thought instinctively of baths, of males and quarrels and a thousand lunatic distracted things like impacts at this speed, and the vane that showed intact in the image on Tirun's screens (but it was not, inside, and that could be bad news indeed.) Urtur. Docking with, likely, kif about. And not a hope of help. Urtur had no muscle adequate to fend off anything. *Poor human fool, we could lose us all here, don't you know? They'd move in, take what they liked, you foremost—* "Come on," she said to the crew at large, who were all tremble-handed at their work. "Break it off. We eat, get some sleep." She caught Tully by the arm. "You come and tell me, huh?"

Chapter Six

The dust whispered on the hull like distant static, above the other sounds—abrading away, Pyanfar reckoned; but their vanes were canted edge-on to it, the observation dome and lenses were shielded, and that was the best that they could do. So *The Pride* exited this fringe of Urtur with a little polish on her hull. They made what speed they could through the muck at system-edge.

Meanwhile—

Meanwhile they crammed shoulder to shoulder into the galley. They had already extended their table with a fold-out and a let-down bench end when na Khym became permanent. Now they squeezed a few inches each and got Tully in, a company of seven now, unlikely tablefellows. But Tully was still wobbly in his moves, his hands shaking as he gulped cup after cup of carbohydrate-laced gfi and nibbled at this and that; while Khym—Khym ate, plenty, for one who had been wobbly-sick half an hour ago. Pyanfar shot glances his way—misgiving (he bade fair to make himself sick) and halfway pleased (he had lasted the rough ride, by the gods, and gone white-nosed as he was to galley duty, and was on incredibly good behavior.) There might not have been another male at table for all the attention Khym paid between his plate and the rotating center-section with the serving-trays.

There was silence at table, mostly—a little muttered discourse as Tirun and Chur and Haral brought their vane-problem to table with them, and worried it like a bone. A little "have this," and "try that," from Hilfy who tried to slip a little more substance under Tully's ribs.

No harrying, no pressure—take it slow, she thought. And: Keep him calm, keep everything low-key ... the while she watched him relax at last, their old friend, old comrade. It was as if he had—finally—come back to them the way he had been, easier and finally letting go.

Time then to talk of things, when he might tell them the truth. Perhaps they had cornered him, pushed him too much, assured him too little. Perhaps he felt the panic in the air and only now felt easy. Perhaps now there would be truth.

"Your House send you?" Khym said suddenly, looking straight Tully's way, and sent her heart lurching past a beat.

Tully blinked that into slow non-focus. "Send?" the translator queried, flat-voiced . . . O gods, trust indeed, wide-eyed innocence. "Send me?"

"I don't know that they *have* Houses," Pyanfar said, and found her fingers flexed and the claws out. Khym *tried* the situation. She knew him. And she knew Tully. Of a sudden the silence round the table was absolute. She wanted to stop it, to shut it off, and there was no way, no way with Khym in bland, smooth attack-mode. Hunting, gods rot him. Pushing for reaction, the crew's and hers. "Don't use big words. Translator can't handle them."

"House isn't a big word."

"Stick to ship-things. Technical stuff. You don't know *how* it comes out the other side."

"Say again," Tully said.

"I asked who sent you."

"# # send me."

"See?" said Pyanfar. "You get a word it won't make sense."

"Name home," Tully said. "Sun. Also call *Sol*. Planet name *Earth*. Send me."

"He *does* talk."

"So," Pyanfar said. Her ears pricked up despite herself. "Sun, is it?"

"Where are we?" Tully asked. "Ur-tur?"

"Urtur. Yes."

He drew a great breath. "Go Maing Tol."

"Seems so. By way of Kshshti. You know that name?"

"Know." He moved his plate aside a handspan and touched his strange, thin fingers to the table surface. "Meetpoint—Urtur—Kshshti—Maing Tol."

"Huh." He had never known much of the Compact stars. Not from them. "Goldtooth teach?"

"Mahe name Ino. Ship name *Ijir*."

"Before Goldtooth got you, huh? How'd you find Goldtooth?"

He looked worried. Or the translator scrambled it. "Go Goldtooth, yes."

"You with him long?"

"#?"

"Were you long time in Goldtooth's ship?"

Perhaps it was the tone of her voice. His eyes met hers and dived aside after one frozen instant, reestablishing contact perforce.

"Where did you meet Goldtooth?"

"Ino find him."

It did not satisfy her. She sat and stared, forgetting the bite on her fork, not forgetting Khym at her elbow. No fight; don't pick a fight, no trouble while Khym's in it. The strictures crawled up and down her nerves.

"You come how long ago?" Geran asked.

"Don't know," he said, glancing that way. "Long time."

"Days?"

"Lot days."

He could be more precise. He knew the translator's limits. Knew how to manipulate it better than he did. He picked up the cup and drank, covering the silence.

Perhaps the rest of the crew picked up the undertones. She thought so. There was not a move at table. Only Tully.

Their old friend.

She reached slowly into the depths of her pocket, hooked the small, thin ring with a claw and laid it precisely on the tabletop. Click.

His face went a shade further toward stsho pallor, and then he reached for it and took it up in his flat-nailed fingers, examining the inside band. His eyes lifted, that startling blue, wide and dreadful.

"Where find?" he asked. "*Where find, Pyanfar?*"

"Whose?" She knew pain when she saw it

155

and suddenly wished the ring back in her pocket and them less public than this. A kifish gift. She was a fool to have suspected anything but misery in it, a double fool; and having started it there was no way to go but straight ahead.

"Mahe got?" he asked. "Goldtooth?"

"Kif gave it to me," she said, and watched a tremor come into his mouth and stop, his face go paler still if it were possible. "Friend of yours, Tully?"

"What say this kif?"

"Said—said it was a message for our cargo."

The tremor started again, harder to control. No one moved at table, no one on left or right. For a long time that lasted, with the dust rattling on the hull, the rumble of the rotation, the distant whisper of air in the duct above their heads. Water spilled from Tully's eyes and ran down into his beard.

"Friend, huh?" She coughed in self-disgust and shoved her plate back, creating a stir and a little healthy living noise. Scowled at the crew. "Want to get that vane fixed?"

"Where get?" Tully asked before anyone could move.

"Kif named Sikkukkut. Ship named *Harukk*. Who did it belong to, huh?"

His mouth made a sudden straight line, white-edged, as he looked down and put the ring on.

It was too small. He forced it. "Need #," he murmured, seeming to have nothing to do with them or here or now.

"This kif," she said, slipping the words past while the shock was fresh. "This kif was at Meetpoint, Tully. He knew you'd come to us from Goldtooth. He knew our way ahead was blocked. What more he knew I have no idea. Do you want to tell us, Tully? Whose is it?"

The blue eyes burned. "Friend," he said. "Belong friend stay *Ijir*."

She let go a breath and shot a look past a row of puzzled hani faces. "So Goldtooth hedged his bet, huh? You come to us. Your companions go somewhere else. *Where?*"

"Kif got. Kif got # *Ijir*."

"Then the kif know a gods-rotted lot more than you've told us. *What* do they know, Tully? What are you up to, your *hu-man-i-ty?*"

"They ask help."

"How much help? Tully—what are you doing here?"

"Kif. *Kif.*"

"What's going on?" Khym asked from her left. "What's he talking about—kif?"

"Later," she said, and heard the breath gust through Khym's nostrils. "Tully. Tell me what's in that paper. You tell me, hear."

"You got take to Maing Tol."

"Tully. Gratitude mean anything to you? I

saved your mangy *hide*, Tully, more times than I ought."

He gave back against the seat. The eyes set again on hers with that tragic look she hated. "Need you," he said in hani words, a strange, mangled sound that confused the translator to static. "Friend, Pyanfar."

"*I* ask him," Khym rumbled.

"No," she said sharply, and felt an acid rush in her gut, raw panic at the potential in that. She brought her clenched hand down on the table and rattled dishes. Tully flinched, and she glared. "Tully, You talk to me, gods rot you. You tell me what those papers are."

"Ask hani come fight ship take human."

"Make sense."

"Want make trade hani-mahe."

"Truth?"

"Truth."

The eyes pleaded for belief. It did nothing for the feeling in her gut. Wrong, it said. Wrong, wrong, wrong. For kif trouble alone the mahe might have asked the *han* direct. Trade—was the lure, and there was something in the trees.

She shifted her eyes past his shoulder to Haral, wise, scar-nosed Haral. Haral's ears canted back and her mustache drew down with the intimation of something odorous.

But there was nothing profitable in pushing Tully. Trust. They had a little of it. There had been a time he had staved off kif for months, led his interrogators in circles despite torture, despite the murder of companions. Tully had held out. More, he had escaped, off a kifish ship. That was no fool. And no one to be pushed.

"Vane," she said with ulterior motives. "Go."

"Aye." Haral moved, shoved Chur's shoulder. Hilfy and Geran shifted to clear the seats and Tully got up.

"Get the galley cleared," Pyanfar said- "Tully. You just became juniormost. Help Hilfy with the galley. Khym—you fetch and carry on the bridge. Whoever needs it."

"I want to talk to you," Khym said, unbudged.

"No time to talk." She turned her head and met his scowl with her own as he stayed put on the bench, still blocking her way out. "Look, Khym, we've got a vane in partial failure. One of us may have to take a walk after it yet. You got a question that tops it?"

His ears went down in dismay.

"Out," she said.

"We could go to Kura, couldn't we?"

"No. We can't. Can't shift course again this side of Urtur—we're in the dust; we've got a vane down. . . .The last course change gods-rotted near killed us, you understand that? I haven't got time to discuss it." She shoved and he moved. She got up and looked back at him, at Hilfy and Tully who were gathering dishes at furious speed. But Khym lingered, a towering hurt. She gathered up her patience, took him by the arm, walked him to the privacy of the bridgeward corridor. "Look, Khym—we've got troubles."

"Somehow," he said, "I figured that."

"Kshshti's mahen-held," she said. "Barely. If the kif have Kita watched they've likely got something in at Kshshti. But there's help there or the mahendo'sat wouldn't send us that direction."

"You trust what they say?"

She looked behind him, where one stark-pale human hastened to hand dishes off the table and close doors.

"I don't know," she said. "Go."

"You don't put me off, Py."

She gave him one long burning look.

"Chanur property," he said. "I do forget."

"What do you want, Khym? I'll tell you what I want. I want that gods-rotted vane fixed. I want us out of here. Are you helping?"

He drew a long, long breath and cast a look over his shoulder in Tully's direction. "Pet?"

"Shut it up. Right there."

The ears that had half-lifted sank again. "All right. That was low. But for the gods' sake, Py, what have you got yourself into? You can't make deals outside the *han*. They'll have your hide. That Ehrran ship—"

"Noticed that, did you?"

"Gods, Py!"

"Hush."

He coughed. Caught his breath. "Chanur property. Right."

"Did you expect different?" She jabbed him hard. It took a lot to get through a male's skin when he had that look in his eyes. "Are they right?"

"Who's right?"

"The stsho in that bar."

His nostrils dilated, closed, dilated, and his nose went pale round the edges. "I don't see what that has to do with it."

"Hilfy back there. You hear a question out of her?"

He looked over his shoulder, where Hilfy was closing cabinet latches, click, slam, click, one after the other; and Tully was folding the table up. He looked round again and his ears were flat.

"Go help Tirun," she said.

"I asked a question."

"No. You *questioned*, and by the gods that's different. You want Haral's rights, you by the gods earn them."

He brushed past her and stalked off bridgeward. And stopped, about half a dozen paces on—faced her, to her relief and her dismay. At least he had not retreated to his cabin. And gods, not more argument.

He stood there. Cold, deliberate protocol.

"Help Tirun and Haral," she said. "The rest of us haven't got a deathwish. That vane's got to be fixed."

That was the way, mention the word. *Dead, dead. Death.* Hit him between the ears with it. Her stomach churned.

"Fine," he said, bowed, turned and talked off, a massive shadow against the lights of the bridge beyond.

She spun on her own heel and walked back into the galley proper, to Tully and Hilfy, who stood idle. "Out," she said to Hilfy, and Hilfy scrambled past her. Footsteps pelted bridgeward.

Tully stood trapped against the cabinets, leaned there with elbows on the counter behind him.

"All right," she said, "Tully, I want the truth."

"Maing Tol."

"I scare you, huh? Maing Tol, Maing Tol. Listen to me. You don't play stupid. You gods-rotted well understand me. You wanted to talk. You wouldn't give me peace of it. So talk. And keep talking."

Maybe the translator garbled that. He had that look.

"Talk, Tully. You want to be friends, by the gods you deal straight with me."

"I sit," he said, and ebbed down onto the mess table bench as if his legs would no longer hold him.

"Truth." She came closer in his silence, leaned both hands on the table and glared into his face. "*Now*, hear?"

He flinched. He smelled of fear and human sweat, like when she had held him, when his heart had beat so hard she could feel it like hammer-strokes. She reached out pitilessly and pinned his arm with claws out. "You risk my crew, Tully. You risk Chanur. By the gods you don't lie to me. Where you come from, huh?"

"Friend," he said.

"You want I rattle your brain?"

He drew several rapid breaths. "Maing Tol. Go Maing Tol."

She stared, at arm's length from his face, stared a good, long while. "You come find me. Need, you say. Need what? You talk, now you talk, Tully. Need what? Number one fool? Where you *been*, Tully?"

"Human space. Want come. *Want*, Pyanfar."

"So you come to the mahendo'sat."

"Mahe come human space."

"*Goldtooth?*"

"Name Ino. *Ijir.*"

She drew a long, long breath. "Doublecrossing

bastard." Meaning Goldtooth, mahen trade and a towering great lie.

"Say again." Blue eyes looked at her with vast worry.

She lifted her hand from his arm and patted his face ever so gently, claws pulled. "Keep talking. More. How did this *Ijir* come into the business, huh? Was it trading in human space."

"Human ship—" He made diagrams on the tabletop. "Human. Kif. Mahe. Not good go so— kif. Three human ship. Gone. Not see. Not come home. Try go stsho. Mahe come-go." He drew route-pictures, mahen traders reaching human space. "*Ijir* come. Say want bring human come talk mahe. Want I come. I, Tully." His mouth twisted in a strange expression. "I small, Pyanfar. Human lot mad. They same send me. I small. Mahe think me big. Want. Take. Human think me make trouble. Shut up, Tully. What you know?" Another intersecting line as *Ijir* moved out of human space toward the Compact. "Goldtooth come. Lot talk, Ino, Goldtooth. Goldtooth want talk me, not talk lot other human, other human lot mad." He drew a great breath, looked up at her as if to see whether she understood his babble, and there was pain in his expression.

"Politics," she said. "And protocols. Same there, huh?"

He blinked, confused.

"Go on."

"Goldtooth want talk me. Want me go Goldtooth ship. I say go find you, you friend, good friend. Not know Goldtooth. Want help. Want you talk these mahe."

"That bastard."

Another blink of skyblue eyes.

"So," she muttered, "the mahe wanted you, huh? And set up a rendezvous. Wanted you. Someone they could talk to. Someone who *would* talk, huh? What about that paper? What's in it? Why Maing Tol?"

"I spacer." Tully's mouth trembled in that way he had when he was upset. "I never say I #, Pyanfar."

"What about the paper, Tully? Whose is it? What's in it?"

"*Ijir* meet Goldtooth, he say make paper—same paper human on *Ijir* got—"

"Copy the paper, you mean."

His head bobbed vehemently. "Same. Yes. Say he take me go find you, go talk stsho, go bring paper Maing Tol, help human—" He held up the hand that bore the ring. "Kif got them. Kif got *Ijir*, got paper same you got—"

"How long time?"

He shook his head. "I don't know." His look grew desperate. "I ask come hani, ask, ask many time. Goldtooth friend? He friend, Pyanfar?"

"Good question," she said, and puzzled him.

165

She reached and patted his shoulder, tapped him with a clawtip. "Safe, understand. Tell me. Why Maing Tol? And why me?"

He shivered, palpably, and reached across the table to grip her retreating hand, ignoring the reflexive jerk of claws. "Big trouble. Lot human ship, lot go Maing Tol soon."

"Across kif space? There's knnn out there! How many ship, huh, how many human ships are you talking about? Three? Four? More than that?"

"Paper say—we make stop kif come human space, take human ship. But Goldtooth say me— Goldtooth say—think now maybe not kif got human ship. Maybe knnn."

"O good gods." The heart sank in her. If there had been a bench under her she would have sat down. As it was she just stared.

"Goldtooth say message got go Maing Tol make stop mahe, make stop kif, go fight—"

"*Fight?* Gods-rotted humanity can't tell knnn from kif?"

"Not."

"*Well, for the gods' sake you know knnn! Did you tell them, did you tell them the difference?*"

"Who I? They don't hear. Shut up, Tully. I'm small person, small, not #, Pyanfar!"

"Gods and thunders."

"Pyanfar—"

"Lunatics!"

"Goldtooth friend?" he asked again. "I do good?"

She stared at him a long, long time and he just looked scared. Scared and on the other side of a half-functioning translator. And the gulf of other minds.

"Goldtooth's mahendo'sat," she said flatly. "And he's got a Personage breathing down his neck. They went to get you, friend, because they wanted trade. I'll bet on that. And those human ships weren't getting through. *Ijir's* no common trader, no way. They wanted to get you to a rendezvous—find out what humanity's up to. That *was* the game. But they found out too gods-rotted much and now Goldtooth's scared. Scared, understand? Kif, the mahe can handle. But if knnn have their small black feet in this—o gods, Tully—you lunatics."

"Got lot ship come—lot, Pyanfar. Got fight kif, got make stop knnn."

"*No one fights the knnn!* Gods and thunders, you don't pick a fight with something you can't talk to!"

Wide eyes looked back at her in distress.

"Where's Goldtooth, Tully? You know?"

A shake of an uncomprehending head.

"Huh." She shoved back from the table feeling her knees gone jellylike. And still that blue-eyed stare was on her. Lost.

Don't go to the *han*, Goldtooth had said; and Beware of Goldtooth—from Goldtooth's stsho ally—

With *Vigilance* in the selfsame port.

Suspicions occurred to her, vague and circular, that the *han* ship might have gotten wind of the clearing of Chanur papers, of mahen money passed to stsho—

—that that ship's presence and Goldtooth's might have had connections Goldtooth would not say ... *Han*/mahen consultations. Stsho like Stle stles stlen, with slippered feet well into it. . . .

And self-interested betrayals, at more than financial depths—

Knnn. Gods, stsho the ultimate xenophobes, and knnn the ultimate reason ... living right next door—living, or traveling, or whatever it was knnn did with those ships of theirs.

Perhaps, hani had whispered, stung by stsho references to the mahendo'sat bringing hani into space to balance kif—

—perhaps a great deal that the stsho knew came from methane-breathers. Tc'a were likely. But had limbless serpents *originated* their own tech?

Or had chi, who might be parasites—or slaves—or pets—to the tc'a? Not likely.

Goldtooth had reason to run scared. And being mahe he had done a mahen thing: he had gone for the contacts that he knew. Same as the whole mahen species had: bring Tully. Go get him. While with trouble in the offing Goldtooth had wanted her. Not the *han*. Not Ehrran. The *han* knew the mahendo'sat, by the gods: it was why the law existed against taking foreign hire. Mahendo'sat went for Personage. For the Known Quantity. They set up powers. Tore them down. Tied hani rules in knots and brought down powers by ignoring them in crises.

Here's unlimited credit—friend. Tell us what you know. Same as they worked on humans.

Send for Tully.

Gods, they'd drained him dry. Even kif had failed at that.

(*I do good?* Tully asked. With that blue-flower stare.)

They had her by the beard, that was sure. Had her, and maybe Stle stles stlen himself.

Until humanity launched ships at the Compact, and knnn objected.

"Trouble?" Tully asked.

She lifted her ears, turned on him the blandest of looks. "We'll fix it. Just go back to your quarters, huh?"

"I spacer. I work." He patted his pocket. "Got paper, Py-an-far."

He did. That was truth. Citizen of the Compact, licensed spacer. More mahen maneuverings. He could not handle controls. He needed a pick to reach the buttons and he was illiterate in hani.

So they locked him up below and shoved him this way and that. He had looked for better from them. Gods knew he must have looked for better.

"*Na* Khym's aboard," she said, feeling the flush all the way to her ears. "*Male*, Tully."

"Friend."

The flush went hotter. "As long as you aren't in the same room, fine. Go where you like. Just stay out of his way. Males are different. Don't argue with him. Don't talk to him if you can avoid it. Just duck your head and for godssakes keep your hands off him and us."

Blankest confusion.

"Hear?"

"Yes," he said.

"Get." She turned him loose and watched him go for the bridge.

She waited for the explosion—realized she was waiting, claws flexed, and drew them in. There was the dust-whisper, high-pitched with their velocity, reminding her of movement, of *The Pride*'s hurtling toward a jump she had to make now.

No way out but that.

The bridge lights were still on, with all of them snatching sleep where they could, going back to quarters for rotating breaks and coming back to the paper-snowed number-two counter, while the dust whispered and the occasional impact of larger fragments hit the hull. ("We'll shine like a new spoon when we get through this," Hilfy had said early on; "We'll be cratered like Gaohn," Tirun had replied, which they were not yet.) The dust screamed now and again, V-differential. Now and again *The Pride*'s particle-sensors and automated systems sent the trim jets into action, little instabilities in G which put a stagger into a walk down a corridor. Now and again *The Pride*'s scan showed her something major and the ship moved to take care of it.

But hani work went on too. And human: a section of the comp still had the working light on that meant Tully was still at it, doing what he could do—working away with linguistics from his terminal in his quarters. He hunted words. Equivalencies. Fought the translator into fewer gaps and spits. Learned hani. That was what he did, far into the hours.

And Khym, shambling red-eyed and shivering from out the corridor—errand to the so-called heated hold: "Got the stores moved down," he said, and cast a worried eye over boards he could not read, at backs turned to him and work still underway. "Go on to bed,"

Pyanfar said. "Hot bath. You've done all you can."

"We're still in trouble, aren't we?"

"We're working on it. Go. Go on. Need you later. Get some sleep."

He went, silent, with one backward, worried glance.

She sighed. Heard other sighs from crew, rubbed her aching eyes and felt a twinge of shame.

"Suppose he secured that?" Tirun wondered.

"He'll remember." But there were his habits in galley—dishes left, a cabinet latch undone. She walked over and keyed in security check. All doors showed closed and a sense of panic still gnawed at her.

On the monitors the numbers still rolled up bleak information. Constant operation. No matter what they tried. They went deeper into the dust, into the well, and station information showed four kif docked, one loose and outward bound, two mahen freighters and six tc'a miner/processors.

Bad odds.

"Gods rot." From Haral.

Another theory failed.

"Go on break," she muttered, back on the bridge the third time, finding Tirun still in the huddle of three heads round the console: Hilfy had changed with Chur; and Haral was back after shift with Geran; while she had stood two straight herself. "Gods rot it, Tirun, didn't I tell you get?"

"Sorry, captain." Tirun's voice was hoarse, and she never looked up from the papers and the moving stylus. "Got this one more idea."

She subsided onto the counter edge, steadied herself through another of The Pride's attitude corrections. She gnawed at her mustaches and waited, wiped her eyes. The stylus scratched away on the paper.

"There's the YR89," Haral said, putting out a hand to point. "If it went—"

"Huuuh." The snarl was hoarse and vexed and Haral got the hand out of Tirun's way. Fast. Scratch-scratch went the stylus.

More silence. The dustscream on the hull grew louder. The Pride corrected. There was a resounding impact.

"Gods rot!" (Hilfy.) Ears went down in embarrassment. She ducked her chin back to her arm on the counter-edge and tried to pretend former silence.

Tirun shoved a strip under the autoreader. The slot took it. Lights rippled as if nothing at all were wrong. Tirun's shoulders slumped.

"Anything left untried?" Pyanfar asked.

"Nothing," Haral said quietly.

"It's a ghosty thing," Tirun said. Her voice cracked. Her ears flagged. "I can't turn it up."

"Stress-produced?"

"Think so. Always possible the unit was rotten. Remember that fade at Kirdu."

Pyanfar heaved a breath and stared at Tirun, reading that grudging mistrust of an unclean system. "We've still got one backup," she said.

"We'll be down to none at Kshshti. Enough for braking. If we're lucky."

Pyanfar thought about it. Thought through the whole vane system. "Back to the regulator," she said.

"You want to replace that Y unit?"

A long, long worming up the vane column, with *The Pride* yawing and pitching under power. A long, dark solo job fishing a breaker out of the linkages, where the system was already in failure. From inside—because the particles would strip a suit.

"No. I want all of us to see Kshshti, thanks." She drew a deep breath. "We put in for repair when we get there, that's all."

Noses drew down. Ears sank.

"Well, what else *can* we do?"

"I'd try the column," Hilfy said.

"Hero's a short-term job, kid." And to Haral: "We go on schedule."

"If it would get us—" Hilfry said.

"I'd gods-rotted put Chur up that thing if it'd work: at least she'd know the system."

Ears sank; shoulders slumped.

"If someone gets killed up there," Tirun muttered, "gods-rotted lot of trouble getting you out of the works. Might fry the system along with you. Captain's right the first time."

"Sure takes out the Kura option," Haral said.

"Huh," Pyanfar said. *"Isn't an option."*

"There's Urtur."

"There's Urtur." She let go a long, long breath and thought about it as she had thought about it the last ten hours. Spend days on Urtur. With five kif, two mahendo'sat freighters and six tc'a who were apt to do anything. Or nothing, while the kif blew them apart or boarded.

"The mahendo'sat," she said, "want us at Kshshti. Goldtooth does. You looked at that scan image? You want to bet Sikkukkut's not passed the word along?"

"Kif got the dice," Haral said. "No bets. You get anything out of Tully to tell us what this is?"

Pyanfar slumped against the cabinet back and stared at Haral. "Big. Real big. You want to hear it? Mahendo'sat tried to get humankind in the back door. Humans lost some ships. I think this *Ijir*'s a hunter-ship. It went in and got Tully—typical mahen stunt. They wanted to figure out what was going on and they wanted

Tully in their hands. He'd talk. He'd trust them. He'd tell them anything they asked."

"O good gods," Hilfy murmured.

"That's not the end of it, niece. Humanity wanted to send their real authorities to the mahendo'sat, I'm guessing, because they had trouble. Mahendo'sat wanted Tully, because *they* have trouble. Here it gets complicated. I think this whole thing's touched off the knnn." No one moved. Eyes dilated to thinnest amber rings. "I think," Pyanfar said, patiently, quietly, "humans failed a promised trade, mahendo'sat investigated, sent a ship—humans from their side blame the kif, and Tully's not high up enough that humanity would've told him much beyond that. He couldn't know the knnn angle. So the mahendo'sat got Tully and rendezvous'd with Goldtooth at some point beyond Tvk, I'm guessing. For questions. Gods know. Tully said the delegation was vexed that Goldtooth wouldn't talk to them; just to him. And Goldtooth took him aboard alone, *Ijir* went for Maing Tol, Goldtooth went gods know where, and meanwhile our papers miraculously got cleared, when stsho had refused us for months, and Goldtooth and we together ended up at Meetpoint."

"So did the *han*," Hilfy said, and Pyanfar looked her way and blinked. The thought leapt to her mind too, two points connecting.

"Stle stles stlen."

"The stationmaster?" Haral asked, hoarse and fatigued, but her ears pricked sharp.

"Might well be. The *han* called for consultation; our papers bought back by one side or the other—*Someone* wanted us in this. Feels like mahendo'sat. Feels like Goldtooth himself. We're his Known Quantity. But so's Stle stles stlen. Theoretically. I wouldn't lay odds on anything right now. *Someone* got things moving. Gods know the stsho took our money to clear those papers, but maybe they took *everyone's*, who knows?"

"Gods-rotted situation," Haral muttered.

"Twice over if Ehrran's in it," Tirun said.

"Where's Goldtooth headed?" Hilfy asked.

"I asked Tully that. He doesn't know. He says. Likely he doesn't."

"He came through here," Haral said. "Kura? Kita?—Kshshti-bound?"

"We *think* he came through here," Tirun said. Her voice cracked. "I'd not lay odds anything's right-side up with that son."

"Bait-and-switch," Pyanfar said. "Gods-rotted mahe's slippery as a kif. No, I don't swear that message wasn't put in before he got to Meetpoint. Or by some outbound agent. Alarm's being rung down from Meetpoint to Urtur to Kshshti, that's what, and we may just think we're the wavefront."

"That knnn at Meetpoint—" Tirun said. "Not forgetting that."

"We can't do anything about it. Except get out of here."

"And stay in one piece," Haral muttered. "Kshshti's a *long* jump."

"We can make it. Even if we blow that vane. Distance may blow it, but it'll help us too: we'll come in with marginal V. We can stop, at worst. At best, it wasn't the Y unit and the vane will hold all the way."

"It may and it may not," Tirun said. "If it's that. One of those goes ghosty, gods, you don't know whether you've got it or not. Ever. It could hold to Kshshti and we could lose it at Maing Tol when we've got higher V."

"One thing I want you to do. Put that whole vane over to backup from the board up. In case we've got a ghost in another unit. Let's just clear all the original systems. Can you do that in four hours?"

"Can," Tirun said.

"Not you. *You* get some sleep."

"I'll get it," Haral said.

"We give up that Y-unit to third redundancy?" Tirun asked. "Could have damaged it when that regulator went backup. If that's sour it'll sure take that linkage out."

She thought about it. *Thought* about going

no-backup-at-all, which was how desperate it was.

"No," she said. "I'll dice with the number two. What we've got aboard—if nothing else—we can't risk on that kind of throw. It'll get us there with something left. That's all we dare try."

"What *have* we got aboard?" Tirun asked.

"Message from humanity to Maing Tol and Iji. Translator. Message from Goldtooth to his Personage. Gods know what that is. About the knnn—most likely." She drew a deep breath and considered the chance it involved the *han*. Alliances. Doublecrosses. "All systems to number two and we jump to Kshshti on schedule. Tell Chur and Geran what we're doing when they come on duty."

"Not the menfolk?"

"Gods, don't worry them. Tell them we fixed it all."

"What —" Hilfy asked ever so quietly, "what about Tully if we go lame at Kshshti? We'll be stuck at dock. Gods know the kif—"

"What we do, imp—We get ourselves to Kshshti and whatever happens, by the gods, we put him in mahen hands. Let *them* worry about him. Hear? They've got two hunter-ships to their account. Let *them* take it." She stood up again. "Get some rest. All of you this time."

"Aye," Tirun murmured in what of a voice she had left. Hilfy stared at her open-mouthed.

"Nothing else to do," Pyanfar said to her. "*Nothing* else. He's worth too much to take chances with. That message is. Understand? We've had it. That vane's got us."

"We go in like this we could be down a week!"

"So we take our damage. We can cover the bill. We've got that. We're done, imp. Finished."

"I could make it," Hilfy said, "up that column and we'd have that unit replaced."

"Wrong. Chur would have to do it. She's smallest. And she's not fool enough."

There was silence but for that. That and the dust.

She got up and walked away, staggered a little as she reached the corridor and *The Pride* corrected course again.

She had another, chilling thought and turned, pointed at Haral. "No way this kid tries it. You sit on her. Someone goes up that column I'll space her. Hear?"

"Aye," Haral said.

No one followed her. Presumably they were clearing up the paper. Closing down. Her eyes blurred with exhaustion and she refrained from rubbing at them as she passed Khym's cabin.

She thought of going to him. She had not—not since Hoas. It was not her time; had not been, then. Such niceties went by the board with them as they had in her world-visits. But sleep would not come easy with the dust, the small shifts of G that went on constantly: and he might be asleep; and there would be questions if she waked him.

Did you fix it, Py?

She opened her own door and walked in, sat down at the desk and methodically cleared the clutter of her own work away.

Course-plottings. Calculations every way she could make them in hopes of getting another dump-and-turn that would turn them off toward Kura and hani space, without breaking them down at Urtur and stranding themselves here with the kif.

None were feasible. And if they were—if they were, knnn notice fell on hani thereafter.

Goldtooth, you mahen bastard. Seeing to the safety of his own, that was sure.

So she handed the package back again: *Here, fool mahe, you take it. Good luck. Run fast.*

And Tully—

She rested her head against her hands. Gods, gods, gods.

Knnn.

And the failsafe that was *Ijir*, whatever else it had been, with its humanity aboard, and just gone backup.

Kif had it, gods help them. Kif would take

them apart, mahe, humans, everyone. Tully
knew, who had spent time in kifish hands,
who had gone to hani for help because he heard
them laugh once, across Meetpoint docks.

Gods rot Sikkukkut and all kifish gifts.

They were out of it, that was all. Whatever
gain or loss there was yet to be made, *The
Pride* had gone her limit. So they should be
glad to be out of it. A vane down. They could
not jump *The Pride* again. They rolled the dice
for Kshshti. That was gambling all their lives.
At Maing Tol the odds went up, that it would
not hold for braking.

Hero's a short-term job, kid.

So what was stung, that they had to give up
and lay back and let others do what hani failed
at?

And hand Tully on alone to mahendo'sat?

"All secure," Haral said, beside her, at her
post. "I take her, captain?"

"I'll take this one," Pyanfar said, and reached
and settled her arm into the brace. She glanced
up at the reflection of the rest of the bridge,
crew in place, Khym in his observer's post.

Fixed, they had told him. And his face had
lightened, trusting them.

Fixed, they had told Tully, who was harder
to lie to, being spacer himself. And he had

182

drugged himself into a haze by now, as his kind had to do.

"Starfix positive, Maing Tol," Haral said.

The dust whined over the hull, constant but thinner now. "Going to dust up Kshshti a bit," she said. "Can't be helped."

Haral rolled a glance in her direction, a stark, stark stare. "Can't be helped," she said.

Sudden silence then, as the jump field began to build and the shields came up.

They rode their luck this time.

Chapter Seven

There were hazard lights blinking urgent alarm, and Haral's voice protesting—

—"Captain—"

—Plaintively, as if she had not heard the beeps and already begun to reach. There was perhaps some mercy in being human and drugged out of one's mind. . . .

"Got it," Pyanfar coughed, though her throat had gone to stone in the long slow leak of time past the instruments, in the inside out of jumpspace. "Location?" One went lethargic, grew fatally tranquil in that dizzy flow where one could do nothing, nothing but watch and take a subjective day moving a finger. There was an itch at the tip of her nose just as important as their collective lives. . . .

But the intellect knew what the will forgot. The mind was primed with a sequence of things she had waited two months to do. The right hand reached the control she had meant two months ago to reach and brought the field up while they still had power, long before they had gotten buoy signal. The eyes sought instruments, diverging lines that had to meet—

The fields of Mahn, yellow in the sun, the woods, the dappled shade. . . .

The vine outside the wall of Chanur, that branched like a river, from one great gnarled trunk; and generations of Chanur had climbed it, branch to branch to branch—

"We're on." That was Geran's mumble confirming destination. "We're in the jump range."

Location: need the vector.

"We're alive," Hilfy murmured. "We're going to make it, going to make it—"

—as if she were utterly surprised.

There it was, that red line trued right on.

"Huh." Pyanfar coughed her throat clear and blinked away the haze.

"Of course we did," Geran said. "Have any doubt, kid?"

There were safety procedures for a ship to follow when coming in from dust-ringed Urtur and they were not following them. They were coming into a system with C-charged dust in their company. Some of it would slip the smaller field of their dump and go through Kshshti system like a hard-radiation storm.

"One more dump," she murmured, pleaded with the ship. "Stand by"—thinking of a ship she had seen die—of a ship which had had a vane shot to flinders, and jumped without a chance in a mahen hell of slowing down.

Nothing to do then but capsule the crew and hope—

She shoved the dump in and felt her eyes roll as the field cycled up. . . .come on, come on, ship, hold it—

More failure lights blinked and held steady.

Branches on the wall. . . .

"Got to be that Y unit," she muttered to Haral, to no one in particular, and had visions of that dying ship again.

None of that crew was alive now. Those the mahendo'sat had hauled down in their capsule and saved—they had died at Gaohn, standing off the kif.

She moved an arm and did a third dump, watching in blear-eyed fascination as the lines on the scopes crept together and merged like silken threads, red and blue, as *The Pride* dragged at the interface and let the bubble go.

Down again, and the wail of alarms calling her back to life.

"Still over mark," Haral muttered. "That's twenty."

"I know. We've got it, we've got it left with the mains." She shoved the jump drive off and sent *The Pride* into an axis roll, canceled G and threw the mains on to finish the job the drive had failed. There was margin left. "Kif. Are there kif? Look alive back there."

"Scan's clear," Chur's voice returned. "Kshshti positive; got the beacon. Stand by course input."

Monitors changed priorities. The course change flashed in, very little off their present heading. She put the bow down and trued up.

"That's luck," Haral said of the course they had been handed.

"Huh," she said. "That's priority for you." Rotational G picked up again as the vector change took effect. "Find out what we lost."

"Stand by," Tirun said.

There was long silence, while comp ran diagnostics under Tirun's hands.

"It didn't hold?" Khym's voice, sounding plaintive and a bit shaken. "Did we lose that vane again?"

"Didn't hold," Geran said. "But we're all right."

"Not leaving here real quick, are we?"

He was trying. And getting harder to deceive. Pyanfar swallowed hard, and took the damage summary as it came flickering to the screen. "We're all right," she heard Hilfy say, which was probably into the com, for Tully. "We're through. We just had trouble with that unit. Sit still down there."

"Blew two holes in final-backup," Pyanfar muttered to Haral, in conversation-tone.

"Gods," Haral said. That was all. And sent Kshshti system image her way, onto all the screens. "Not much, this place."

"Huh."

It was not. A dull orange sun with only moons for company, moons and a station. Small mining, sufficient for its needs. Some trading. Mostly mahendo'sat maintained it because it would be someone's, situated as it was; and best it should be theirs, when it was a connection on a route straight for Maing Tol from Kefk, inside kif space. With a shipyard facility, thank the gods.

"Lot of traffic," Pyanfar muttered, picking up the com chatter. "Gods-rotted lot of traffic to be out here at this hole."

"Kita," Haral reminded her.

"Kita for sure. Word got spread uncommon fast, didn't it? Or we lost more time than we ought in that jump."

"Huuuhn." No comment. Not here, not now. Not with Khym on the bridge.

Twenty stars were *The Pride*'s regular ports of call. Not Kshshti. It was not a port any hani sought.

"Nasty little place," Geran muttered from back along the counter. "Real nasty."

*   *   *

There was time. There was time for a great many things as *The Pride* came limping in toward Kshshti—

Time to hear the chatter of the station before their wavefront reached station and station's then-wave reached them: the chitter and wail of methane-breathers in confused conference, the clicking sounds of kif whose uncoded remarks were on ordinary kifish business, terse and uninformative. No hani voices. No sign of hani at all.

"Station answering," Hilfy said as that wave came in. The feed was routine, coldly business-like transmission. It might have been any approach to a mahen station, less lively than some.

"Queer quiet," Haral muttered. "I'd've expected a curse to a mahen hell and back again, the way we came in."

"Huh," Pyanfar said. "Bet you to a mahen hell all of this is set up from the start. We're expected and they're not rattling this thicket, no."

That got a look from Haral. Not a happy one.

So they glided closer and closer to Kshshti with the noise of methane-breathers whispering over com.

Rimstation. Border station. Kif claimed the star; mahendo'sat had built the station and held it with the tc'a and chi, whose mining had no particular profit. Nothing at Kshshti did . . . except its nuisance value to kif ambitions across the line.

"Where's that shiplist?" she asked of Hilfy. "I want names, imp."

"I'm still trying," Hilfy said. "Station says they've got computer trouble."

"Sure they do. Like the board at Meetpoint."

"Beg pardon, aunt?"

"Gods-rotted lot of malfunctions lately. Get that list. Tell them read it off by voice and cut the nonsense."

"Don't know what we can do," Haral muttered beside her. And that was truth. The vane systems boards flickered steady disaster under Tirun's probes. It was all down. Everything.

"We'll manage," she said, "something—" but her gut was knotted up in one unceasing panic. She fished the repair authorization out of safe-keeping and shifted to put that in her pocket, braced for arguments with mahen officials. There would be outcries, howls, delays if she could not face them down.

And if there was no ship for Tully, if there were the wrong kif, and no help—

Not leaving here real quick, no.

"List is in," Hilfy said.

"To your one," Haral said and put it to the screen.

14 *Iniri-tai*: Maing Tol
 9 *Pasunsai*: Idunspol
 7 *Nji-no*: Maing Tol
30 *Canoshato*: Kshshti: insystem
29 Nisatsi-to: Kshshti: insystem
 2 *Ispuhen*: Maing Tol: repair
32 *Sphii'i'o*: V'n'n'u
34 T'T'Tmmmi: N'i'i
40 *A'ohu'uuu*: T t'a'va'o
49 knnn
50 knnn
51 knnn
52 knnn
10 *Ginamu*: Rlen Nle
20 *Kekkikkt*: Kefk
21 *Harukk*: Akkt
22 *Inikktukkt*: Ukkur
 8 *Ehrran's Vigilance*: Anuurn
15 *Ayhar's Prosperity*: Anuurn
 3 *The Pride of Chanur*: Anuurn: enroute

"Gods," Haral muttered.

"Party, huh?" She drew down her mouth as at a bad taste.

"*Kekkikkt*. Remember that one?"

"Couldn't forget. A whole list of good news, isn't it?"

"Got help, at least."

"Got help." She scanned the mahen section again. "Insystemers and short-hoppers. Ever hear of *Iniri-tai*?"

"No."

"*Pasunsai?*"

"No. Neither of them."

"Gods rot, there's supposed to be a hunter ship here."

"Got *Vigilance*," Haral said dryly.

"Huh." She rose to the humor, but there was ice at her stomach.

"What do we tell them?"

She remembered what she had told them at Meetpoint, the final message. *Kif on our trail. No explanation possible.* "Something inventive. We'd better."

"Ayhar," Tirun muttered between her teeth. And that was the second good question.

"That scrapheap never beat us here on the Urtur route, that's sure."

"How'd they know?"

"Want to guess?"

Haral made a sound in her throat, not a pleasant one.

"Rhif Ehrran's got a lap pet."

"What do we do?"

"Huh. I'm thinking about it." Meaning she did not know. Meaning there was nothing they could do but bluff and Haral already knew that much. *Vigilance* had gathered itself a witness, that was what—footed the bill to divert a merchant carrier like *Prosperity* off its normal run.

They had dumped cargo at Meetpoint, same as themselves.

And *knew* where to intercept them. Same as *Harukk* had known.

Gods, were they the only ones running blind in this business?

"Stsho? Stle stles stlen?

Gtst knew Goldtooth's plans.

If *gtst* had talked—

"Captain," Hilfy said. "Tully's asking to come up."

More questions. Pointed ones. She drew a deep breath and downed the panic. "Tell him yes. Tell him—" —*watch his step*. But he knew how to move in a ship underway. He had felt the uncertainty in their dump, had understood more surely than Khym had that they were in trouble, and what kind they were in—that they had escaped dying outright. But they were lame—at Kshshti. With the kif.

Now what, now what we do, huh, Py-an-far?

Tully did not take long about it. Pyanfar turned her chair from his reflection overhead to the solidity standing in the doorway.

He looked worried. He glanced about him, scanned the monitors with an eye that knew what it was looking for, that could read more off the graphics than he could understand in words.

"Safe," she said to him. "We're safe in Kshshti. Got help here. Big hani ship."

He nodded. He did hope. That was in the

look he gave her. But something else was in the slump of his shoulders as he turned and sought the seat Hilfy offered him, observer, beside her post.

Quiet, thank the gods. She was ashamed of herself, remembering that he never did go to masculine extremes. Professional. It was hard to remember that, that Tully, whatever else he was, was not prone to hysterics. *There*, she thought, *Khym. That's how. That's how it's done. You can do it—*

The way she had believed it once, having voyaged with Tully, so that she hoped—

Khym was looking at her now, one hard, unforgiving stare.

Sure, Khym. It's fixed.

Tully, perhaps, had never fallen for that lie in the first place.

And Khym had, perhaps, just seen that shiplist.

She turned back to controls. Blinking lights and mahen chatter had no accusations.

The metal speck that was Kshshti became a star, a globe, resolved itself into torus shape in the vid; became an aggregate of plates and flashing lights as *The Pride* moved in and fell into rotating pattern with the wheel.

"In lane," Haral said. "Autos on."

"Take her in." Of a sudden the hours mounted

up like leaden weight. She spun about and faced the bridge as a whole, saw Khym sitting there with his elbows on the console facing the scan.

Tully's pose was much the same. But he turned to face her, with that haunted look he had worn for days.

"We'll get that repair done here," she said. "Kshshti can handle it."

Hilfy looked her way. So did Khym. And Khym's stare was dark.

Another lie? she read the backslant of one ear, the flare of nostrils.

Her own pulse raced. She held herself in place, silent, with nothing to say to either of them.

Lies and lies and lies.

"When we get in," she said to Hilfy, looking straight at her, "I want a mahen courier in here. I don't care who it is. Dock manager will do. Don't shake things up, but get us someone who can get us someone else. Shouldn't be hard. Suggest we've got a cargo difficulty."

Khym sat there. It occurred to her that in his life he had never told a witting lie . . . being downworld hani, dealing with hani and believing in the *han*. And it had never occurred to her that in dealings off Anuurn she had had many faces—one for stsho, one for mahendo'sat. She was more hani with the kif.

196

"It isn't Anuurn," she said across the bridge in a low, hard voice. "Nothing's Anuurn but Anuurn itself, crewman, and we aren't home."

Maybe he understood that much. She saw a slight flicker in the eyes.

"Pyanfar," Tully said. "Maing Tol. Go Maing Tol."

She put the com plug into her ear. "I understand," she said. He was scared. Terrified. "Quiet, hear? We got you. We'll work it out. Fix, understand?"

He said nothing, neither he nor Khym.

"Gods rot," she muttered, and got up. "Take her in, Haral." She stalked off aft, caught the safety grip and looked back. "I'm going to clean up. Tirun, you wash up; I want you with me. *I want that courier, niece.*"

It was not an easy thing to manage, a cleanup during dock approach. She had inhaled a bit of water and stung her nose, but that meeting was its own kind of emergency—to be presentable as possible, formidable; and there was not, here, the time to spend on it.

She overdid it, if possible—wore her finest red breeches, her most resplendent rings. She reeked of perfume. *That* was interspecies courtesy; and it was strategy, to drown subtle cues to sensitive alien noses.

Face the bastards down, by the gods.

It was *The Pride* at stake. And with it—

The Pride nudged her way into dock, smooth, smooth glide now; a last warning from Haral and another shift of G as all ship rotation ceased, only spin-match carrying them now. The sensation of fifty pounds extra weight eased off. She held on to the recessed grip by the cabin door, trusting Haral's skill, and dock came softly, a thump against the bow, a clang of grapples going on, the steadying of G force at a mahen-normal .992 as they became part of Kshshti's wheel.

She gave her mane and beard a final combing, twitched the left ear's rings into order. The sudden silence of the ship at rest gave an illusion of deafness: the constant white noise had ceased.

"Aunt." That was Hilfy from the bridge. "I made that contact. We've got a customs official on the way."

"Good." She clipped a pocket com to her waist, tucked a pistol into her pocket—gods, no way for an honest hani to do business. But Kshshti, as she had said to Khym, was not Anuurn, and the universe was a lonely walk among species that had been at this hunt long before hani came.

Fix the rotted vane at Urtur; crawl up the column, indeed. Hilfy Chanur would have. Would do, when she inherited *The Pride*. Hilfy would make high and wide decisions, take the straight course, not the devious.

Perhaps she had done that herself once. She tried to remember. Perhaps age dimmed the recall.

She thought not. No, by the gods.

Young fool, in charge of her ship. Not for by-the-gods years yet. But the thought appalled her . . . to go back to Chanur, sit in the sun and waste away. Haral, Tirun, no youngsters themselves, to give up their posts to bright-eyed youngsters who thought everything was simple—

Gods.

She latched the drawer tight, and walked out, a little rubber-kneed in Kshshti's heavier G.

"Captain." From the pocket com, Haral's voice. "Message from *Vigilance*. Rhif Ehrran's at our dock."

"Oh, good gods."

"They want the lock open."

She put a claw in the pocket com. "Where's that customs officer?"

"On the way. That's all we know. Stall?"

She thought about it. Gave it up. There was no need starting off hot. "No. Let her in. Due courtesy. You and Chur and Khym stay on the bridge and keep your eye on things. Hilfy: galley. Geran and Tully, half an hour to clean up and trade watch with first shift. Move it." Crew was tired. Exhausted. Gods knew how much rest they would get. Or when.

"Aye," Haral said. "They're about to hook up the accessway."

"At your discretion."

She took the lift down, the while the ship-to-station connections whined and clanked away against the outer hull, the thunk! of lines socketing home, the portside contact of the access tube snugging into its housing on the hull.

Tirun joined her, swung along with a visible weight in her right-hand pocket and not a word of expectations.

Kshshti, after all.

"Ehrran's out there," Pyanfar said.

"Heard that." Cheerlessly. "Figured blackbreeches would be quick about it."

There was the final thump, that was the seal in place.

"Stand by," Haral said.

"Ker Rhif," Pyanfar said—took up a pose facing the *han* deputy and her black-breeched crewwoman; not insolent, no. Just solid enough to invite no farther progress down the corridor.

"Ker Pyanfar." Rhif Ehrran took up a like pose, arms folded. Armed, by the gods: a massive pistol hung at the side of those black silk trousers. The crewwoman carried the same. "Sorry to trouble you this early. I'm sure you've got other things on your mind."

Pyanfar blew softly through her nostrils, comment enough.

"What caused the damage?" Ehrran asked in that friendly, official way.

She pursed her lips into a pleasant expression and glared. "Well, now, that's something we're still looking into, captain. Likely it was dust."

"You want to explain that last message at Meetpoint?"

"I think it's self-explanatory. I meant it. It would be a lot better if you avoided us right now. We've got a problem. I don't pretend we don't. I don't think it ought to involve the *han*."

"You feel qualified to decide that?"

"Someone has to. Or the *han*'s in it. I hadn't wanted that."

"You hadn't wanted that."

She refrained from retort. It was what Ehrran wanted. It was all she needed—if anything lacked at all.

"Where do you plan to go?" Rhif Ehrran asked.

"Nowhere, till I get that vane fixed."

"Then?"

"Maing Tol. Points beyond."

A silence then. "You know," Rhif Ehrran said, "you've had a lot of experience out here, a lot of experience. Do I have to tell you the convention regarding hiring a ship out?"

"You don't. We're not."

"You're sitting in a border port with your tail

in a vise, Chanur. Are you still going to brazen it out? I'm giving you a chance, one chance before I suspend your license on the spot. You get that two-legged cargo of yours down here and turn him over."

"You're not referring to my husband."

Ehrran's ears went flat and her mouth opened.

"I didn't think so," Pyanfar said. "Who sent you? Stle stles stlen?"

"See here, Chanur. You don't negotiate with me. I've got a *han* ship eight light-years into the Disputed Territories because I figured you'd foul it up, I'm likely to get my tail shot up getting out of here, and I'm not in the mood to trade pleasantries. I want the alien down here. I want him wrapped up and ready to go, and be glad I don't pull your license."

"We aren't carrying any alien. You're talking about a citizen of the Compact."

"I'm aware of the fiction the mahendo'sat arranged. Let's not argue technicalities. Get him down here."

"He's a passenger on my ship. He has some say where he goes."

"He'll have no say if this ship has no license."

She drew a long, slow breath. The world had gone dark all round, excepting Rhif Ehrran's elegant person. "There's Compact Law, Ehrran. I trust you'll remember that."

"You're on the edge. Believe me that you are."

She stood there with her heart slamming against her ribs and the light refusing to come back. She was aware of Tirun there, at her side. She could not see her. "Where will you take him? To the *han*?"

"Just leave that to us."

"No. You're talking about a friend of mine. I can be real difficult, ker Rhif. And we're not in hani space."

There was long, frozen silence. Rhif Ehrran's ears flicked then, breaking the moment. "You're a fool, Chanur. I can't say I don't respect your position."

"Where's he going?"

"Trust me, Chanur, that things go on in this universe somewhat remote from your interests. Suffice it to say that this is not a unilateral action."

"Gods rot it, he's not a load of fish!"

"If you have such concern for his safety, captain, I'd suggest you distance you from him and him from you—considering the condition of your ship—and let me get him out of here."

She looked away, found no solace elsewhere. Glanced back again. "We'll bring him."

"I'll send a car."

"Someone of my crew will take the ride with him," she said quietly. "By your leave. He's not going to like this."

"I assure you—"

A dark figure appeared in the corridor, at the accessway: Ehrran's ears twitched round and body followed as Pyanfar reached for her pocket, but it was mahendo'sat, not kif.

"Customs officer," Pyanfar said.

"Advice," Rhif Ehrran said. "This is Kshshti. Not Meetpoint. If you can get this ship running, get back to Urtur and get on to Kura. Fast. If she won't stand it, sit tight."

"Same advice you give *Prosperity*?"

"*Prosperity's* on *han* business. Leave it at that. *Stay out of things that don't concern you, Chanur.*"

"I hear you. I hear you very well."

"The car will be here in an hour. I don't want any foulups."

"Understood, captain."

Ehrran inclined her head in scant courtesy, collected her crewwoman and departed the corridor, past the mahendo'sat who turned and stared.

It was a small, worried-looking mahen official who slouched past the departing Ehrran with a backward look. Mahen female, this, a clerical with the usual clutter of clipboard and signatures and seals and notebooks hung about her chest; but the belt which held up the kilt about her rather pot-bellied person had the badges of middling authority.

Then the gut came moderately in and the

head came up—no miraculous transformation, only the suddenly sharper look of this disreputable individual.

"Voice, I," she said.

"Huh," said Pyanfar, laying back her ears. She set her hands on hips, drew a neat quick breath, tried to reset her wits for another frame of reference. Gods. A Voice, yet. No dockside official. "Ehrran know you? *Whose* Voice?"

A second look back, this one taller and disdainful. The Voice—if Voice it was—would have no name, no particular identity, and yet a considerable one, being alter-ego to some Personage, speaker of the unspeakable, direct negotiator. She straightened round again. "Voice stationmaster Kshshti. Stationmaster send say you number one fool come in like that."

"No choice."

"More fool deal with fool." The Voice gestured over her shoulder, where the Ehrran had vanished. "Where cargo?"

Pyanfar made a deprecating gesture toward the self-claimed Voice. "Where authorization?"

The mahe drew out one small object from her belts, a badge inlaid with gold and the Kshshti port emblem. "You keep this cargo aboard."

She laid her ears down, pricked them up again. "Look—"

"Keep. Not permit this transfer."

Pyanfar tucked her hands in her belt, turned a frown Tirun's way and looked back again. No time to start shouting. Not yet. She gestured toward lower-deck ops. "Look, you want go sit down, Voice? Get drink, talk?"

"What talk? Like got big cargo, got damage, got make foulup whole business?"

"*Look* Honorable." Now it was time to shout. "*The Pride*'s no gods-blasted warship, got no weapons, hear? I risk my ship twice, got damage, and I got the promise of your government to make it good." She pulled the authorization from her pocket and handed it to the Voice. "We got downtime, got cargo lost—"

"We fix."

It was like leaning on a wall and feeling it go down. She was off her balance an instant, staring into those dark, earnest eyes.

Then it made sense. She drew in a breath and twitched her ears back in the beginnings of negation.

"Meanwhile," the Voice said, "you stall this fool deputy."

"No. Not possible."

"You want help, got."

"You bet I got. Got authorization." She retrieved the paper from the Voice's hand and waved it under the Voice's nose. "Un-con-ditional. Code Hasano-ma! That mean anything to you?"

"We not permit this transfer."

"Well, take it up with the deputy. *I* can't stop it. It's my license. You understand that?"

The Voice came close, tapped her on the chest with a dull-clawed forefinger. "Hani. You we know longtime. This other fool we got no confidence."

"I can't do anything."

White rimmed the dark eyes. "You get number-one repair job, make quick. Want you back in action, Pyanfar Chanur. You listen. We got right now no ship here stop this bastard. Got delicate situation, got stsho upset—you know stsho bastard, know hani got young fool, old bastard stsho lot smart, lot timid, got own interest. Not say not-friend. Got own interest. Our interest got you fix up. You fix *han*."

Her jaw dropped. "Good *gods!* what do you think I am?"

"Maybe we talk, huh?"

"There's nothing to talk about." She waved a hand aft. "That's the Y unit out. The Y unit took the main column linkage. When the linkage failed—"

The mahe waved her own lank black-furred hand. "Get you fix, you take this cargo."

"I'm telling you you can't get that vane fixed fast enough. Two hundred, three hundred work hour fix that vane. We sit here we got kif positioned all round this system. Plenty time for that. Mahe, we've got *knnn* loose!"

"God—!"

"Not our fault. Mahendo'sat set this up, all the way. Your own precious Personage at Maing Tol. We got routed here. Number one usual mahen foulup, like Meetpoint, like got Kita blocked, like desert me with no support—"

"Ship come. Meanwhile get you fix. Lousy hani engineering, huh?"

"Gods rot, you route a ship through Urtur and throw a course change at it and see how it holds!"

Minuscule mahen ears twitched. The nose wrinkled and the Voice lifted a deprecating hand. "Technical not my business. Personage say: Find damage, fix, send this fool away quick before got kif organize. We fix. You hold this cargo."

"Can't do!"

"Want repair?"

The breath strangled her. "I'm due repair, you bastard. I've got the paper says so. I can't stall the deputy. . . ."

The Voice frowned. Her small ears folded, twitched as she looked up and jabbed again with the finger. "We take care this cargo. We take him station center, big inquiry, lot fluff. Get you fix, bring back cargo—twenty hour."

"Can't be done in twenty hours."

The mahe lifted one finger. "Bet?"

She stared at the mahe, thinking treachery,

thinking double-cross; and all the same her pulse raced. She threw a look at Tirun, saw her cargo chief/engineer with that same wary, heart-thumping thought.

"They'd have to replace the whole gods-rotted tail to make that schedule," Tirun muttered. "No patch job."

"Got good system," the Voice said. "Better. *Mahen* make. Match up you systems no trouble. Twenty hour, you run. We fix *han* deputy. We confiscate this cargo. Let deputy go Maing Tol make complaint."

"Gods, you know what you let me in for?"

"How much already, hani? You think. How much you got?"

"We'd still have kif." She gnawed a hangnail and stared at the Voice.

"Always got kif."

"You know a ship named *Harukk*?"

"Know. One bastard."

"He's been with us since Meetpoint. He knows what we've got. Ship named *Ijir*. Our backup. It's gone. Kif have got it."

"Damn, hani!"

"Kif got whatever it had. They know whatever it knew."

The mahe's mouth made a hard line as she looked down and up again. "You run fast, hani. We get you fix, you burn tail get hell out Kshshti. Maybe arrange small accident this *Harukk*.

C. J. Cherryh

Maybe skimmer bump vane, huh? Maybe multiple collision.''

"All three? You want kif feud?"

"Raindrop in ocean, hani. You make deal?"

She gnawed her mustaches, looked at the deck plates, looked up at the mahe. "Deal. You handle the deputy. You stop her. Caught between local government and a *han* order—I can't very well contest a confiscation, can I—if it gets here first."

"We get car. Take custody." The mahe drew a watch from amid the clutter of her belts. "Time now 1040. You expect action, maybe— half hour."

"I want a Signature on that repair order."

Small ears twitched. "You doubt word?"

"Records get lost. I'd be in a mess later if that happened—wouldn't I?"

"So." The mahe wrinkled her nose, made a grimace more hani grin than primate, whipped up a tablet. She scribbled and affixed a Signature. "Repair authorize, charge Maing Tol authority. Got. You satisfied?"

Pyanfar took it, waved a hand toward the outbound corridor. "Speed, huh?"

"Twenty hour," the mahe said, fixed her with a hard stare that held something of mirth in it. Then she turned on her heel and walked off toward the outbound corridor.

Pyanfar drew another breath, inhaled the

mahe's lingering perfume. Blew it out again and looked at Tirun.

"Got a chance," Tirun muttered.

"Gods know what they'll pin on our tail. Or what they'll stand by when the inquiry board meets. We just agreed to get shot at. You know that?"

"Better odds than ten minutes ago."

"Huh." But her heart was still pounding against her ribs. It was hope, unaccustomed in the last two years. *The Pride*, back in prime condition. Finish this job, get the hold loaded on credit at Maing Tol before the other bills came in. It was a chance, one chance—and if the human mess settled down and the human trade materialized, if *that* came through—She waved an arm at the exit. "Shut that. We've got kif out there."

Meanwhile—meanwhile there was one difficult thing to do.

The smell of gfi went through the bridge, ordinary and comforting; voices drifted out of the galley, noisy and normal. But Haral was back at her post, damp from a hasty shower, and turned a solemn look back while Pyanfar slid the tablet's Signature codestrip into comp.

Comp talked to ship-record, to station comp, back and forth in a rapid flurry of codes. "Checks out," Pyanfar said, while Tirun came and draped an arm over her sister's seatback, two sober, weary faces. Haral had heard. There was no question about that: Haral always listened when there were strangers on the deck.

"Tully listen in?" Pyanfar asked.

"No."

"Where is he?"

A nod toward the galley. *"Everyone's there."*

"Huh." She drew her shoulders up as against some cold wind and looked that way. She tucked her hands into the belt of her trousers. "Come on. Both of you. Let the damage list go."

They followed, two shadows at her back— *Cursed lot of nonsense,* Pyanfar thought, screwing her courage up. Gods, where was common sense, that breaking one small bit of unpleasantness upset her more than facing down the *han*?

There was noise, chatter, Khym's deeper voice wanting something from the cabinet— "Sit down, Tully," Chur said. "For godssakes, *na* Khym— Hilfy, where's the tofi got to? Can you find it?" And glanced around at Pyanfar. "Captain."

"Sit," Pyanfar said sharply, stilling voices, the tofi-search, the opening and closing of cabinets. Geran came and put a cup in her hand. "You too. Sit down, Khym." —as he made one last foray into a cabinet. He snatched a substitute and subsided scowling into the middle of the benches, shaking the spice into his cup and concentrating on that while others found their seats left and right of him.

Pyanfar braced herself at the galley corner where stable footing existed in-dock, foot braced at the edge of the shifting step-up of the gimballed table section. Khym sulked, in general foul humor, and pretended full occupation. She leaned there, sipped the liquid and felt the warmth coil through a boding chill at her stomach. Others were still, not the rattle of a spoon, only a shifting as Tirun and Haral nudged Tully over and slid into the benches.

"I'll make this fast," Pyanfar said. "I've got to. Tully, is that translator picking me up?"

He touched his ear, where the plug was set. Looked at her with those bright, worried eyes. "I hear fine."

She came and sat down on the jumpseat, leaned her elbows on the table, the cup between her hands. She faced all of them. But Tully most directly.

"You'll know," she said, "we never did fix that thing at Urtur. Shut up, Khym—" before Khym could quite get his mouth open. "Tully, there wasn't a way to fix it. Hear? So we made it in. One vane is gone. Takes time to fix. Understand? Now we got a little trouble. There's a hani here wants to take you on her ship. You understand? Hani authority."

The pale eyes flickered with—perhaps—understanding. One was never sure. Fright: that, certainly. "Go from you?" he asked. "I go? Go new ship?"

"No. Now listen to me. I don't want them to take you. This is a mahen station. Mahendo'sat, understand? Mahendo'sat take you to the center of the station, keep you safe, fix the ship. Twenty hours. You understand? They're going to take you with them into the center of the station."

"Kif. Kif here—"

"I know. It's all right. They won't get near you. The mahendo'sat will bring you back when we're ready to move. This way we keep the other hani from taking you to their ship. We keep you safe, understand?"

"Yes," he agreed. He held the cup in front of him, in both his hands, looking as if he had lost his appetite and his thirst.

"Got to move fast, Tully. Get down below. Take whatever you need. Clothes. A car is coming."

"Car."

"No nonsense this time. You'll be under guard all the way. Not like the stsho. Not like Meetpoint. Mahendo'sat have teeth."

"One of us," Hilfy said quietly, "one of us could ride along. Make sure they understand him."

There were a lot of unspoken questions around the table, a lot of worried looks from hands who knew what damage existed in the vane. No one was questioning.

"Listen," Pyanfar said, moving the cup on the table out of her way. "Truth: twenty hours. We're going for a first-class job. Whole new assembly back there."

"Gods," Geran breathed in reverence. Chur blinked; and Hilfy stared.

"They say twenty hours. They want us headed out of here for their own reasons. Now move it. We've got to have him down at the dock in ten minutes, packed and out."

"One of us ride along?" Chur asked.

"You and Hilfy." So the two of them had always fussed over Tully. Keep them both happy. "Armed. This is Kshshti."

"I'll go," Khym said.

She glanced his way with a furrowing of the brow. Honest offer. Feckless lunacy.

"If there was trouble," he said.

"No."

"If—"

"No." She stood up and tossed the cup into the disposal. "Get it moving. Nine minutes."

Crew hurried. Haral took Tully in tow, her hand hooked about his elbow, and headed for the bridge.

"Pyanfar," Khym said, working his own way out from between bench and table. "Pyanfar, listen to me."

"If you want to sulk go to your quarters and get out of the way."

"Is it Ehrran?"

"*I haven't time.*" She brushed past his arm and headed for the bridge, spun on one foot as she heard him following and brought him up short. "Use some judgment, Khym."

"I'm trying to help!"

She gave him one long desperate look, and watched his expression go from anger to desperation too. Anguish. She sorted a dozen jobs. All of them took skill. "You want to help, I want Kshshti data pulled from comp. Go do that." She spun about again and headed bridge-ward, for the papers she had under security.

That had to go. It was all one package, Tully and that envelope. If Ehrran knew about Tully she likely knew he came with documents. And all of it had to go into mahen custody. Fast. She could keep the deputy off the bridge: the law gave her that.

But since the kif hit Gaohn, since a great many changes had happened in the *han*—

One took no chances. Gods knew what *Prosperity* would swear to. It had gotten to that. Distrust of foreigners. Distrust of hani who defied the conventions. Foreign ways, they said. Hani males outside Anuurn: the keepers of the home, learning there were things outside the *han*, friends stauncher than other hani, outsider-ways of thought.

She reached the bridge, opened the security bin beside Haral and took out the precious packet—committed treason by that if not before. She slammed the bin shut.

Haral looked round at her, her scarred face quite, quite calm.

Khym was there too, just watching, from the side, as staunchly downworld in his own way as Ehrran's clan.

Worried. And silent now.

"Got something coming outside," Haral said, whose eyes and ears were partly *The Pride's* from where she sat. And whose discretion was absolute. "Two minutes, captain."

Chapter Eight

She headed down the corridor from the lift in haste, keyed the airlock to inside-manual and looked back as Hilfy and Chur and Geran came hurrying along with Tully in their midst.

"Car's on the dockside," Harral advised them from the general address. "You operating that on manual?"

"I've got it," Pyanfar said, touching the pickup by the lock controls. "Just keep a sharp lookout up there."

The four arrived, Tully dishevelled looking and disreputable in a white stsho shirt half tucked into the blue hani trousers. The shirt was far too big, the trousers too small; and for luggage he clutched a white plastic sack of the kind they used for utility—a change of clothes, toiletries, gods knew what they had thrown together for him in so short a time.

"Got the translation tapes?"

"Got," Tully answered for himself, patting the bundle.

"Here." She handed him the packet. "Tuck that in too. For the gods' sakes don't give it to the mahendo'sat."

He knew what it was. She saw the disturbed look, the doubt.

"Go on," she said, and triggered the inner lock. It hissed open with an exhalation of cold air. "Chur, Hilfy, you watch it. You watch it coming back. Don't you walk it. If they don't give you a car, you call and I'll see they do. Tell them priority. Tell them Personage."

"Right," said Chur.

She walked into the lock with them, pushed the button for the second door on alternate-set, so that the first closed behind them. She took no chances. Not now. The yellow accessway gaped like a ribbed gullet. The chill hit like a wall. "Hurry it."

"Pyanfar," Tully said of a sudden, and turned and balked. She put a hand on his back and propelled him ahead of her.

"Come on, come on, Tully. It's all right." She walked by him with her crewwomen trailing after, kept her arm at his back and kept him moving down the accessway. He was cold already. She felt the stiffness in his movements as they hit the slant and headed down to the rampway. "Won't be long. Bodies will heat up the car." —Chatter to keep him distracted. She saw the gray of the docks like docks anywhere, the pair of vehicles with the strobes flashing. "Translator's going to be out of range awhile, but they'll get you hooked up again when you get to station central. There's an outside chance—a small chance, understand?—it might be more than twenty hours. *Might* be, might be—they might have to shift you to some mahen ship. I don't think so—"

He balked again as they came down the last few steps, turned and gave her a panicked look.

"Captain," Chur said from behind, sharp and urgent: she heard the engines at the same time, looked toward the sound down the dock.

Another car, headed their way in a great hurry, from up-dock.

"Gods rot," she muttered, grabbed Tully by the arm and pulled him on. "*Fast*, Tully." The mahendo'sat in the cars got out, excepting the two drivers, one curly brown, a tasunno mahe, smaller than the others and rare this side of Iji; an officer and four others the gods-knew-what race of generations-back spacers, black and tall and bearing badges and sidearms on the usual harness. Not friendly-looking. Like one black wall. Tully balked again, looked about in panic as the moving car hummed up and braked, resisted again as two of the mahe grabbed him and pulled him toward the open door of the second mahen car.

"Pyanfar!" he cried.

Hilfy started forward, but Pyanfar caught her arm and held her as the number-three car door slid down and three Ehrran crew got out in haste.

"Hold it," the senior said. "Hold it there."

Pyanfar shrugged and faced them. She had let go Hilfy's arm, and everyone had stopped— the mahe trying to get Tully into the car, the Ehrran who had bailed out of their vehicle.

"Go on," Pyanfar said to Hilfy, and moved the hand at her side. "Chur, Hilfy. It's all right. Sorry, Ehrran. You've been preempted. Station-master's intervened."

"You," the foremost Ehrran said, gesturing at the mahendo'sat. "Where's the authorization?"

The mahe officer said something in one of Iji's manifold languages, waved a hand. The rest pulled Tully into the car and Chur and Hilfy piled in after. Doors began to close.

"Chanur," the Ehrran said.

Pyanfar gave a second shrug, displayed empty hands. "Out of my control."

"That's your personnel."

"Just to keep him quiet on the way. You'll have to take it up with station offices."

There were limits. Cursing a captain to her face was one; calling her a liar was another. The Ehrran did neither, but it was in her eyes, that were lambent brass. The mahen vehicles snugged up the doors and began to move. Ehrran cast a wild look that way, waved an arm at her crewmates and they dived back into their own car.

"Evidently the Ehrran haven't got a com in there," Pyanfar observed to Geran, who had stood fast by her left. "Gods be!"

The hani vehicle swerved wildly about and cut close to the mahendo'sat, dropped back as the mahendo'sat refused to be passed on the narrow dock.

"Cheeky lot," Geran said.

"Won't go well out here. Gods-rotted black-breeches thinks it's Anuurn. Ought to be interesting when they get news to their captain, oughtn't it?"

Geran turned a quizzical look her way

"I rather imagine they had trouble getting a car," Pyanfar said. "For some reason." Up the row there was another swerve, visible as the cars went up the curving deck, headed for the curtaining tangle of lines that would cut off the view. "Gods rot—"

"They're crazy," Geran said.

"Come on," she said, spun on her heel and headed up the ramp, with quickening long strides.

"Put me through to *Vigilance*," she said when she hit the bridge, not out of breath, not quite, but blowing through her nostrils. Geran was still with her, equally disarranged.

"Got that on vid," Haral said with quiet satisfaction, the while Khym stared in confusion and Tirun moved past his seat to reach com. "That maneuver going out."

"Sharp," she said. Haral smiled and powered her chair back round to business with the damage check.

"They don't answer," Tirun said, half turning in her seat. "No response."

"Log that. Call the station office and file a protest."

"Hazard to our personnel?"

"That'll do." She drew a quieter breath, hands on hips. Looked at Khym and saw a gleam in his eye she had not seen since Mahn. She stood a breath taller, walked over to lean over Haral's shoulder. "Next thing's that repair crew. Any sign yet?"

Kshshti docks passed in a blur of gray and brown, of dingy fronts obscured by the shielding of the car windows as the vehicle hummed along, buzz-thump-thump as the soft tires hit the joints of unshielded deck plating with manic speed in time to Hilfy Chanur's heart. She leaned to look back again as far as the shield-dimmed car window afforded: the Ehrran vehicle had fallen in behind them, no longer attempting to pass, but staying close on their tail. Tully's leg pressed hers on the left, the three of them occupying the back seat with Chur on the far side. Two of the mahen guards sat in front with the driver. The escort car filled much of the forward view, they ran so close to its tail: the strobe atop that lead car limned objects and the three mahendo'sat in front in unreality and blocked out the outside so that it had no color. Beside them office fronts and gantry machinery passed in a blur.

"Easy." She felt a shiver from Tully and patted his leg as she straightened around to look his way. "Safe, Tully. It's all right." The translator had stopped working as they passed out of range. But some words he understood on his own. "Safe, hear?"

He nodded, glancing distractedly her way. He had his plastic bundle clutched firmly in his arms and they sat close to him to keep him warm. The white flash from the front of the car glanced off his pale skin and pale hair and turned his nervous movements into something surreal.

"I—" he began, and the car lurched, swerved, threw them all forward and left with a suddenness that brought the rear of the escort car up in Hilfy's view as she turned her head, the car, the mahendo'sat driver fighting to turn, the guards flinging up arms to protect themselves as the car slewed into angled impact, glanced, hooked itself perversely into the escort car's torn body and kept slewing round, grating metal as a tire stripped off the rim and jolted over deckplates. Things blurred, snapped clear in a howl from the mahendo'sat, and a fist slammed them; the back of the seat flew up in Hilfy's face and she grabbed for Tully as her head hit the padding with the shock of explosion whumping through the air and the whole car tilting and slamming down again.

"They're firing!" Chur yelled and that reality got through to Hilfy's brain, sent her hand clawing for the gun in her pocket, numb-fingered from a shock to her elbow somewhere in the spin. The car had stopped. The forward window was cracked. The driver was slumped; both guards were alive. . . . "Stay inside," Chur was yelling from the other side as one guard worked at the door on that side. A shock hit the car and blossomed in a fireball beyond the cracked front window and Hilfy got the gun out as the stench of ozone roiled through the door in silver smoke. The door opened on manual, slammed down as the smoke poured in and the mahe sprawled as he went out in a pop of weaponsfire through the smoke: his comrade fired from inside and another shock hit the car, fire bloomed, deafening.

"Hilfy!" Tully dragged at her as cold air hit from the other direction, as Chur got the door open on the sheltered side and bailed out of the car. Hilfy flung a look in the other direction, pasted shot after shot at the flutter of black kif robes amid the smoke, intending to go when she had stopped that.

But alien hands seized the waist of her trousers and skidded her sharply backward across the slick seat even as she fired. An arm whipped round her waist and jerked her from the door backwards as she got off a last few shots. Tully tried to carry her, but she twisted free, got her feet on the ground and ran for herself, Tully beside her, Chur—

Another shock blossomed by her, and she was flying through the air, the deck coming up under her hands and under her face as something heavy came down on her and sprawled.

She was running then after a blank space, her legs working, not knowing how she had gotten there or where she was going until the gray of a girder came up and hit her shoulder and she spun, flailed for balance and caromed into Tully, arms about him as she decided on

227

cover and kept falling, crawling then, along the base of the gantry over deckbolts. She gripped the hard edge of the base rim, hitched herself along, lay still then. Smoke roiled along the overhead where red alarm strobes flashed, staining girders and smoke alike. Sounds were distant, through the ringing in her ears. She felt small distant pains, saw Tully's face twisted with exertion and with pain. "Chur?" he said, twisting on his elbow to look back. In panic: *"Chur?"* And Hilfy rolled over to look through the obscuring smoke, wiping her eyes and trying to see and hear.

"Chur?" she cried.

The red-gray smoke gave up a momentary view of tangled vehicles and other wreckage, of running figures, of fire from various quarters. She heard the dim chitter of kif commands, flinched as a shot came their way and reached to her pocket for the gun, but it was gone.

"Hilfy—" Tully cried, and pulled her further back as kif poured past them to take up position.

"O gods," she breathed. "We're behind the wrong gods-rotted line!"

Shots popped off the wall behind them and ricocheted wildly. She ducked down and in the first pause in fire she grabbed Tully by the shirt, scrambled up and ran with him while the smoke held—but that smoke was not dissipating as it should, the fans were not working, and it dawned on her battered skull that they were cut off, shut down: section doors had sealed.

"Where?" Pyanfar shouted into the com as if volume could help, aware of Tirun and Khym and Geran at her back and a great silence elsewhere on the bridge. "What 'stay still'? You gods-rotted incompetent—Where around the rim?" —Babble poured into her ear. She whirled round as her eye caught movement, saw Haral's running arrival on the bridge and waved a furious hand at her crew. "Arm! Move it!"

"Got section seal go," the mahen official was saying into her ear. "Got no chance kif get away, you wait report—"

"You authorize us past that seal. Hear?"

"Office got no authority—"

"Get it!" She cut the official off in midword and shoved her way past Khym. Geran had the sidearms out of the locker. "Get the rifles," she said. They had them. It was illegal, a defense they never admitted to port authorities they had.

"Aye," Haral said, and ran.

"Pyanfar—" Khym said.

She put the lock on controls, spun about and ran. Khym was with them and she had no desire to stop him. Not in this.

*   *   *

The huge section doors were shut, red and amber strobes on their surface spearing through the wafts of smoke that reached even here. Sirens wailed and echoed in the vastness of the docks. "They're shut, they're sealed," Hilfy gasped, blinking smoke-tears and half-carrying the human who half-carried her, the two of them weaving past the clutter of dockside bins and chutes as they tried to get the break they needed to get past the line of fire. "We can't get out—Tully, stop!"

Shots broke out from a new direction. She dragged him off his balance. They both staggered, thumped into the echoing side of a bin and she landed hard on her rump as Tully collapsed with a gasp. Flesh stank. He rolled over, clutching at his arm and she kept pulling at him, claws hooked into his shirt as she worked toward the corner—

O gods, that there be shelter there—

There was an alleyway of a kind, a recess for freight loading, a door with a white light over its recess. SERVICE ACCESS, said a battered sign, ROHOSU COMPANY. Beside it, mahen graffiti, obscurely obscene. She tried the door; but it was locked like every other door along the row once the emergency had sounded. She rang the bell; battered at the unyielding steel. "Open up, gods rot you! We're hani! Let us in!"

No answer. Tully babbled something. Sirens.

She heard them too, far down the dock. She sank down by him, pried his hand from his arm and grimaced at the wound the dim light showed, black edged and bleeding hard. She grabbed the tail of his shirt and tore a wide strip of cloth off, pressed it tight and put his hand on it, ripped another strip off to tie it with.

"Easy," she breathed, senseless chatter to keep him from panic. "Easy, you're all right, all right, hear?"

He slumped back against the wall, his face gone to waxen color. The hand of the wounded arm shook and the tremor spread to the rest of him as he began to go into shock. But he listened, his eyes on her whenever she looked.

"Listen," she said, "listen, station's onto it now. And The Pride—they'll have heard by now. The captain's doing something, you can bet she'll get us help—Pyanfar, understand?"

"Pyanfar come."

"Bet on it. All right, huh?" She got the bandage around his arm, put his hand on it to hold that. She snugged the knot tight and he mumbled something in human language. No translator. The translator-tape—

—in the bundle of clothes. With the papers. Back at the wreck. With Chur—

"Hilfy—" He stiffened, eyes fixed toward the exit of the alley. She turned her head.

231

Shadows moved in that red-dyed smoke, paused and conversed outside, a gathering of black robes, tall, stoop-shouldered silhouettes.

Tully edged aside, out of the light the door cast. She moved too, as carefully as she could, as far as Tully did, and put her arms about him to hide his pallor with her own redbrown hide as much as she could within the shadows. She felt Tully shivering; felt her own stomach knotted up when she recalled kif eyesight.

They were night-hunters by preference; and Tully—white shirt, pale hair, paler skin—

She kept her arms clenched about him.

And saw that conversation outside their refuge break up, the kif start to move.

One stopped and looked their way.

"Open that gods-rotted door!" Pyanfar yelled, and used the rifle butt on the guardroom spex, so a scared mahendo'sat in the section-control yelled back threats from the other side. *"It's clear from the Personage!"* she yelled. *"Open that section-seal!"*

"Au-to-matic," the yell came back through the com-transfer, in mangled pidgin. Mahen station. Half the personnel never managed fluency in pidgin.

"Personage!" she yelled back in mahen Standard.

Gibberish came back. This one spoke dialect.

*   *   *

Black-robed shadows filled the alleyway, dark, featureless, except for the wan light of the bulb in the low ceiling of the door recess and Hilfy gathered herself to her feet. Tully struggled and she helped him by his good arm to give him that chance at least.

"Run if you can," she said in a low voice, thinking perhaps she could break a hole for him. But he knew so few words. He pressed closer to her as the kif gave them less room. He would try to fight—blunt-fingered, without any advantage, without even speed to outrun a kif. And it was Tully they wanted: alive. She had no doubt of that. "Got claws," she said beneath her breath. "You don't. Run, understand?"

The kif moved closer, keeping their circle. "We'll not hurt you," one said. "You're in the wrong place, young hani. Certainly you are. If you had a gun you would have used it, would you not? But we aren't your enemies."

"Who?" She perceived the origin of the voice: the speaker stood out among the rest, taller, finer-robed, and she guessed the name as she edged into Tully, trying to keep open space about them as the kif moved and shifted.

"Sikkukkut. From Meetpoint. You remember me, young Chanur. I have no wish to hurt you, either one. And there are far too many of us. Come, be reasonable."

The kif moved, all of them at once. "Run!" she yelled at Tully, spun and swung and kept swinging as her claws carried a kif headon into the wall. "Run, for godssakes, run—"

Black cloth obscured her vision, cleared as Tully pulled one off her, and she rattled that one's brains.

But kif claws pulled Tully by the shoulder, and grabbed him by the arm.

"Gods blast!" she cried qnd tried to get that one off him, but two kif got her arms and a kifish arm came hard about her throat.

The door thundered back on chaos, the flash of red lights on smoke the fans refused, the sweep of floods, the lunatic strobe-flash. "Gods," Geran muttered. The center of the trouble was evident, a knot of flashing white lights stabbing into the smoke far up the dockside. Pyanfar started running first, rifle in both hands—"No, wait—" from the mahen official who had gotten the door open. "Hani, got wait!—" But Geran was pace for pace with her and gaining—fleet-footed Geran, whose sister Chur was in that mess.

A laser shot streaked the smoke. Pyanfar brought the rifle up and fired on the run. Geran did the same, not with particular skill, but with dispatch; and more fire came behind her, with the mahen official screaming for them to take cover.

Khym shouted, something: the heights distorted it, twisted it into a blood-crazed roar. A volley of smoke-bounced shots came back from kif near the wreckage and Pyanfar dived aside, remembered Khym behind her with one heartstopping fright and rolled to cover his blind rush.

But he came skidding in beside her, gasping, with the pistol quickly braced up hunting targets as Tirun reached their cover. Geran and Haral had tucked in with the mahendo'sat next a stack of cans: shots spattered the plastic and those three ducked.

Then a flurry opened up from the other side, and for a moment the pop of projectile fire rang everywhere off the overhead: mahen voices yowled distant satisfaction and she put her head out, sprawled back again because shots were wild and going a dozen ways about the wreckage and up the dock to their position.

Geran got off three quick shots from her side, Haral another burst. "That's mahen fire!" Haral yelled, seeing something from her vantage; and Pyanfar ventured another look, saw fire going the other way and pelted out of cover the last long sprint for the wreckage, from which cover a steady spatter of fire went out aimed the other way.

C. J. Cherryh

Mahe braced in among the tangle started at
their arrival, and hani among them turned about
with backlaid ears.

Ehrran.

Pyanfar slid in among them, grabbed an
Ehrran shoulder and shook it as Geran arrived,
and the rest of the crew. "Where's Chanur?"
Pyanfar shouted into the Ehrran crewwoman's
backlaid ears. "Where, gods rot you!"

The Ehrran pointed mutely to a hani lying
on the deck and Pyanfar's heart lurched over as
Geran scrambled that way, to her sister's side.

"Where's the rest?" Pyanfar yelled, and a
larger hani arm appeared from behind her and
seized a fistful of Ehrran beard. *"Where are
they?"* Khym shouted, and the Ehrran waved a
frantic hand toward the dock at large.

"—Ran—they ran—Somewhere out there—"
Pyanfar let go her grip with a shove and
abandoned the Ehrran to get to Chur.

Chur was alive. They had propped her head
off the deck and the wound that had spread
blood all about was hard-sealed and glistening
with plasm that stopped further bleeding. Geran
bent over her, just holding her hand, looking
more than scared.

"How is she?" Pyanfar asked.

"She hurts," Chur said for herself, past
scarcely moving jaws. Her eyes were slitted.
"Where's Hilfy—Tully?"

"We don't know. Where'd you lose them?"

A weak move of Chur's head. A try at pointing. "Got out," she said. The pointing was nowhere in particular. "Don't know."

Pyanfar looked round at the others who hovered near. "That packet. Tully had it in his hands. Hunt the wreck."

"Got," Chur said thickly, reached feebly behind her head, delirious, Pyanfar thought, until she recognized the thing Chur's head was lying on. Chur tried to pull it. Tully's plastic sack.

"Gods," Pyanfar said with feeling. "Geran. Stay with her. You hang onto that. They'll get an ambulance in here real soon."

"Not Kshshti," Chur said. "*Pride*."

For a moment Pyanfar failed to understand her, then gripped her arm. "No way we leave you here. Got that?"

"Got," Chur said, and let her eyes close.

"Stay with her," Pyanfar said to Geran. "We'll find them." She stood up, keeping low, for there were still shots flying, drew Tirun and Khym and Haral off to the mahen position. She seized one by the arm and pulled him about. "Hani. Seen hani?"

"No got," he said.

"Alien?"

"No got."

She edged back again, cast about amid the confusion of arriving emergency vehicles, the thunder of PA above sirens, each confounding the other. *Evacuate*, she made out. *Evacuate, evacuate—unsafe—*

—getting the non-involved clear. She hoped. Possibly the whole sector of the station had gone unstable in the explosions. In the mahen-language shouting and the noise of the sirens there was no knowing. She put her head up, for firing had stopped, ducked down again as her own crew pulled her down, but there were still no shots.

"Think they're through out there," she said, and seized Haral by the arm. "Get Chur into an ambulance. Geran's not to leave her. Whatever."

"Right," Haral said; he turned to leave and froze, so that Pyanfar turned to look too, where hani had appeared among the emergency vehicles, some black-trousered, several blue, the first sight of which lifted her hope and the second dashed it.

"*Ayhar*," she spat, and hurled herself to her feet. "*Ehrran!*"—for Rhif Ehrran was in that group, and she headed for them in mingled wrath and hope, dodged round a stretcher crew and a fire-control team headed into the wreckage. Hani faces turned her way, Banny Ayhar and Rhif Ehrran chiefest of them.

"Chanur!" Ehrran shouted, headed her way. "By the gods, Chanur, you've really fouled it up, haven't you?"

She slowed to a walk, with long, long strides. A hand caught her arm and she jerked free.

"Captain," Tirun begged her. "Don't.

She stopped. Stood there. And Ehrran had the sense to stop out of her reach. Tirun was on one side of her, Khym on the other.

"Where are they?" she asked Ehrran.

"Gods if I know," Ehrran said, hand on that pistol at her side. The whites showed at the edges of her eyes. "Gods rot it, Chanur—"

"Be some use. We need searchers. They may have taken cover somewhere, anywhere along the docks."

Ehrran flicked her ears nervously, turned and lifted a hand in signal to her own. "Fan out. Watch yourselves."

"Move," Pyanfar said to her own, and they did.

Hilfy moved a finger, a hand, discovered consciousness and remembered kif, with the kif-stink all about her. She tried the whole arm, both arms, a deep panicked breath, and opened her eyes on a gray ceiling and bare steel and lights, with the memory of a jolt she had not fully heard, with her arms tangled in something, her legs pinned—*the wreck—o gods—*

She turned her head, a dizzy haze of lights, a bright spot of light with kif clustered round something pale on a table, something pale and human-sized.

She heaved, met restraints that held her to a surface. Blankets wrapped her arms about, and they had her fastened about that. She heard another clank of machinery, shieldings in retraction, all the familiar sounds, watched the kif cast an anxious look up and go back to their work—*Clank! Thump!*

Ship sounds. It was the grapple-disengage. The kif stayed at work, clinging to the table on which Tully lay when the G stress shifted. There were hisses, the click of kifish speech. She shut her eyes and opened them again and the nightmare remained true.

Pyanfar stopped and looked about her, swung the rifle about as she heard someone coming in this zone of wreckage and shot-out lights. Hani silhouette against the lighted zone.

"Captain," Haral cried, and the echoes went up. "Captain—" Her first officer gasped for breath and stopped, leaning on a gantry leg. "*Harukk* just left dock. Mahendo'sat just sent word. . . ."

She said nothing. Nothing seemed adequate. She only slung the rifle to her shoulder and started running for the center of the search, for what help there was to find.

* * *

They had left. "Tully," Hilfy said. The G stress was considerable, and it was hard to breathe; the kif had beat that out the door, gone somewhere for protection, but they had left Tully lying there on the table, no blanket, nothing against the cold. "Tully—"

But he did not move. She gave over trying to rouse him. They had patched the worst, she reckoned. They were headed for long acceleration, for jump, and they wanted their prisoner to stay alive that long.

She, she reckoned, was quite another matter. Against Chanur, quite a number of kif had a score to settle.

"Going where? She built the map in her head. Kefk, likeliest. Kefk, inside kif territory. They could do that in one jump.

The whole ship jolted. *Hit*, she thought with one wild hope that someone, somehow, had moved to stop it; but the G grew worse then, incredibly worse. The ship had dumped cargo, no, not even cargo: she remembered *Harukk*, the sleek wicked lines of her docked at Meetpoint. It was the false pods that had just blown, and stripped *Harukk* down to the hunter-ship she was.

Nothing could catch her now.

"How long ago?" Pyanfar shouted at the messenger, and the tall mahe backed up a step.

"Soon ago, soon." The mahe laid hands on his chest. "I messenger, hani captain, got com shot up, come office Personage give me same, say bring you."

Pyanfar took a swing at nothing in particular, turned away and found Rhif Ehrran in her path.

"Well, Chanur? Got any brilliant plan?"

"If you weren't down here on the dock, if you hadn't left the only ship fit to chase them sitting crewless, you gods-rotted fool—!"

"To do what? Chase a hunter-ship to Kefk? You're the fool, Chanur. There'll be a full report. Believe me that there will."

"Py, don't!" It was Khym who got her arm in time and dragged her back, so it was too late to do it at white heat. She straightened herself, stared at the Ehrran whose crew had moved in to back their captain.

"Captain," a mahe said, moving in. "Captain, Personage want see, quick, please quick. Got car."

She shoved the rifle at Khym, turned and followed the mahe across the littered deck. She was aware of Haral with her, Tirun, Khym hastening to catch up.

"Chanur." A hani voice, a portly hani moving up from the side. "Chanur—" Banny Ayhar caught her arm and tried to stop her.

She flung the hand off. "Get out of my way, Ayhar. Go lick Ehrran's feet."

"Listen, Chanur." Ayhar caught her arm with force this time and thrust her bulk in the way. "I'm sorry! You want passage?"

She stopped dead and stared at Banny Ayhar's broad face.

"She hire you?"

"No."

"Who did?"

"See here, Chanur—"

Pyanfar walked off.

Chapter Nine

The lift let them out where Tully and Hilfy should have gotten to, in the upper security levels, where guards looked nervous at the appearance of a clutch of blood-stained hani armed with rifles, and one of them a male.

But doors opened for them unquestioned, doors upon doors of Kshshti's utilitarian architecture, gray steel, heavy security, armed guards at intervals.

Stars and dark: Pyanfar lost the sight in front of her for that, remembrance of the kif hunter-ship in dock at Meetpoint, sleek, deadly, fast; of a ship outbound to Kshshti nadir and the jump range at a greater and greater fraction of C. She went there the guard motioned, went where doors parted.

The last let them into a dim chamber with a plasteen division, with violet light beyond. On the white-lit side, a desk and two mahendo'sat. On the violet one, a huge serpent-form, which moved and shifted restlessly before the waist-up glass.

Tc'a. The sight of the methane-breather shocked her to an involuntary stop. The barrier looked frail, the presence hani were accustomed to see only on vid and dimly, showed detail that made it seem all too imminent: wrinkled, soft-leather skin with phosphor-glow in the gold, eyespots large as a fist, five of them clustered round a complex trifold mouth/sensor. The tongue darted, constantly. The body shifted to this side and that, which tc'a always did.

"Esteemed captain." The Voice spoke, uncharacteristically subdued. "I present the Personage Toshena-eseteno, stationmaster this side Kshshti; the Personage Tt'om'm'mu, stationmaster methane side."

"Honorables," Pyanfar murmured. The tc'a alone deserved the plural, several times over; and gods help psychologists.

The leathery serpent-shape loomed closer, twisted to peer through the glass with its five orange eyespots. A wailing came through, five-voiced, from a brain of multiple parts, as a monitor below the glass displayed the glowing matrix:

TC'A	TC'A	HANI	HANI	MAHE	KIF	KIF
CHI	CHI	STAY	STAY	STAY	GO	GO
UNITY	UNITY	ANGER	ANGER	ANGER	GO	GO
STAY	STAY	STAY	STAY	STAY	GO	MESSAGE

"Thank the tc'a Personage. *What* message?"

"Kif." The mahen Personage rose slowly from the desk, robes falling into order, severe robes unlike the display of Personages elsewhere. He held out a paper with his own hand, and she took it. "This come," the Personage said, not through the Voice, "from *Harukk*. All three kif ship outbound. We got two mahe ship chase."

"Shoot?"

"No shoot."

She held a small, horrid doubt whether they should have refrained, hostages or no. For the hostages' sake. If it were *The Pride* in pursuit— but she pushed that thought away. Unfolded the paper.

Hunter Pyanfar, it said. *When the wind blows one should spread nets. Mine was fortunate for us both. Should your sfik insist to meet with me, Mkks is neutral ground. There you may reclaim what is yours.*

"He's got them," she said for the crew's benefit. She gave the paper to Haral. *Mkks.* Disputed Zones. Not Kefk, in kif territory.

Bait. Where she could reach it.

"I make order," the Personage said, "mahe ship track this kif. Go Mkks. Try use influence."

"*Influence*. How much influence, when a kif's got what he wants?"

The Personage made a small, casting-away gesture. Pyanfar stood there with her pulse hammering in her ears and no trust at all. Nothing, where they crossed the mahe's interest.

"You follow this kif?" the Personage asked. "Or you go Maing Tol?"

Which gets my ship fixed, Honorable? But she did not say that. She cast a look toward the glass where the tc'a dipped and wove aimless patterns. Back then to the mahendo'sat in his ascetic robes. "You have a suggestion?"

The Personage lasped into mahen language.

"Hani captain," the Voice said, "kif use proverb mean he got result from confusion someone else. Maybe not plan. Got maybe other motive. This Sikkukkut—" The Voice shifted footing and put her hands behind her. "Forgive. Not got polite hani word. *Hatonofa*. He look get number-one position."

"I know the word. I don't know this kif. *No one* knows a kif, but another kif."

Another exchange between Personage and Voice.

"Personage," said the Voice, "want make delicate this. I confess lack skill."

"Say it plain. I'll add the courtesy."

"Ask what else you got this kif want."

"I don't know."

The tc'a made a sound.

CHI	TC'A	HANI	HANI	KIF	KIF	KIF
STAY	WARN	DATA	DATA	WANT	GOT	WANT
TC'A	KSHSHTI	MKKS	MKKS	MKKS	KEFK	AKKT
FEAR	WARN	DIE	DIE	TAKE	TAKE	TAKE

"Information," Toshena-eseteno translated that.

"What's the *Kefk* and *Akkt* mean?"

The screen went dark and stayed that way.

"What's it mean?" she asked the mahe.

"Not clear." The Personage walked to the glass and laid his hand on it. "Not always clear, tc'a colleague. Warn you. Got warn you. Crew—already work repair you ship. Where go?"

She gnawed her mustache. "Twenty hours."

"Maybe do better."

The screen lit again. The serpent wailed.

CHI	TC'A	CHI	KNNN	HANI	HANI	MAHE
TC'A	HANI	HANI	HANI	SAME	OTHER	OTHER
KSHSHTI	KSHSHTI	KSHSHTI	KSHSHTI	KSHSHTI	KSHSHTI	KSHSHTI
MKKS	MKKS	MKKS	MKKS	MKKS	MKKS	KSHSHTI
SEE	SEE	SEE	SEE	GO	DIE	STAY
DANGER	DANGER	DANGER	THREAT	DANGER	DANGER	DANGER

"What threat?" Pyanfar asked. The matrix had potential to be read in any direction. The computer picked it out of the harmonics and no sequence was certain. "Knnn? *What* hani die? Present or future?"

The tc'a reared back from the glass.

AVOID AVOID AVOID AVOID AVOID AVOID AVOID

"Is that the answer or the reaction?"

The tc'a dipped and weaved. A chi skittered up into view from below the glass, a hani-sized bundle of rapidly moving sticks phosphoresced in the violet light. It clambered up the tc'a wrinkled side and clung there, touching with frenetic quivers of its limbs.

The Compact's sixth alleged intelligence. Or a tc'a symbiont. No one had figured that out.

DANGER DANGER DANGER DANGER DANGER DANGER DANGER

"Still, be still." The mahen Personage lifted his hands to the violet glow, turned about against the light. His ears were back. The light glistened in a halo about him; his profile was shadowed, featureless.

"One broke out of Meetpoint," Pyanfar said. "Knnn. Tc'a too. There was trouble there. Haven't seen it since."

"Knnn come, go. No one ask."

"Might be here, you mean."

"Knnn business. Not talk this."

"They snatched the human ships."

"*Not talk this!*" The Personage turned to face her, totally shadow now.

She flicked her ears and lifted her head in one long grudging breath. "Apologies." A second, shorter breath. The air seemed close. "I'd better go, Honorable."

"*Where you go?*" the Personage asked. "Maing Tol? Mkks?"

"You want to tell me which?"

"I say, you not listen, true?"

Not dull-witted. No.

And not, adding up the asked and not-asked, not knowing everything Goldtooth had planned or done. Maybe the wavefront of that information was one lonely hani ship. Or maybe Maing Tol had not trusted Kshshti security.

Coils within coils within coils. To pull the snake's tail one had to know which end was which.

"I got orders," Pyanfar said, "mahe who gave me this job. He trust. You?"

The Personage said something the Voice did not render, and turned and gazed at Tt'om'm'mu. The tc'a and chi were otherwise occupied, the chi busy waving its limbs over the tc'a's leathery hide. Speech, maybe. No oxy-breather knew.

The mahe turned round again. "You go where choose. Got no bill, no dock charge. Kshshti give."

"Gratitude."

The mahe joined his hands in courtesy. The tc'a Tt'om'm'mu—remained occupied.

"Hurts," Chur murmured. Her eyes cleared somewhat, looking up at them clustered about her bed. "Want—" The rest of it faded out.

"Sedation's pretty heavy," Geran said, leaning forward from her low stool at the bedside to brush at her sister's mane. Pyanfar nodded, hands within her belt. Geran had gotten the news outside the door, knew the contents of the message. "Good treatment here. Kshshti medics get a lot of practice."

It was a joke, desperately delivered. Eyes still closed, Chur gave a twitch of a smile, as forced as the joke. "Get me out of here, captain. Godsrotted dull port."

"Get your rest." Pyanfar leaned over and closed her hand on Chur's arm. "Hear? We'll be back."

"Where's Hilfy? Tully?" Chur's eyes opened, far sharper than she had thought. "You find them?"

"We're working on it."

"Gods rot." Chur moved, a stir of her whole body. "*Where are they?*"

"Go to sleep. Don't move about like that."

"Something's wrong."

"Chur." Geran slipped a hand in and held

her arm. "Captain's got work to do. Go back to sleep."

"In a mahen hell. *What's the news?*"

There was no lying about it. Not to Chur. Not likely. The blood pressure would go up and up. She would worry at it. "Mkks," Pyanfar said. "Kif snatched them both. One Sikkukkut. Says he's talking deal. Wants us to go to Mkks to meet him."

"O gods."

"Listen." She held Chur's arm, hard. "Listen. It's not hopeless. We've got help from the mahendo'sat. We'll get them back. Both."

"You going to let the mahendo'sat do it?"

She hesitated on that answer. Gave it up for the second truth. "Haral and Tirun and I. We can handle *The Pride.* They're going on the repairs."

Chur's ears went down against the pillow. Her eyes were shut. "Promised. You."

"Can't do it. Can't do it now."

"Tomorrow. I'll be there. At the ship. Geran too."

"You rest."

"Huhhhhnn." Chur's eyes flashed open. "Patch will hold. I'll stand jump just fine. Captain."

Pyanfar stood back, met Geran's eye.

"See you at the ship," Geran said.

Pyanfar laid her ears back. "Listen." She set a hand on Geran's shoulder and drew her aside.

253

"We can handle it, much as we can do. Gods-rotted place to be left. Stay with her, huh?"

"Then what?"

Shipless. Two hani, stranded. She had no answer for that.

"See you," Geran said.

One hani left behind. No better. Chur without Geran. They had never been apart, never looked to be. It was a final shock, in what sense remained unnumbed.

"See you." She dropped the hand and turned to gather up Tirun and Haral. Khym stood by the door. No rifles. They had left those outside with a nervous stsho medic and scrubbed up in a washroom. But the stench of smoke still hung about their clothes. Strong soap and smoke. The smell turned her stomach. "Come on. Better let her rest. —Chur. You take it easy, hear? We'll fix it. Trust us for it."

Asleep, she reckoned.

"Captain." Geran bent beside the bed and picked up a white plastic sack. Washed, since Chur had had it beneath her head. "It's in there. Packet's intact."

"Huh." She took the white bundle and tucked it within her arm. Kif would have killed for it, would have wiped the station to get it—if they knew. The stationmasters themselves had not known. Knew comparatively little, all things considered. "Thank her, huh?"

*   *   *

She laid the sack on the bridge counter, lacking the heart to delve into the personal things. She drew the packet from it and checked inside.

Intact. Rumpled papers. Recordings protected in their cases. She put the lot into security storage, closed the coded latch.

Sounds reverberated through the hull, horrendous sounds from aft as skimmers performed their work and cut away the stern assemblies. The shocks went through the very frame as a third of *The Pride*'s length was sheared away.

"Py. Captain."

She looked up and back. Khym was standing there.

"You didn't mention me—when you talked about crew going to Mkks."

"Khym—"

"I can fetch and carry. I can scrub galley. Lets skilled crew free. Doesn't it?"

Protective instincts rose up. Another image did. Khym's arm between her and the Ehrran; Khym, whose mind had gone on working when hers quit.

"Good job," she said, "that business on the docks." She walked past him, patted him gently on the arm.

"Captain."

Not *Py*. . . . She looked back, saw rage, and hurt.

"For godssakes don't dismiss me with *that!*"

She stood there, trying to recall what she had said or done. "I'm tired," she said. "I'm sorry."

He managed nothing, no answer.

"You want to go," she said, "gods rot it, you're in. Get killed with the rest of us. Happy?"

"Thanks," he said flatly. In a hostile tone.

She turned and walked off. It was the best way, when his tempers got obscure. Gods defend him. Fool.

He was fond of Hilfy, that was what. Age got on him and he doted on daughter-images, remembering his own. Theirs. Tahy. Who had been no defense to him against her brother. Hilfy respected him. Called him *na* Khym. Fixed special things for him and pampered him the way he was accustomed.

Gods rot.

She reached the galley, delved into cabinets and threw gfi into the brewer, feeling the wobble in her knees. She had not cleaned up, except the scrub at the hospital. She did not care to now, wanting only something on her stomach.

"Fix that for you?" Khym offered, having followed her. "Sit down, Py."

Her arm tautened to slam the unit lid down. She lowered it carefully and looked around, bland as he was. "Galley's all yours."

"How much did you put in?"

"One."

He added more, going quietly about his business. So he had created a place for himself, and truth, if he freed up crew on this one, he was useful.

Whatever they were doing to the tail rose to a distant shriek.

"Py." He offered the cup and she took it. He poured the rest, capped them, to deliver where Haral and Tirun were.

But Haral showed up, bathed and with her blue coarse breeches still showing wet spots, her mane and beard hanging in ringlets. She had a paper in her hand. "That mine?" she asked of the gfi, and laid down the paper in front of Pyanfar. "That came in."

Pyanfar looked at it. Sipped thoughtfully at the gfi.

Ehrran's Vigilance, *Rhif Ehrran captain, deputy of the han, Immune, to* The Pride of Chanur, *Pyanfar Chanur captain, chief vessel Chanur company:*

This will serve as legal notice a complaint will be filed regarding breach of Charter, section 5: willful disregard of lawful order; section 12: hire of vessel; section 22: illegal cargo; section 23: illegal arms; section 24: discharge of arms; section 25: actions in breach of treaty law; section 30. . . .

She looked up as Khym left on his errand. "They missed the illegal system entry."

Haral gave a short, dry laugh and sat down. *The Pride* shuddered to operations aft, and the humor died a rapid death.

"We answer that?"

"Fills the time." She drew a deep breath. "Sleep, rest, plot course. We take for granted they'll get us out of here."

Haral's eyes drifted to the clock. Hers too, irresistibly.

"Tully," Hilfy murmured. The Gforce kept on. Her nose bubbled with every breath; some blood vessel had popped inside, adding misery upon misery. Her hurts throbbed, and might be pouring blood, but she could not tell and the cocooning blanket would soak it up.

Tully was still out. She talked to him periodically, in the chance he should have waked, to let him know one friend was with him. But he did not respond. Possibly they had taped a drug patch to him to keep him under. Perhaps he had just failed to come to. Instincts wanted to call for help and other instincts remembered what would come and told her to keep her mouth shut and let him go if he could.

They were headed for jump. And if he were awake he would be terrified.

So was she, when she let her attention wander to herself. When she did that she hoped there was a ship or two chasing them that would let off an unexpected shot before they got to jump, and solve their problems at one stroke.

Think of anything but the place where they were going.

Think of Pyanfar, who was likely taking the station authorities apart and telling them what to do about it, which thought gave her a surge of hope; and Haral—she pictured Haral sitting in that chair whose upholstery she had worn out and turning round just so, with that unflappable calm that never broke, not even when in her first tour she had made a dangerous mistake.

Want to fix that? Haral would say.

O gods, she wished she could.

The thrust died of a sudden, just died, in one stomach-lurching shift to inertial.

Prep for jump.

"*Harukk's* left," Tirun said, when the word came in. "That's 43 minutes light, station-center. Pursuit ship relayed image. Jumped . . . about an hour and fifteen ago."

Timelag, Tirun meant: reporting time was in that, what ship scan could pick up and relay, beating the beacon report by a few minutes.

Pyanfar nodded, kept working on the course plottings, a great deal of it futile until they had the readout on the new rig. When it got finished.

When.

"That's affirmative on Mkks vector."

"Huh." Her hands shook. She flexed her claws out and in and powered the chair about, taking a look at the work aft, which their dome camera was fixed on. She flinched inwardly at the sight, The Pride stripped of her familiar outlines. There was a new unit moving in. They had the transmissions from the pusher. And getting ship and tail unit joined was only the roughest beginning of the matter, a matter of preparing disconnect-ravaged surfaces for new welds. Hard-suited workers showed like sparks in the working floods, like a swarm of insects where they had backed off for that unit's arrival. Service-com frequency was never silent, crackling with chiso, the mahen patois that bridged their scores of languages, easier than trade-tongue for mahendo'sat.

"I'm going to get some rest," she said, for the smothering weight of all of it came down at once, and getting herself out of the chair and down the corridor loomed as a major undertaking.

"Call Haral up when you have to."

"Aye," Tirun said. Not an expression, not a question what they were going to do or how.

She appreciated that.

Time did twists now. In one fashion she could relax, because for the next stationside several weeks Harukk and its company were in the between, in the compression of hyper-light, where everything was in suspension and nothing would start again until the Mkks gravity well took hold. Two weeks at least, in which everything was stopped. No pain. No fear. Nothing, til they came out again.

But Tully needed drugs for that gravity-drop, needed them like stsho needed them. Perhaps kif knew this. Perhaps they cared to keep him sane.

Better, perhaps, if he was not.

She waked, suddenly, caught at the edge of the sleeping-bowl and realized she was not falling, despite the thumping of her heart. She rolled and looked at the clock and punched the lights on and the com connection. The hammering was silent. That had waked her.

"Bridge, gods rot it, it's 0400!"

"Aye, captain." Haral's voice. "Nothing's going on. Thought we'd let you sleep."

"Uhhhnn." She leaned her elbow on the bed-edge. "That tail set?"

"They're welding now."

"They're not going to make that deadline."

"They've got techs working on the boards already. They're pushing it."

"Gods." She let her head down on her arm, feeling as if a wall had come down on her yesterday and some of the bricks still lay there. Lifted it again. "How's Chur?"

261

"Geran called, says she's doing all right. They both got a little sleep."

"Huh. Good."

"Got a call from *Vigilance*. They got our paper. Ehrran's chewing sticks."

"Good."

"Got a pot of something fixed in galley."

Her stomach rebelled. "Fine." She passed a hand over her face, rubbing her eyes. "I'm coming." She punched the com off, rolled out and sat on the bed edge trying to convince her legs to work.

Gods, Hilfy. Tully. *That* settled back on her shoulders. There was the packet in the security bin. There was Tt'om'm'mu's writhing shape in its violet glow and the mahendo'sat, together against the glass (*don't ask about the knnn*) and mahendo'sat making vital connections on her ship, when mahendo'sat incompetency had let kif do as they pleased.

Incompetent? Kshshti stationmaster, and no better than that?

Suspicions had tramped her subconscious half the night, rose up in memories of dreams of a kif in the shadows of that room. Of delicate connections in the column links, some mahen technician carefully making a sequence of mistakes that would send false readout to the boards. Gods, what if—

A body could go crazy on what-ifs. Like

treachery from Goldtooth from the start. Like *Vigilance* being in the right—for hani interests. Like Chanur on the wrong side of matters and about to become expendable in some mahen intrigue.

Or traitorous.

She got up, showered, dressed in a subdued way, a pair of old breeches she saved for rough work. No earrings but the plain ones, such as any spacer wore.

Khym had done much the same, in a pair of silk breeches that had seen the Meetpoint riot and would never be the same. He met her in the galley with gfi and a dish of something overspiced—not good at cookery either. But the job got done and the stuff was far from fatal.

"Good," she said, to please him, and coupled with that was the ugly thought that nothing mattered much, beyond Mkks. Tomorrow. *Their* tomorrow, and their next tomorrow, when they would come out the other side of jump.

How much time-gain for a hunter-ship like *Harukk* and its ilk? Days faster than *The Pride* at absolute best. *Harukk* would be in port at Mkks as much as a week by the time *their* day-after-tomorrow came, and they spent time working up to dock at Mkks, and all the attendant nonsense. If they got that far.

She shivered, swallowed an overspiced last mouthful and washed it down with gfi. Her ears kept going down despite herself. She pricked them up. Looked Khym's way. "There's a procedures list in comp," she said to him. "Checklist."

"Got it," he said, displaying a paper on the countertop. Gods, efficiency. She poured the whole matter out of her mind and got up and walked off.

Maybe—*maybe* the kif would hold off in Hilfy's case, until they had used the bait for everything they could get. Not Tully. No. Not with a chance to pull information about all humankind from him, and a week to do it in. The first time kif had had their hands on him he had had a word or two he could speak, and a handful more he could understand, and never admitted either to the kif.

Now he could get a hani sentence out. And Sikkukkut had fluency.

"Captain," Haral said when she walked out on the bridge. "Got a request from the repair chief. They want to get column access from inside. I told them go ahead. I'm opening lower deck for that."

"Get their security down there." The thought of outsiders straying at random through *The Pride's* interior workings set her nerves on edge. But they were out of personnel. Out. Totally.

"Second item," Haral said. "A freighter turned up about 0300 last watch in approach to 29.

Our scan's been down. It just turned up, blink, on station output, at the one-zone. I didn't think it was worth waking you, but I queried station. They identified it as *Eishait*, said it came in during the *Harukk* business and security had it scan-blocked. I queried *Prosperity*. They had their scan shut down. They're too far round the curve for the cameras to help. I put in a call to *Vigilance*, begging your pardon—"

"They get it?"

Haral dipped her ears. "They said, quote, they had no authority to release information. I suggested they wake their captain. They suggested I wake you."

She drew a tight slow breath and leaned against the counteredge nearest the doorway.

"At that point," Haral said, "it was committed to dock and I figured there wasn't all that much to do about it that fast. Stationmaster's office stuck by the *Eishait* story. I called *Prosperity* back and suggested one of them take a walk down that way."

"Should have waked me, gods rot it."

"*Prosperity* agreed. They say it's all security down there. Can't get past. Our work crew never stopped back there, no sign of any concern while that ship was inbound. Meanwhile there's nothing kifish on com. I think it's a mahen hunter."

"Not friendly of station not to say. Wouldn't you think?"

"Worries me," Haral said. "Whole gods-forsaken place worries me." Her eyes shifted minutely aft, by implication including the repair work. Back again. "You still want that mahen security on our access?"

The breakfast lay uneasy at her stomach. "Put them on it. They're all we've got. And log those exchanges."

"They're logged." Haral powered her chair about and punched into the station comlink. "Kshshti central, this is the watch officer, from the bridge, *The Pride of Chanur.* . . . Get me dock security."

Pyanfar stood away from the counter and looked left as Tirun came shambling in half asleep and nodded a courtesy.

"Morning," she said to Tirun. "Chur's doing fine. Get some breakfast."

"Huh," Tirun said, and went, blindly trustful. Down on lowerdeck they had a lock about to open.

Pyanfar sat down in Tirun's place at bridge ops, conscious of the pistol she kept in her pocket, its weight swinging against her leg. She started locking doors, putting the lift on key/bridge operation only, sealing every hold access but the necessary one that would get work crews to *The Pride*'s vitals.

"Security's coming," Haral said.

*   *   *

Mahen workers came and went, an occasional splatter of bare running feet, a rush of black and brown mahen bodies in the lower corridors carrying this and that item the techs wanted—honest mahendo'sat, Pyanfar convinced herself. She came down to see the faces, to judge reactions, and the earnest look of the workers reassured her. Their speed reassured her, and the surprised reflexes of respect. Some recognized her, blue breeches and all as she took the tour through ops, where mahen techs ran checks. Above, aft, the first new vane panel was moving up in the careful grasp of a pushership, and suited mahendo'sat prepared the column to receive it.

It was a hundred ten panels wide to the old ninety and looked monstrous large. The old drive could not have pushed it. The old drive, *The Pride*'s old heart, had gone off in the clutches of a mahen pusher and a new, mahenmade unit was coupled to the ship's alloy spine, struts recoupled—as good amputate a part of her, and put back some fancy foreign part. She watched the floods sparkle bright off the panel rim and glisten off the black panel surfaces as the pusher turned. A shiver prickled up her back, worry about telemetry complications, systems that might not mesh and set them further back, despite the Voice's assurances. Topside, Tirun ran calculations and more calculations, had the third, this time sulphurous request in for raw specifications on the individual units. . . ."*Make soon,*" the reply had come back from the supervisor, "*give composite.*" And when Tirun objected that: "*Got get security clear give that information.*"

"*Good gods!*" Tirun had screamed into com. "It's part of our *ship,* you gods-rotted lunatic!"

"I make request," the supervisor said.

Meanwhile the panel was moving in, and mahendo'sat ran their own checks in ops; and things felt—marginally in control. Not just the unit back there on the tail. The bill. The finance.

Nine tenths of *The Pride*'s physical value, excluding her licenses and rights—and mahendo'sat picked up the tab.

Foreign hire. *Vigilance* had made that charge already. They were down there logging everything. There would be inquiry.

The *han* would have questions.A lot of questions. If they lived through Mkks.

She turned from the screens, walked past a cluster of *chiso*-babbling mahendo'sat who had their own instruments linked into auxiliary sockets on the ops board, headed out in the hall for fresh air. They had the place chilled down for the mahendo'sat. The hall was frigid. A cold draft wafted in from the lower lock, with the flavor of Kshshti docks, oil and old beer and mahendo'sat as she passed that corridor. Workmen in their orange coveralls came in, some went out. She pursued her way to the lift.

Hilfy. The thought came nudging in whenever she let it, and she pushed it away. "Captain," mahe said. "Come."

She stopped, blinked at the workman who beckoned her to the lock, opened her mouth to refuse that imprudence, but the mahe had flitted around the turn again, hasty as every mahe was hereabouts.

Some gods-rotted supervisor with questions. Her ship. Her access. She refused the jangling of her nerves and went after the workman. But her hand was in her pocket as she walked into the lock.

No one. She spun a look over her shoulder, looked back again as something dark came into her way, mahe-tall and spacer-ringed with gold.

Her finger tautened, hand cocked to aim through cloth and all. *"Pyanfar!"* the mahe cried, flinging up both hands; and the finger stopped.

"Jik!" she gasped, and her heart started up again. The mahe still held his hands up till she had gotten hand from pocket. "Where'd you come from?" And then she knew. "That's *Aia Jin* in 29, isn't it?"

"Same." Jik still looked nervous. "Make quick come here. Got trouble, huh?"

She looked him up and down, this lank solitary mahe with enough gaud in his dress to turn a hani envious. "Jik." It seemed half the troubles in the universe fell off her shoulders. "O gods. About time. *About gods-rotted time, hear me?*"

He flung up his hands again, pleading for quiet. She grabbed him by the arm and pulled him back toward the lift. "Come in here like this," she muttered, fishing up the key. She stuck it in. "Dressed like that." The lift doors hissed wide. "Get in." She snatched him inside, this mahe a third again her size. He leaned against the lift wall as it shot them up topside and the door shot open.

Khym was in the hall. His mouth fell open at the sight.

"Jik," Pyanfar identified him. "My husband, Khym. Old friend. Goldtooth's partner. Come on, Jik."

Chapter 10

Nomesteturjai was his name: captain Keia
Nomesteturjai. Jik to tongue-bound hani, this
thin, anxious-looking mahe. "Sit," Pyanfar said
and, spinning the com-post chair about, backed
Jik into it. She leaned on the counter and one
chair arm with not an arm's length between
their noses. "Where's Goldtooth?"

"Not know sure."

"What, not know?"

Jik's dark eyes shifted uncomfortably at that
range. "Think near Kefk."

"*Kefk!*"

"Not know sure." The eyes shifted back and
forth, bloodshot-rimmed. "Not good make
guess."

"Gods and thunders, what are we in?"

"You go Mkks?"

She stood back. "Khym. Get him a hot drink, huh?" Gods. *Him.* A weary twitch went through her nerves, a panic rage at biology.

But: "Aye," Khym said and went. Pyanfar sat down on the counter edge. Haral settled one hip on the console near her station, to keep an eye to things, Tirun slouched onto the padded arm of observer two.

"We talk," Pyanfar said. "Real slow. You understand me."

"Not sleep," Jik said, wiping a lank, blunt-clawed hand over his face. His shoulders slumped. "God, lousy course change Urtur system."

"It took us out," Pyanfar said. "Come on, Jik. What's going on out there? Hilfy and Tully are headed for Mkks, Chur's in hospital, they're dicing up my ship, the Personage says he's sorry and don't discuss the knnn I've had on my tail."

The arm went stiff in mid-motion, eyes fixed on hers. "Knnn."

"Out of Meetpoint. Maybe to here. I don't know. Kshshti stationmasters are nervous as stsho. What's going on?"

"Got kif take human ship. Human lot upset."

"*Knnn* take human ship, gods rot you, tell it straight! And I've got other news. Ship named

272

Ijir. The other courier with other humans. Kif got it.''

"God." He leaned back against the leather seat, arms on either rest, and looked at her. "How you know?"

"Message from Sikkukkut an'nikktukktin. Same as got Tully and Hilfy."

"He got *Ijir?*"

"Don't know."

Jik let go a deep long breath. His reddened eyes traveled up again as Khym padded in with a tray. Khym offered him the first, stiffly courteous, and Jik took it without a flinch. "We not meet. Both Gaohn station."

"Huh," Khym breathed, a grinding in his throat. But his ears came up with interest. He passed cups around, kept one for himself and settled, silent—gods, decorous—on the arm of the com-station seat, empty tray aside on the counter, quiet as Haral, as Tirun.

"Hunter ship," Pyanfar said for Khym's benefit, while Jik drank gfi and wrinkled his nose, shuddering as he drank. Gfi was not a mahen favorite, but it was substance and Jik seemed to need that. The strength looked to have drained out of him as if he had run a long, long time. "Best pilot in mahen space," Pyanfar said, not lying. "You talk to the stationmaster, Jik?"

Weary eyes lifted, guileless. "Go station center, talk." Another sip of gfi, another small shudder and grimace at the taste. "Got ask you—Pyanfar. Where packet?"

She drew in a long, long sip of her own cup. "What packet?"

Jik swallowed hard. The gfi was hot and tears sprang to his eyes, which acquired a heat of their own and a hard glitter of thought. "Bastard," he said. "No game."

"It isn't. When they get my tail back working, huh? You know, it occurs to me with *Aia Jin* in port they might take me off priority. They got hunter ship, huh? Not need hani now."

"Fix."

"Sure, they will."

He sat there a moment, breathing in and out and a good deal more rapid going on behind his eyes. "You got packet, huh? Kif got Tully, you got packet and you go Mkks. What want? Give both to kif?"

"Maybe trade."

The least uncertainty crept into his expression. "No. You no do." It became fear. "You got too much smart, Pyanfar."

"No," she said, gazing deep into his eyes. "I got friends. *Don't I, Jik?*"

He drew a breath. "You give packet. Damn, hani! You try hold this thing, Kshshti authority board and take!"

"Stationmaster doesn't know it exists. Does he? Not Eseteno, not Tt'om'm'mu, not our pink-slippered cutthroat Stle stles stlen. But you know. And the fewer know it exists, the better. Don't you think?" She jabbed a claw at him. "How'd the kif know to move that quick, to set up an ambush on the docks? How'd we get set up, huh?"

"You say stationmaster?"

"You say kif make lucky guess?"

"I know this Eseteno. No. No, Pyanfar. Not. He honest, long time got post. Trust him."

"All right. That's one. But how far down the line does honest go? How much does it take? Kif got some security agent's relatives, make deal, huh?"

Jik's dark face was very sober, ears down. "All time possible."

"Maybe same got agent repair crew, huh?"

"Kif want you go Mkks. Want blow ship there got lot chance. Not need sabotage."

It made sense. It was the cheerfullest reassurance she had had since the docks blew up. She drew her mustache down, thinking on the odds.

"Give packet," Jik said. "Got go Maing Tol, this packet. I ask. Number one important."

"Goldtooth's observations, is it? His report— what's going on out there in kif space. Knnn stuff too."

Jik's small ears went back. "You got no profit make guess, Pyanfar."

"I make deal. I trust my honest mahe friend.

275

That repair crew stays on the job and my engineer gets specs on those parts number one quick."

"Got."

"Got authority, do you? Lot of authority, same as Goldtooth."

Jik's ears twitched. "Some thing yes."

"Some thing, huh? You want this packet, you go with me to Mkks."

"Hani, I guard you tail at Gaohn!"

"Guard it at Mkks and you get the packet."

Gently: "You bastard, Pyanfar."

"You same kind bastard. You say, you do. I know this."

"I go Mkks," he said.

"Get the packet, Haral."

Haral moved. Jik leaned back into the leather cushion and watched, bestirred himself to take it when it came, this largish several-times crushed envelope with a dark stain at one corner. "All here?" Jik asked.

"Everything they sent me. What are you going to do with it?"

"Try find honest captain."

"In this port? Stay away from the hani."

"A?" He looked her in the eyes and the ears sank slowly before they came up again. The face had no fool's look, not now. "Trouble, huh?"

"Lot trouble."

"You come."

"Come where?"

"Come with. We talk these hani."

"No."

Jik stood up. "I go. Sure thing we talk. Want share?"

"Gods rot—*Gods rot it, I've got enough trouble!* Leave my name out of it!"

"They got jealous, huh?"

"Look, look, you earless lunatic, there's laws, there's regulations I already break—The *han's* after my hide, you understand me? Chanur's got troubles! You want to hand them *proof*, huh? It's illegal for me to work for foreign government, understand? *Against the conventions!*"

"You carry cargo government give."

"*That's* legal. Gods rot it, you know the distinction. *You* trade, what time you're not up to no good—"

"So you carry cargo." He lifted the packet. "Same legal."

"Look, look, Jik—old friend. They're looking for an excuse. They want find trouble, understand? You'll get us skinned, all of us."

"What choice got? Pyanfar, good friend, got no choice. Packet got go."

"Send it with the tc'a!"

Ears flicked. "No." Short and sharp, a small flicker in the eyes that rang alarms. "Not number one good idea, Pyanfar."

277

More alarms. Methane-breathers, with their own interests. Tt'om'm'mu rearing up behind his glass, violet and murky phosphorescences.

"You come," Jik said. "Maybe better you be there, huh, stop stupid mahe say wrong thing these honest hani?"

"No! Absolutely no!" She got up, flung off across the bridge, waving her arms and dislodging Khym from her path. She looked back again. Jik still stood there with the packet in his hands and that Tully-look on his too-narrow mahen face.

"Pyanfar." He held up the envelope.

"No," she said.

"Chanur," the Ehrran said, Rhif, rising from a much-scarred and grimy chair. KSHSHTI PORT AUTHORITY the office said on the outer door, in four different alphabets with letters missing. CONFERENCE in three: the hani line had fallen off altogether and left only brighter paint behind, misspelled.

"Ehrran," Pyanfar said. And with a glance at the other hani captain in the narrow room: "Ayhar." Jik closed the door behind them both and they were all alone with each other.

"You?" Ehrran asked of Jik. "The Personage send you here?"

"No," Jik said quietly, with unflappable good nature. "I ask Personage send you."

It shot straight through Ehrran's guard and Pyanfar got a quick furtive breath and swallowed it quick, straight-faced, watching the Ehrran's face.

Quick re-thinking, by the gods. Rhif Ehrran drew herself up, mouth not quite closed, and then it did close, and the Ehrran stared closely at this raffish-dressed mahe.

"Sit," Jik said, "captains, I ask you."

Pyanfar pursed her mouth and sat, watched first Banny Ayhar lower her portly self into a grimy seat and then fastidious Ehrran, who looked as if she had a mouthful of salt and no idea where to spit.

"What I got ask," Jik said, taking his own seat at the battered table, in this despicable little office, "what I got ask—" He laid the rumpled envelope on the table. "Need courier."

"Who needs?" The question got out past Ehrran's well-groomed mustaches. "I'd like to see some Signature, if you don't mind."

"A." Jik bent a lank wrist toward his kilt belt, deftly whipped up a small folder, spun it across the table. "That good?"

The Ehrran picked it up as if it had been charged, extruded claws to pull the two leaves apart, and read something there that brought her head up and her ears to level. She mutely flipped the holder closed and spun it back again.

Jik replaced it. "Know you," he said. "Rhif Ehrran. Where you course?"

"*Han* business."

"A. Maybe got same business lot trouble kif. Maybe got invoke treaty."

"Maybe you can get Chanur to do your work."

"Maybe invoke treaty. Need you, Ehrran."

Ehrran's eyes smoldered. One claw came out, traced a pattern on the tabletop, a clean green line amid the grime. "I've got business, mahe."

"So. Maybe got. I got. Got hani citizen with kif. Got hani shot up, a? No, I tell you, ker Ehrran. You in mahen space, inside mahen agreement—" Jik held up one blunt-clawed finger, forestalling a word from the Ehrran. "You here, a? I call other side treaty, got number-one emergency, got need ship run courier—"

"You want to buy other hani?"

"*Gods rot—!*" Pyanfar straightened and a dark-furred mahen arm landed slam! on the table between her and the Ehrran.

"I make request," Jik said. "Of-fi-cial, a? Treaty stuff. Now, we got cooperative agreement, agreement like I tell you, Ehrran. You got say yes, say no. You honor treaty?"

The ears were flat already, the fine fair nose rumpled, the eyes ruddy amber. "What do you want?"

"You on hunt. Tell you this hunt go Mkks."

"*Mkks!*"

"Mkks, hani. Got other thing Ayhar do." He shoved the packet skidding at Ayhar's startled grasp. "You got priority undock, captain. You got. You run damn fast. Know you. Know you, Banny Ayhar. You got lot year, lot smart. I know, huh?"

Ayhar's ears sank. Her eyes showed white rims. "Where?" Ayhar asked.

"Maing Tol."

Banny Ayhar drew the packet up in her hands, drew her mouth down taut, not without a shift of her eyes Ehrran's way. But Ehrran never looked. "No trouble," Ayhar said, all quiet.

"Good," Jik said. "You go. Go fast, ker Ayhar. You not talk, you not wait. Got six my crew see you get car, see you car get ship. Dock crew already work get you out."

Ayhar stood up, the envelope still in her hands.

"You not open," Jik said.

"Gods be feathered if I want to," Ayhar muttered, and looked this way and that ... delayed then, with a look back. "Ker Pyanfar. You want that crewwoman ferried out?"

"No," said Jik ahead of anything. "You run. Run hard. Not ask why. You not got safety. Not got choice."

"See here—" But it faded. Whatever Ayhar had meant to say faded out. She looked a moment at Jik and turned then, the envelope in her hands, and vanished out the door.

Ehrran had gained her feet, ears flat. "Chanur," she said, "out."

Pyanfar leaned back and fixed Ehrran with a cold stare. "I'll stay, thanks. I *can* sit proxy to Chanur's interests. Or is the mahen captain more privy to *han* business than a member is? I'm here to witness. Formally."

Ehrran drew a long, long breath, and her eyes were dark-centered. Perhaps she considered the recorders. "Kshshti's already had one security breach. . . ."

"*My crew*, my niece, my passenger, Ehrran. You want to talk to me about security breach—"

"We'll settle that. Elsewhere. This action of yours—" Ehrran looked at Jik, with no more pleasant face. "My course is Kefk."

Jik waved a loose, limp hand. "Now Mkks." The hand returned to his hip above the gun and rested there. "Ten, maybe twelve hour. You think got business Kefk. No. Lousy place, Kefk. You no go."

"To do what? To do *what* at Mkks?"

"You stay my tail, a? You dock left. Dock right, Chanur. Three number one bastard go take walk Mkks docks, a?"

There was a long, long silence. Ehrran stood staring, hunter-fix. "Right," Ehrran said. "Ten hours. I'll trust this gets authorized higher up, *na* Jik."

She walked out, flat. The door whisked shut. "Pyanfar," Jik said, and gestured that way, in Ehrran's wake.

"Huh." Pyanfar got up with a grimace, collected herself and followed Jik outside, where three of his crew waited, all of them gaudy as Jik himself, even toward raffish; guns carried openly. An abundance of gold chains and armlets, and one had a knife.

"All done," Jik said, laying a hand on her shoulder, "got fix good, a?"

"Sure. Sure, fix." She looked round at him with her ears back. "Expensive fix, friend. She won't forget."

"Got soul like kif, that hani."

"Number one right. *What* business? What's she after?"

The hand squeezed, a pressure of blunt claws. The mahe's dark eyes wrinkled round their edges and looked only tired. "This Ehrran hunt hani ship. Not you, no, she got rumor got hani work many side this thing. *Han* lot upset. This Rhif Ehrran, she want this renegade real bad. Think maybe you, a? *Han* lot crazy. They don't like the stsho make sudden clear paper, bring you to Meetpoint. Got lot suspicion, the *han*. I tell you, Pyanfar, you got go home talk sense these hani."

"*Who* cleared those papers up?"

Jik pushed her doorward. She braced her feet. "Who, gods rot it?"

"Goldtooth talk good stsho, got same treaty, a?"

"Stle stles stlen."

Jik rubbed the bridge of his nose, where an old scar showed gray. "Same got Ayhar."

"*What* 'same got Ayhar'?"

"Stle stles stlen. Got somehow station damage charge, a? Got big bill, Ayhar. Stsho seize Ayhar cargo."

"O gods."

"Lot scared, Banny Ayhar. Stsho send here, direct route, run courier old bastard Stle stles stlen. Same come *Vigilance*. Same Stle stles stlen got long talk Rhif Ehrran after you leave Meetpoint, a?"

"That eggsucker!"

"One scared hani, Ayhar."

"Gods rot. What's *gtst* after?" But ideas occurred to her. A certain bill. A detailed report to the *han* sent by way of *Vigilance*.

And another thought muddled past, about timing, information and mahen interests.

"You came from Kura, huh? Sure, you did."

Jik held up both hands. "Maybe come Meetpoint. Forget these detail."

"Gods rot it, can't *somebody* tell the truth?"

"Lot truth."

"Sure." She jerked her arm as he laid a hand on it to move her on, and he gave her all her reach for distance between them. "Sure," she said. "Maybe fifty-fifty, huh? What happens now when I get outbound? Maybe have an accident?—Sorry, old friend? Repair crew made a mistake? Hope you enjoy the trip? *Gods rot—*"

"No. Swear to you." Jik held up his hands again and dropped them. "Say message come to Kshshti. I get same here."

"Who sent you here?"

"Mahen agent, a? Got here, there agent, same hani, same kif. I not say more, Pyanfar. See? I one time try tell truth, got big trouble."

Ayhar? she wondered. Gods, no. Not Banny, not that lot. They loved their liberties too well.

Methane-breather? *T'T'Tmmmi* had come in from Meetpoint. She had seen it on the list. It was still in port.

Tt'om'm'mu's spy, reporting to methane-side of Kshshti? Circles upon circles. It sent a cold, cold feeling to the stomach.

Knnn. But *no one* talked to knnn. No one could—excepting tc'a.

"You come," Jik said, mistaking overload for acquiescence, taking her by the unresisting arm, flinging his over her shoulders. "Get you safe back ship, Pyanfar. Got time maybe catch sleep. Tell you truth . . . I come Kura way, lousy long run. Sleep make you better, a?" He squeezed hard, dropped the arm again as they came out into the general offices and walked through. Mahen crew hastened to open the outside door. Station guards stood with rifles beside the waiting car.

Kura. Kura was in hani territory. And Ehrran had folded fast when she had a look at the authority in that small wallet Jik had at his belt. Ayhar—Ayhar had been folded before she got there, ears down.

Scared. Plenty scared.

She got into the car at Jik's side in back, surrounded by mahe whose musky flavor got past the perfumes. A guard caught her eye, one curly-furred and smallish, and alarms rang.

"That one," she said to Jik, digging claws into his knee, "outside—"

"Name her Tginiso," Jik said, ducking his head to look past her out that window. "Eseteno aide."

"She was with the car when Hilfy went. Her fur's not singed." For a moment the air seemed very close, the scent of mahendo'sat all-enveloping, and she knew who she was talking to, hunter-captain, mahe with mahen interests very much at stake. She felt Jik's arm shift across the seatback.

"Move," he said to the driver in the mahen tongue. The car leapt forward with a burr of the motor, wheels bumping on the plates like a panicked heartbeat.

Not a word from Jik, only a shifting of his eyes from one side to the other, watching everything along the sides.

Pyanfar watched him, among the rest. Friend. Companion. Along with Rhif Ehrran.

The car thumped along, dodged pedestrians.

Jik took out his pistol and thoughtfully took the safety off in his lap, no small piece like her pocket gun, no, nearly as long as his forearm, with a black, wicked sheen. The mahe on the other side drew hers and kept scanning the surrounds, the whisk of gantries past, of lines, machinery, canisters, all places for ambushes.

Berth five passed. Jik spoke to the driver in something mahen and obscure. "We go close," Jik said. "Want you go fast up ramp."

"Gods rot it, my whole lower deck's occupied."

He pressed her knee. "Same good get you safe in ship." The car veered: a ship access and guards loomed into the way and the car veered again, bringing the door even with the access. The door flew up and Pyanfar scrambled out with Jik and the crewwoman close behind.

Up the ramp then, a slower pace, the long, chill walk through that yellow gullet with the L bend to the lock. Pyanfar looked back, looked round again as they reached the lock and Jik laid a hand on her shoulder.

"Safe. Safe here."

"Sure. The stationmaster's handpicked aides—"

"Listen. I know you safe."

"You know. What's in that ID, Jik? Who are you? Who are you working for?"

Both hands settled on her shoulders. There was nowhere to look but dark mahen eyes, a plain mahen face. "You got watch on you deck, understand, got number one good watch."

"Who? What are you talking about?"

Jik's lips went tight. "Mahe take orders somewhere else. Same good tech, a? Not make mistake."

"Like that aide? Safe like that?"

"I fix."

That left cold after it. Jik lifted his hands from her shoulders, held one finger up.

"Then," Jik said, "get good sleep."

"Ayhar's jumped," Khym said, who sat monitor on com, and the board checks paused for the moment. He scribbled furiously on the lightpad and his florid scrawl came up on screen three as Haral punched it through, a string of numbers meaningless to him, but he got them down with speed.

Heading, velocity, strength of field.

"It's on its way," Tirun muttered, and Pyanfar felt a twinge of relief as the full scan input went to the number two: no pursuit.

There was a tc'a out. *T'T'Tmmmi*. Outbound on the same heading, none too quietly.

TC'A   TC'A   TC'A   TC'A   TC'A   TC'A   TC'A

. . . its
transmission said, with ship-function babble in all its harmonics, a tc'a ship fully occupied with tc'a business and the speaker thinking

only of its/their jobs. Tc'a did not lie, so the story ran, could not. Once a tc'a began to output, the underminds had to be there or the harmonics failed and the whole matrix fell into gibberish.

So someone non-tc'a had reckoned, from what gtst thought tc'a had claimed, a hundred years ago.

She went back to work, running checks through the systems, resetting failsafes and running them again and again, putting comp through one and the other simulation as it reprogrammed itself.

"Pride." Khym's low voice, answering some call, in the profound silence, the click of keys, the sometime shift of a body in a leather seat. "First is busy. Can you—" The shift of a heavier body. "Ker Tirun. It's *Vigilance*. They want a crew member."

Tirun muttered something and took it. "Gods rot," she said. "You don't need to go up the line for that, Ehrran .... That *was* a crew member."

Pyanfar turned around.

"Fine," Tirun said, and punched the contact out. "That's a confirm on the Ayhar jump."

Pyanfar said nothing. There was nothing to say. Tell Khym to stand his ground and ignore a request for higher authority? But next time it might be something that truly had to get someone more knowledgeable. Log the discourtesy? Who would read it but the *han*?

Khym was busy already, a look of concentration on his broad, scarred face the while he listened to station chatter that flowed past him like so much babble, sorting for anything of interest, anything of tc'a or knnn, anything of kif or mahendo'sat. Doing the best he could.

In Hilfy's vacant post.

Pyanfar turned back again, twisted in her seat a third time as she heard the lift work down the corridor.

"Captain!" Tirun spun her chair as she did, as she came out of her chair reaching for her pocket and Khym was out of his place.

"Identify." Haral had usurped com function to her panel and keys clicked to freeze locks, but the lift door opened all the same.

Hani. Hani and smallish and one of their own.

"Geran," Pyanfar muttered, and the gun went back. No rejoicing, not from any of them. It was not that kind of time, an hour to go and Geran out of place.

"Something wrong?" Pyanfar asked as Geran walked onto the bridge. "Chur all right, Geran?"

"Left her below, snugged in."

"Gods and thunders!"

Geran shrugged, padded over to main scan, rested a hand on her seatback and looked round again, ears at half, and obduracy in the stare she gave back. "Don't like to cross those docks, captain. Scary place out there."

It took a good long moment of even breathing to cope with that.

"Geran—" in a tone quiet enough to warn a chi. "We've got one hour, one gods-rotted hour to get things sorted out. You two—"

"Captain, please." Geran's voice sank to the same level, but all wobbly. "Chur'd kill me for saying it, but she's scared. Gut-scared. Being left here—the ship and all—where'd she be? What good's two of us—here? By ourselves? Where's home, but *The Pride*?"

Something superstitious settled into her own gut, nothing reasonable. "Look. We're not after suicide, hear me? Jik's in port. He's got *Vigilance* on our side for what she's worth. We're going to Mkks to do some good. Hear me? Now get Chur back where she belongs."

"She is. Same as me." Geran's claws sank into the chairback, tendons stark on the backs of her hands. "What's all this new stuff worth with half a crew, huh? Chur can walk—walked across that dock out there from the lift, she did, just fine."

"Good gods."

"The plasm took; the wound won't tear. Got her packed in real good and the time-stretch'll give her a good few days to heal. Might be on her feet by the time we get to Mkks—"

"The gravity-drop'll kill her."

"No. Not Chur."

She folded her ears down and Geran stood her ground, meant to stand it, gods knew. And they needed that pair of hands. Needed hands that could fit hani-specific controls, fit a hani crewwoman's space. "Gods rot," she muttered and walked off the other way with a wave of her hand. "Bring her topside. Put her in my cabin. Put her close to us. Pack a med kit in there."

"My cabin," Khym said. "She can have mine."

"Do it."

"Thanks," Geran said, all heartfelt. "Thanks, captain."

"And get yourself back here. We've got a tight schedule, huh?"

"Aye!" Geran scrambled and took Khym with her.

Pyanfar looked at Tirun and Haral. Tirun's face carefully showed nothing; Haral's was toward the boards, occupied with business.

"Odds just went up," Tirun said, "captain."

"We need crazy people on our side?" She threw herself into the chair, powered it about again, feeling a shameful comfort to know one more seat was filled. The lift hummed, Khym and Geran going down to see to the transfer.

"Getting a confirmation from *Aia Jin*," Haral said, who still had com. "Getting a readoff on course. They're putting us out gods-rotted deep in the well."

She looked at the figures that flashed onto monitor one. "Huh." She keyed that data set into the simulator and watched the lines tick across the screen, affirmative, affirmative, can-do. It was still *The Pride*'s boards, but something alien answered from aft, up the circuit-synapses through the metal spine. "Huh." It made her nervous, in a way that camera-view did not, that picked up the wider vanes, the rakish lines of the vane-columns. That was plain to inspection. The heart and core of it was not, that added some twenty percent to their unladed mass and threw varied percentages into the figures of moving that mass. Old familiar reckonings went by the board. They had to lean on comp entirely, trust it without the dead-reckoning knowledge what the answers ought to be, when it told them *The Pride* could make a jump that she could never in a mahen hell have survived half a week before.

"We go with it," she said.

Continued in

THE KIF STRIKE BACK

Appendix

Species of the Compact

The Compact

The Compact is a loose affiliation of all trading species of a small region of stars who have agreed by treaty to observe certain borders, trade restrictions, tariffs, and navigational procedures. It is an association, not a government, has no officials and maintains no offices, except insofar as all officials of the various governments are de facto officers of the Compact.

The hani

Native to Anuurn, hani may be among the smaller species of the Compact, but the size range, particularly among males, is so extreme that individual hani may overreach and outbulk the average of other, taller species. Their fur is short over most of their bodies except for manes and beards. It ranges in color from red gold to dull red brown with blackish edges, and in texture from crimped waves to curls to coarse straightness.

Hani were a feudal culture divided into provinces and districts a few centuries previous to the events of *The Pride of Chanur*. They had well-developed trade and commerce when they were contacted by the spacefaring mahendo'sat (qv) and flung from their middle ages, with its flat-earth concept and territoriality, into interstellar trade.

The way of life previous to that age had been this: that individual males carved out a territory by challenge and maintained it with the aid of their sisters, currently resident wives, and female relatives of all sorts, so long as the male in question remained strong enough to fend off other challengers. Actual running of the territory rested with a lord's sisters and other female relatives, at least a few of whom, if he was fortunate, would prove skillful traders, and whose marriages with outclan males would form profitable links with the females of other clans. Such males as lived to become clan lords were sheltered and pampered, kept in fighting trim at the urging of their female relatives, and generally took no part whatsoever in interclan dealings or in mercantile decisions, which were considered too exacting and stressful for males to cope with. The male image in most households was that of a cheerful, unworldly fellow mostly involved in games and hunts, and existing primarily for the siring of children and, in time of challenge, idolized for those natural gifts of irrational temper and berserker rage which would greet the sight of another male. The females stood between him and all other vicissitudes of life. Much of hani legendry and literature, of which they are fond, involves the tragic brevity of males; or the cleverness of females; or the treks and voyages of ambitious females out to carve out territory for some unlanded brother to defend.

Under the management of certain great females, vast estates grew up. Certain estates contained crucial trade routes, shrines, mountain passes, dams—things which were generally the focus of ambition. Certain clans formed amphictionies, associations of mutual interest to assure the access of all members to areas of regional importance, which was usually done by declaring the area in question protected. Out of such protected zones grew the concept of the Immune Clan; that is, a clan whose hold over a particular resource must not change, because of the need of the surrounding clans to have that resource managed over the long term by a clan with experience and peculiar skill: such clans devoted themselves to public service and dressed distinctively. Immune males enjoyed great ceremonial prestige and were generally cloistered and pampered, while the sons of Immune houses were without hope of succession except by the death of the lord by natural causes. To attack an Immune male was a capital offense, bringing all the area clans to enforce the law.

This form of regional government proved successful in bringing Enafy province, where the Llun Immune had its seat, to preeminence in the great plains of the Llunuurn River. Enafy province spread its influence through trade into other regions and other amphictionies sprang up, some less benevolent. The concept of amphictiony spread to other continents and races and, while other cultures survived, generally they were small, or so divided that they managed little growth: the Enafy and Enaury of Anuurn's largest continent spread their culture by trade and occasionally by intrigue and by marriage and alliance.

Into this situation came the mahendo'sat, who chose for their landing site the Llunuurn basin, as the most extensive river system on the planet and the area with the most developed roads and habitations. Because of this selection, initial contact happened to be with the largest and oldest amphictiony, in the lordship of na Ijono Llun.

Na Ijono's sister ker Gifhon Llun went out to meet the intruders, since they were neither hani nor (as Gifhon assumed incorrectly in several cases) male. By the time she understood what she was dealing with, dealing had begun, trade had been offered, and the world, without Gifhon's clearly realizing it for some years, had forever changed.

Other amphictionies felt threatened by this relationship of Enafy province to the mahendo'sat and the elevation of the Llun clan from supervisors of the dams of the lower Llunuurn tributaries, to supervisors of a starfaring shuttleport and station. The mahendo'sat played one against the other and snared all the hani leaders into trade.

The hani amphictionies, however, whether or not it accorded with mahen intentions (and perhaps it was the intent of the mahendo'sat from the start) began to deal with each other in the concept of a much larger amphictiony, one with Anuurn itself as the Resource which had to be protected.

So the *han* was created, the council of councils, the heart and center of hani government, microcosm of the world in which alliance, province, clan and Immunity still played their role—as, indeed, *han* has another meaning as a collective meaning All Hani. Theoretically every hani lord was ceremonially part of the body: some actually attended and addressed the assembly. The seats, one to each clan, belonged to the female heads of household, or, in practice, to any senior female in the vicinity of the several meeting halls, one of which existed and exists in every province. The *han* is thus composite, and only infrequently holds a true general meeting, the location of which is subject to intense negotiation.

Hani relations with other starfaring folk were not generally positive. The stsho (qv) were not in accord with the mahendo'sat intervention on Anuurn: their motives might be judged to be several—unwillingness to see the mahen sphere of influence increase; the fact that they and the hani shared a territorial border; their distrust of all virtually exclusive carnivores based on their experience with the kif (qv); their fears of instability in the Compact; or other reasons which like minds might comprehend. The kif understood the arrival of the hani on the scene as opportunity, in the exercise of which they were driven back by mahendo'sat and hani combined. The opinion of the compact's other species was never solicited nor received.

Hani territory included originally Anuurn system. The name of their home star is Ahr. The planets of Ahr system are, in order: Gohin, a hot and barren world without atmosphere; Anuurn itself; Tyo, a cold, barren world partially terraformed for a hani colony; the gas giants Tyar and Tyri; and frozen Anfas. Gaohn station was built by mahendo'sat in orbit about Anuurn and turned over to Llun, whose males were the only hani males ever to leave the surface. Kilan station was built in orbit about Tyo, never particularly prosperous; and Harn station was built as a shipyard facility.

The Chanur Family

A very old clan of Enafy province, occasionally obscure but more often involved in the amphictiony of Enafy under a series of ambitious leaders, Chanur sprang into considerable prominence as one of the first clans to see the benefits of offworld trade.

Kohan Chanur is current lord: his principle mates are Huran Faha, Akify Llun, Lilun Sifas. Actual manager of the estate is his aunt Jofan Chanur par Araun. His sisters are Pyanfar, Rhean and Anfy Chanur, whose mates are of clan Mahn, Anury, and Quna respectively, and who captain the ships *The Pride of Chanur, Chanur's Fortune* and *Chanur's Light*. His daughters are: Hilfy, by Huran; Nifas, by Akify, among others; and two sons (exiled).

Araun is a tributary clan, rated as cousins to Chanur; other cousin clans are Tanan, Khuf, and Pyruun. Jisan Araun par Chanur was mother to Haral and Tirun through an obscure tributary clan lord from remote Llunuurny, long since defeated and replaced by a male Haral and Tirun declined to support, leaving him to his numerous if unambitious sisters. Nifany Pyruun, Jofan Chanur's blood cousin, is birth-mother to Chur and Geran and a son in exile. She is administrator of Chanur offices in the port authority.

Kohan's most recent defense of Chanur was against Kara Mahn, son of Pyanfar Chanur and

Khym Mahn. Mahn, a nonspacing clan in the
Kahin Hills nearby, remains an uneasy neigh-
bor with Kara in Khym's stead, and his full
sister Tahy at the head of Mahn's financial
interests.

Hani language and religion

There was not, of course, one language, but the
Enafy dialect of the Llunuurn valley became stan-
dardized as the language of commerce and diplomacy. With considerable resistance it was adopted
as the language of the *han* and is the only language heard offplanet.

The language was the vehicle of the spread
of Llunuurn culture planetwide and carries it
into space.

Terms of respect are: *ker*, title of a high clan
woman; *na* title of a clan lord; *par* maternal daughter of a clan. *Nef* is the title of an ex-lord, who is
no longer entitled to be called by the name of his
clan.

Hani terms of disrespect involve uncleanness;
age (eggsucker implies one too old to hunt moving game); disavowal by clan (bastard is an inac-
curate translation, since legitimacy cannot be at
issue in a matrilineal descent); the deities; the
condition of the ears, which tell a great deal about
one's efficiency in self-defense. More peculiar is
the use of *feathered*, an impious reference to a
hani religious debate; and *son*, as in *gods give*

you sons; since male offspring do no work and are exiled at puberty to return and attempt to take over the estate in their prime, a house with many sons is in constant turmoil.

The Mahendo'sat

Among the tallest species of the Compact, tending to ranginess and length of limb, the mahendo'sat have fur ranging from sleek sheened black to curly brown, with all gradations in between. Their claws do not retract, and are more a tool of utility than a weapon. They are omnivores, native to Iji, from which they control a considerable territory. Their neighbors on the one side are the hani, on the other the kif, with whom they share some territory in dispute.

The mahendo'sat have more than a hundred languages native to Iji. Their own lingua franca is *chiso*, which not all mahendo'sat speak; and very many mahendo'sat have never succeeded in learning even the simplified pidgin that they popularized during the hani contact. Ironically, this species which pursues both art and science for its own sake and which is continually engaged in research of all kinds, cannot translate either into or out of its own set of languages with any degree of accuracy, which some might suspect indicates more than apparent idiosyncrasies in psychology as well as physiology.

The fact that the pidgin is mostly hani rests on

several facts, most of them having to do with the mahendo'sat's inability to translate their own tongue. First, mahendo'sat and stsho were already in communication with great difficulty through a bastard tongue involving kif, who spoke stsho. Second, when hani came into the picture, hani proved able to learn kifish and stsho and with their long experience as traders, evolved a pidgin hani that blended with the current pidgin and virtually supplanted it. This proved something even mahendo'sat could handle, and which kif had less trouble with than they did with stsho. So the mahendo'sat took to it with relief.

As for the inner workings of the mahen culture, even the species name exists in some uncertainty. Mahe is generally singular, sometimes plural; and mahendo'sat actually seems to stand for the species collective mentality, or the species as an entity, or for some concept which refuses translation as nation or species. The term *han* in its application as the collective of the hani species is clearly a reflection of mahen influence in the formative phase of hani world government.

Mahendo'sat are often collectors, which they have in common with stsho; but mahendo'sat are most interested in natural objects and make elaborate gardens, an art which they taught to the hani, whose gardens nevertheless maintain a hani-like plainness and agricultural practicality. Mahendo'sat on the other hand are devoted to design and derive philosophical meaning from the growth patterns of their carefully tended trees. Mahendo'sat also keep pets, a trait they share with stsho and perhaps tc'a (qv) but mahendo'sat are likely to keep difficult ones and to lavish care on exotics.

The history of the mahen species is one of pocket kingdoms, continual religious ferment, mysticism, leaders with self-claimed credentials rising to some purpose and vanishing in what may have been a tradition of such vanishments. They are greatly concerned with abstracts and courtesies, symbol and hidden meaning.

Modern and ancient mahen authority rests on Person, involving dignity and charismatic appeal, and interlinking Personages in an elaborate chain of command in which one appoints the next, but in which a higher Personage may be brought down by the malfeasance or error of an appointee. Mahendo'sat set great store by this indefinable quality and esteem it where found, to such an extent that they likewise choose to honor or ignore members of other species with complete disregard of those species' own concepts of authority. Personages are of either of the species' two genders, usually of mature years. Personages come in many ranks and levels of authority, but all are attended by a Voice, a person usually of the opposite gender whose apparently self-appointed task it is to represent the Personage and to utter unpleasantness which the Personage is too serene to deal with.

The mahen social unit is complex, revolving around personage: mating is at apparent random, but Person has a great deal to do with it. Young are traded about with apparent abandon, but this also has to do with the bonds of Person, and the desire to expose the young to good influence or superior instruction.

The mahen government currently rests with a Personage at Iji whose serenity is untroubled; but in the fashion of mahendo'sat, this and the entire form of government are subject to change without notice.

The Stsho

The stsho, native to remote Llyene, are a pale, hairless species, trisexual hermaphrodites, one of each triad bearing young: but that same individual may exist within another triad as a non-bearer. Stsho refuse to explain.

They are omnivores of great sensitivity and fragility. Their limbs break easily. Their very personalities fragment under stress, which seems to serve as a social absolution. It is very impolite to recognize a stsho who has changed persona, or as stsho call it ... Phased. An individual seems to go through many Phases in life.

They trade. They are aesthetes and enjoy subtle distinctions in taste and sight. They have forty-seven different words, for instance, for white.

Like hani, they prefer bowl-structures for chairs

and beds. Their elaborate architecture is apparently random and universally pastel in color.

They are the only natives of Compact space who need drugs to survive jump.

They permit no intrusion of oxygen-breathing species within their territory, but they are utterly incapable of enforcing this except through their relationship with the unpredictable methane-breathers who divide them from kif territory. They share one border with the hani; methane-breathers come and go within their space; and to their considerable distress they have discovered humans are at their backs, on the side of stsho space nearest Llyene, which is a mysterious and forbidden world.

They were among the first spacefarers in the region, anomalous, because their primary policy seems to be to acquire the widest possible area about their homeworld from which strangers are excluded. Certainly they did not seem to go to the stars to make contact with outsiders. Or perhaps some experience lies in their past which has made them what they are. Stsho allow no real information about stsho to leak out of their space, which greatly vexes the curious mahendo'sat.

Legendarily Llyene is a treasure world of fantastical wealth. It is certain that stsho trade is lucrative in all directions, and that they are the source of a great deal of technology that the mahendo'sat turn to various purposes.

The Kif

Kif are tallest of the species of the Compact, very lean and having virtually no body fat. They are mostly hairless, except for a close-growing strip down the midline of their elongate, long-snouted skulls—which is seldom visible, as kif go robed and hooded and seldom bare their heads. The skin is gray and soft, if very tough and much wrinkled, and hot to the touch of hani or mahendo'sat. They are agile and strong; their claws are retractable and very sharp. Their eyes are usually red-rimmed: they prefer very dim light. What their genders are is a matter of guesswork. They may have two, but outsiders often use *it* of a kif in complete uncertainty, and *he* by convention which the mahendo'sat began: kif use he and occasionally she of themselves, but whether this precisely reflects a mahen/hani style gender distinction or something more like the stsho is still uncertain. Kif give few clues to aid the guesswork.

Kif got into space independently, through an arms race, and acquired starflight through contact with tc'a, whose wisdom in this other species question.

Kif are totally carnivorous, incapable of swallowing anything very large. Two independent sets of jaws exist within the snout, one to bite, another to reduce the intake to pulp and fluids. They prefer live food, and actually have rather delicate appetites: they are repulsed by carrion and could not easily handle cooked meat.

Color does not play a part in their decor, which is generally utilitarian and often black and gray. The light in their dwellings is quite dim. They have keen night vision, and indeed much of their homeworld dwelling is underground, though some mahen scientists have disputed on the basis of the kifish eye (smaller than the eyes of other nocturnals on other worlds) whether the species did not in fact originate as a diurnal hunter and change its lifestyle in the remote past. As kif do not share data with mahendo'sat, and stsho and hani have no interest in the question, it goes unanswered. Curiously kif do practice art, which seems confined to objects of ordinary use, weapons, cups, boxes and containers, which are embellished in tactile patterns. They place little value on mass-produced goods and great value on objects they believe to be unique, or on consumables such as rare and endangered species or uncommon liquors. They do appreciate intoxicants of various kinds but are the most moderate of known species in their consumption: individual kif who have become intoxicated have been killed outright by their companions.

Kif are facile linguists, great mimics, and in particular speak fluent hani, as well as their own several languages. Their homestar is Akkt, their homeworld Akkht, which outsiders often confuse, and reputedly both mean *home* or *homebase*, since *home* as understood by kif has the connotation of a place to which one repairs to gather one's forces for the next season. When they discovered outsiders, the shock and subsequent period of organization enabled a few leaders to seize power on Akkht, and eventually let the spacefaring kif seize power over Akkht entirely.

Kif have historically had little organization, usually engaged with each other in disputes and continual snatching of property from weaker kif. They have the concept of *sfik*, or face, in which the stronger will hold to a thing and defy all comers. The more attractive and unique the prize, the greater the *sfik*. Their interest in art perhaps revolves around this; of particular *sfik*-value are consumables or perishables which may be destroyed or used at any moment and for calculated purpose to frustrate the enemy. Taking such a thing is difficult and of great value, and there are also legendary destructions of great and valued objects.

Along with *sfik* there is also *pukkukkta*, which has no true translation except as a devastating blow to a rival.

Usually the kif operate as individuals or as crews, in which one kif is supreme, and weaker kif, if not protected from this one, are at least protected from other kif.

Sometimes a kif rises to a position of supremacy in which others fear to challenge him and in which he gathers great fear and support from those about him. Such a kif is a *hakkikt*, which kif say means prince. A *hakkikt*'s existence usually means a period in which outsiders will have trouble with kif. There is a growing expectation among kif that a *hakkikt* will arise to unite all kifish worlds into a power the rest of the Compact cannot withstand.

Tc'a

Tc'a are serpentine beings, leathery gold, methane breathers, native to Oh'a'o'o'o. They have a multipartite brain that thinks in matrices and communicates in harmonics. The mouthparts are toolusing. They can bulk a dozen times the weight of a mahendo'sat and bear several young at once, without apparent attention to the process, which has happened in the middle of conversations. They do trade, and mine, and what they think remains tc'a business. They usually run the methane side of stations in the Compact, since so far as anyone knows they are the only methane breathers interested in doing so. They are associated with chi and knnn (qqv), and while a great deal is known about tc'a comings and goings and while they take no aggressive action against any species, virtually nothing is known about the tc'a mind or the history of the species, except that they were in contact with the chi before they met the stsho, and were extremely early spacefarers.

Chi

Chi are neon yellow sticklike beings who (which?) move with great rapidity and often seem to be in total panic. "Crazy as a chi" is a hani proverb widely understood.

It is uncertain whether chi are associates of the tc'a or pets. Chi can run ships but are erratic navigators and it is virtually certain they did not invent their own technology. Tc'a are not found without chi, though occasionally chi may nest in communities into which tc'a do not appear to go.

Natives of Chchchoh, chi regularly accompany tc'a into the most hazardous mining areas. No oxygen-breather has ever reported visiting Chchchoh. Tc'a will not permit it, for what reason is unclear. It is known that chi reproduce by growing a second brain at some point midway along their bodies. Additional leg segments follow; then fission, and the newborn chi races off independently. Gender with a chi is therefore of questionable application. Activities have been observed which may be mating, but this is uncertain.

Knnn

No one knows the name of the knnn homeworld. No one knows if their ships have names—except perhaps the tc'a or the chi, who do not say. No oxy-breather is even sure which star they come from, except that it is on the underbelly of the Compact, and suspicion centers around one star known to be a hub of knnn activity.

Knnn look like black nests of hair-snarl with spider legs. Packrats of the galaxy, they breathe methane and sing long involved songs over ships' radio. They are (perhaps) miners and (one supposes) traders, but their idea of trade (as best the tc'a could communicate with them) is to dash onto station or ship, and exchange what they've brought for what they want or what they take a fancy to. In the bad old days, knnn simply gutted ships. They go in swarms or solitary, and their ships are the only ships known to change vector in jumpspace. They have a jump boost and turn maneuver that is impossible for oxy-breathers. They are not popular. One can only talk to them through the tc'a, who can get a kind of general translation—if you can understand the tc'a's seven-part matrix-sentences.

Knnn ships observe no lane regulations or instructions, and no one is about to challenge them on the point. It is suspected in some quarters that the knnn may have been the origin of much of the technology of the Compact. No one except the stsho knows whether the stsho actually devised their own technology, and perhaps stsho in general do not know: certainly they do not comment on it.

Knnn were unknown at Anuurn until Pyanfar Chanur brought them there. Her people are not grateful.

C.J. CHERRYH
THE ALLIANCE-UNION UNIVERSE